Take me

To Luke.

Hope you enjoy

Tony Sherwin

To my Daughters

Kate and Rachel

With love.

Chapter 1

The carriage doors were slamming shut and people were running up and down the platform to and from the train. Mary sat in her seat watching everyone in such a hurry going about their business and trying to catch the correct train or looking for loved ones who had come to meet them. She was comfortable in her seat having prepared her paper and coffee all ready for her trip to Carlisle where her car was waiting at the station. Mary had been in London to deal with some unfinished business that she and her husband Frank had been dealing with prior to them moving back to the north of England. It was the finalisation of the sale of one of the properties they still owned. Now that had been taken care of she could concentrate on the farm they had purchased. The train started to move slowly up the platform out of Euston station, Mary noticed how dark everything looked, tidy but dirty, years of grime still evident from the steam and diesel days of rail travel "That's stations for you, they all look dirty, I suppose" she thought as she watched casually at what was happening out there while taking a long drink of her coffee. It seemed a while before any greenery appeared but then London is a big city to get out of and as It was the beginning of spring the countryside was starting to come into colour which gave her a good feeling that summer was on its way. The journey home was uneventful. Mary enjoyed her quiet time with her paper and the crossword. "8 down, extra-terrestrial, 9 letters," she thought for a while. "Of course, Astronaut" as she filled in the spaces. Mary looked around and noticed that opposite was a smart young woman, obviously quite successful judging by her clothes and a chap sitting reading his book across the aisle. She noticed a happy couple sitting opposite, laughing and chatting and thought to herself that she and Frank were once like that, not a care in the world when they were together. The man leaned over to the woman and gave her a passionate loving kiss. "How lucky you are, Franks not done that for a while" Mary thought. She dreamt that her life would change one day into love and excitement but realised that this was a long shot. The journey to Carlisle took about 3 hours but to Mary it seemed to go quickly and she enjoyed her time alone people watching and reading her paper. After a while though she did start to settle and become drowsy and decided just to shut her eyes for a while and chill out. She must have nodded off for what seemed a while and heard a voice say 'wake up miss, your stop is approaching.' It was the ticket man, reminding her that they were stopping at Carlisle. The train pulled in and Mary collected her things and got off and started to walk to the exit. It took Mary about 40 minutes to drive to the farm which was hidden in a picturesque valley in the hills out in the countryside. There was a little town close by which serviced their needs with shops of varying types and quite a good nightlife. As she drove down the lane she saw the sign "Gregory's Farm" on the gate post. She didn't know why it had that name but she liked it so decided to keep it. The sign was very old and a little broken but she liked the antiquity of it. Sometimes while working she wondered who Gregory was and what tales he could tell about the farm. She turned in and drove down the track to the house and as the land rover pulled up it created a dust cloud from the dry earth. She got out, waving her hand to move the dust away from her face and collected her bags from the car. As she walked in she called out "Hi Frank, you about?" There was no answer. "He must be in the field," she thought, as she dropped her bags and kicked her shoes off had a stretch and clicked the kettle on before stepping outside to find Frank. Mary was 45, blonde, attractive and approx. 5'2" and was a busy farming girl who was married to Frank Scott. She had no children and because she felt so unsettled in her marriage didn't want any. Even with these doubts Mary was still very enthusiastic about the farm and loved working with the animals. Frank was a quiet man, 47, average build, good looking but with no real interests, as long as the work was done and he had a beer in the evening he was happy these days. They met while working in London. Both had good jobs in estate agency and property development before moving back up to their roots in the north. When the farm came on the market they both agreed that city life was no longer for them and decided to take a chance on something less pressurised that would take them back to nature. The farm she ran with Frank was self-supporting with cattle for milk, chickens for eggs and some sheep and Mary also had her horse Shiloh, a 17 hand cob, black and white or known as a Pinto like an American Indian horse from the Wild West, and a black Labrador called "Monty". The couple did quite well at market and really wanted for little in the way of material things as they'd had the fancy clothes and comforts in the City and lived a simpler life now, but without these things Mary realised that they were still quite lucky compared too many. They both had their own ideas about how they would like to see a little expansion to the farm but were happy to let it move at its own pace. They were not desperate to move forward quickly as they were not short of money because property was so much cheaper up north. They came out with a good profit on the London home and after the purchase up here had a nice amount left in the bank. Frank drove down the track in the old small tractor, an old grey Massey Ferguson, old, noisy, rusty but reliable and good enough for their needs. Frank found this fun to use and sometimes they both got on and had a ride around the farm boundary just for fun. Monty ran ahead of the tractor straight to Mary making a tremendous fuss of her.

"Oh hi, you're back" Frank said, jumping off the tractor

"Great to see you, how was your trip" he said while giving her a welcoming hug.

"All sorted, paperwork's signed and gone, no need to go down again for some time now, fancy something to eat" she said feeling hungry herself, "Sounds good" he said rubbing his stomach.

Mary loved to cook but rarely got the chance to show her true skills these days so meals were always a bit quick to prepare, but they ate well. "John will be here early in the morning with the tanker to fetch the milk," Frank said. "Can we make sure that first thing we put the cows out? You know what a racket that tanker makes" Mary smiled: "I'll make it my first job, Come on Monty, let's get a bite" she said as they both headed to the house. Monty wagged his tail in happiness. The next morning as Mary stepped out onto the veranda with her coffee she was taken aback by how good the start of the day looked. The sun was rising over the horizon and there was a lovely mist covering the ground, "Almost heavenly" she thought. "I'm so pleased we made the decision to come back to the north". Mary had done as Frank asked and moved the cows out into the field so they wouldn't get upset by the noise of the tanker when it arrived. At that moment John's tanker made its way up the driveway and ground to a halt by the barns, scattering dust and exhaust fumes. Mary was always amused by this as John was always as dirty and as scruffy as the tanker "Morning John," she said. Bacon sandwich before you start?"

"You know me so well dear" he replied as they walked to the kitchen. Mary liked to make a fuss of him He was a widower having lost his wife only a year earlier, so she always made him a sandwich and a brew. How are things Mary, are you still enjoying life in the country? "

"Yes very much so thanks, it's good to see it coming together. I wouldn't want to go back to city life now after being here. It's so lovely and we're becoming to feel real locals now "said Mary.

"How's Frank feeling about it?" he asked. "Oh he says very little, but I can tell he's enjoying it, he's so lost in his work and has little time for anything else" Mary said "Including me" she thought. John and Mary chatted while John ate his sandwich and had a welcoming brew. Afterwards John got started on loading the milk. It took a while but when John finished he popped in to say goodbye. Mary and Frank waved him off as the old lorry made its way up the track. The rest of the day went by without Mary and Frank seeing much of each other due to the work each of them had to do, but as the sun went down they made their way back to the farmhouse. Monty was sniffing the grass on the way down while Mary pondered what she could come up with for dinner "Sticky honey chicken with paprika and salad, simple," she thought, "I'll do that, It'll be nice". "Come on boy, let's run" she said rubbing his head, and the two of them had a little race to the house, Monty won, of course! Following dinner they sat and chatted about the day, exchanging thoughts and experiences about their duties, what made them laugh, what they thought could be done better in different areas, Frank liked this evening chat as he felt without this they would lose sight of their direction for the farm's future. "Won't be long," Mary said. "Just popping back to the barn, need to check on the mornings feed for the chucks. Slipped my mind with everything else going on today, come on Mont" the dog scurried away to catch up with her. Frank nodded to her as he poured himself a beer and flopped into his chair with the paper. It was dark, the moonlight made the roof of the farmhouse glisten as though wet although it was a lovely warm summer evening with no cloud cover. Mary was walking back to the farmhouse having dealt with her chickens in the barn and she took a slightly longer path as it was a nice evening. The grass was quite long on this path and Mary liked the feel as it brushed against her jeans and ran through her fingers. As she approached the house she sat for a while relaxing in a rocking chair at a table on the veranda, her hand hanging down stroking Monty who was at her side. She spent a while gazing up at the lovely moonlit sky as she often liked to do. "I love nights like this" she thought. After a while she got up and went to the kitchen to make herself a drink before going to the bedroom to change into a dressing gown and showering. Feeling refreshed she stepped back onto the veranda with a bottle of wine and made herself comfortable in the rocking chair. Frank stepped out and sat in the chair opposite with a beer and his book. It was a warm, sultry summer evening. Mary let the dressing gown fall open a little to cool down but not to expose too much of her chest. She was naked under the gown, which fell away exposing her right leg. Mary had a lovely figure and she knew it, a figure that many men would chase. It was a mystery to her why Frank just didn't seem interested.

"How's your beer," she said to him, trying to strike up some sort of conversation

"Too warm, but ok" he replied.

"I put some in the fridge for you earlier, you obviously missed them," she said, trying to sound caring. "Really? I'll go and have a look" he said as he jumped up and went inside. "Wish he was as keen as that to get to me" Mary thought with a smirk. She did care for Frank a great deal, but for some reason the spark had gone out of their marriage and it had become hard work at times. She had made many efforts in the past to try to revitalise it, but to no avail. She felt that it was getting all one-sided. The night sky was beautiful, not a cloud to be seen and because of where they lived there was little light pollution making the stars carpet the sky with their bright sparkle. Mary let her mind wander and looked out into space. She loved the night sky and would spend hours in the evening just gazing out in awe. She wondered if anyone was out there on other worlds that were as bored as she was. Must get a telescope, she thought!

The next day following a couple of hours work Mary and Frank met for breakfast and chatted about the day's plans.

Then Mary jumped into the land rover for a quick visit into town for some shopping. Food in the fridge was getting low. While there she came upon her friend, Kath, walking towards her. "Hi Kath, great to see you, how's things?" she asked

"Hiya hunni, not too bad, come on I'll buy the coffees, we've not spoken for a while" Kath said as they walked to the trendy little coffee bar "Michaelangelo's" round the corner.

Although Mary wasn't dressed for trendy coffee bars she didn't resist the temptation to spend time with her friend. Kath was 36 an artist who was married to Rob, a lawyer. The girls spent some time chatting about their lives, love and general home life and just enjoying a good catch up.

"How's Frank? Is he still fired up for you?"

"Don't be silly, I've decided he's either celibate or gay" Mary said and they both laughed. "Let's hit the wine bar tonight Mary, we've not been out for ages and you need to get away from the farm now and again, there's a folk band on tonight." Kath was excited about her idea!

"Ok, meet you about 7.00" said Mary with apprehension. What would Frank say about the short notice of a night out she thought, I suppose he'll be ok.

That evening after tea Mary told Frank she was going out for an hour or two with Kath " Ok " he said " Hope you have a good night " Mary was not really surprised by Franks relaxed air. She stood in the shower remembering how Frank used to join her here, how they used to have fun when they were younger and first met. She let the soap wash over her, rubbing her hands over her body longingly. Going through the wardrobe she carefully scanned her dresses as it was a warm evening and she wanted to feel comfortable and was able to pick a sensible summer dress that was a little revealing but tasteful. She felt well when dressed up and rather feminine, something she'd not felt in a while as her usual clothes were now jeans and wellies. As Mary walked into Monty's an air of confidence swept over her, remembering how it felt when she was single and on the dating scene. The place was alive with young people laughing and having a good time. "Mary, we're over here" Kath's voice shouted across the room. A group of people were around a table, people who Mary recognised but had not seen for a while. Alan, a good looking young man about Mary's age pulled a chair out for her and beckoned her to sit by his side. She was flattered. "Red wine please, a Merlot" she said to the waiter "certainly Madam" he replied with a smile. "I've not seen you for ages Mary, you look lovely," said Alan. Mary felt warm, a compliment, and the first in a long time. The waiter returned with Mary's wine, she thanked him and noticed what a lovely glass the wine was in, quite unusual, it was a goblet with a fine red line down inside the stem, almost as if the wine went right down there to the base of the glass. It was very pleasing and looked quality. "It's the farm, Alan, It keeps me and Frank busy, not something you can just drop when you feel like it" she pointed out to him. "However I have to say it is so nice to be out again. I feel free" and she smiled and waved her arms in the air. Alan looked at her in a way which indicated he liked what he saw. He admired her lovely legs and figure and her noticeable cleavage which left little to the imagination, she noticed this, and Mary liked the thought of being found attractive by someone "How is Frank," said Alan "No-one sees him these days either."

"He's ok, just has his head down with work, wine bars are not really his scene now, only cattle markets and auctions" Mary sat and thought about Frank for a moment and realised that he had distanced himself from everyone, not just her, and was lost inside himself these days. "All the people here know him and would give him a welcome and be pleased to see him as they remember how he used to be an outgoing man and was fun to be with" said Alan "I know, and he probably would enjoy it if he made the effort," said Mary in a flat voice."Come on Mary, let's get the dancing going." Kath was on a high, really enjoying herself. Shoes were kicked off and the girls let their hair down and had fun. It had been a long time since Mary had had so much fun, although she did feel a bit guilty that Frank was alone at home. Alan joined them on the dance floor with his jacket off and a lovely party spirit ensued. Towards the end of the evening a slow tune came on, Alan took Mary's hand and held her close as they slowly moved on the dance floor.

"Don't be a stranger" he said to her.

"I know, I won't" she said "It's good to be out"

"What are you doing with yourself now Al?" She enquired.

"I work for a company called Technoscope, It's an American company so I work worldwide but I'm here because we're working on the new observatory up in the hills fitting the radio telescopes in position and aligning them with the computer systems. It's quite complicated and we're going to be working on them for a while, so I'll be here myself for quite a while. We'll soon to be able to look into the depths of darkest space from up there." He seemed excited about his project as he spoke.

"I love the night sky, I sit outside when I can and gaze up in wonder at what's out there, I'll get a telescope one day, I've promised that to myself as a treat" Alan was impressed at her interest "Why not come up one evening when we're up and running with the telescope, it'll be quite a while before the observatory itself is finished but you'll be able to see through the telescope and how it works with the computers. I'll let you know when we're ready"

"I'd really like that Alan, thank you, I will" Mary felt that Alan was genuine and was not trying to come on to her, she had known him a long time and although she knew he liked her he had always remained the gentleman and did not feel threatened by him. He was single and seemed more interested in his career than he did in marriage. She felt excited at the thought of looking through a professional telescope though "wow, this will be cool" she thought to herself!

Mary really enjoyed her evening with friends and was sorry it was coming to an end so soon but Alan offered to walk her to her car. She liked Alan, he was a kind caring man, but there was little sexual spark. When they arrived at the car she kissed him on the cheek and they gave each other a warm hug, and said goodnight before making their way home.

Chapter 2

Mary's car made its way down the dark lanes which led to the farm. She saw the lights on the gateposts and turned in, a short drive up to the farmhouse and she was home safe. Mary put her key in the door, opened it and walked into the lovely hallway of the old farmhouse. The house was in darkness apart from a small lamp in the hallway. Mary stood with her back to the front door and took a moment to admire her welcoming home. Wood panels on the walls adorned with lovely pictures and the most beautiful Minton Hollins tile floor - a credit, she thought, to the Potteries where they were made. Frank had retired to bed, so she made her way to the kitchen, kicked off her shoes and poured herself a large wine. She had only had one drink earlier as she was driving; now she felt comfy as she was home and could relax. Monty was stretched out on his back in his basket, Mary reached down "Hiya mate," she said and tickled his belly. He wagged his tail in delight. After a while and feeling tipsy by now, Mary made her way upstairs and into the bathroom where she undressed and studied herself in the mirror, happy with her figure. She took her nightie and started to put it on then paused, thought for a moment then took it off and put it back on the chair, switched off the light and walked slowly naked to her bed where Frank's eyes were closed. But she knew he was not asleep. The light from the window lit one side of her body as she gently slid in beside Frank, pushing her naked form up to him and wrapping her arm around him. "Have you had a good night with your friends" Frank mumbled "Yes, it was good, but I'm not sleepy yet" as her hand rubbed his chest and she kissed his shoulder. "Try counting our sheep for a while, night hun" Frank said and the snoring began! "Great, goodnight to you too" she thought with an air of frustration. A few days later Mary walked out to Frank who was busy repairing fences in the lower field to take him some lunch and a fresh flask of coffee. It was a lovely day and she was dressed in a shirt tied at the waist with short cut-off jeans. She looked very 'countrified'. "I've been thinking" she said "Let's have a dinner party, we seem to be losing contact with our friends and they did ask about you. It would be good to catch up." He could see Mary was enthusiastic about her idea.

"We've not done that for ages, we could do, I suppose, but who would you invite? "

"I'd start with all the people who don't know you've become a miserable git" she couldn't resist and she giggled as she said this and walked away smiling broadly with a spring in her step. Frank just looked at her with a puzzled expression, shrugged his shoulders then got his sandwiches out. She knew exactly who she would invite. Frank came in later that evening looking very tired "Any chance you can help me to finish off the fencing tomorrow, It's become a bigger job than I thought" he said while scrubbing his hands. "Of course I will, we'll soon crack on with that, soon have it done" Mary said with enthusiasm. They had tea and chilled out on the back porch as it was a warm clear night, "Fancy a beer while I'm getting my wine" Mary said as she stood up and started walking towards the kitchen "Lovely, thanks" Frank said as he sank into his seat. Mary came back and passed Frank his beer, the tin was very cold and condensation was running down it onto Frank's hand He stared at it for a moment before pulling the ring. Mary sat down and poured herself a large white wine, sat back and looked into the sky. The stars were really bright that night and she was able to pick out the aircraft lights adding their little bit of red and green colour to the black sky. "Do you think there's anyone out there Frank?" she said enquiringly "What would anyone want in our fields at night?"

"No silly, I mean out there, in space, little green men, E.T, UFOs, like Bowie's Major Tom, or that chap in the old movie The Day The Earth Stood Still" Mary said while staring out into the darkness. "No chance, I think we are the only ones about, we'd know about it by now if there were. Why the hell would they want to come here anyway?"

"Curiosity maybe" Mary said before relaxing back in her seat. A little while passed and Frank was asleep in his seat. Mary's casual gaze picked up a little light in the distance. Assuming it was a plane she just let her eyes follow it for a while.

It seemed to be getting a little closer but it was small and she could see no detail at all. Then she realised that it was not a plane and it was an unusual colour, bright orange, "strange" she thought? Mary stood up and watched it till it disappeared behind the trees, "How weird "she thought. Next day while in the field with Frank she told him of the sighting "Frank, I saw something strange in the sky last night"

"Really, what did you see?" he said "It was a bright light, sort of orange colour, too far away to see detail but it was weird" Mary replied thoughtfully.

"How many wines had you had" he smiled.

"Oh get lost you, I know what I saw" Mary said giving Frank a playful slap. "I'm off to make us lunch, back in a while." Mary made her way back to the house. "Come on Mont, dinner time" the dog scampered after her. While Mary prepared lunch she remembered mentioning to Frank about a dinner party, this got her mind working "Maybe Saturday if everyone's free, let's see there's Kath, Rob, Alan and me and

Frank. That will do as its short notice," Mary thought. She picked up the phone and called Kath "Hello ghostbusters" said Kath in a silly voice fooling around. "Hi it's Mary. Are you and Rob free for dinner on Saturday at our place" she asked "We most certainly are hunni, what time?" Kath asked.

"About 7.00 if that's ok" said Mary "Any chance you could find out if Alan's free as I don't have his number "Will do, I'll let you know" Mary put the phone down. "Better get his lunch to him" she thought.

They managed to finish the length of fencing and were both really pleased with their efforts for the day. As they walked back over the fields the sun was beginning to set and Mary realised that she still had work to do with the animals which had been left due to the fencing job. She realised it would be a late tea this evening. By now it was 9.30pm, the evening was getting dark and she had almost finished her jobs when she looked up at Shylo, "Oh come on boy, it's too nice tonight for you to be in, how about going out into the field tonight. You can watch the stars with me." It was as if the horse understood he was going out as he seemed to get excited. Mary walked him back up the track to the top field. The night was very quiet apart from the sound of Shiloh's hooves on the ground. She opened the gate and let him free. Off he ran enjoying himself, knowing he had a sturdy field shelter if he did feel like cover from the wind and cold. The bars on the gate dropped down to secure it in position; Mary checked and was happy that her boy was safe for the evening, she stood leaning on the gate watching him for a little while as he had a run around his field, scaring rabbits along the way. She turned to make her way back down the track and froze on the spot. In the darkness of the clear summer sky was the orange light again only this time it appeared to be closer and heading her way. "What the hell is that" she said to herself. She stood and watched it move slowly over the sky. "I wonder if anyone else can see this" she thought to herself. Very slowly the light started to disappear behind the hills and soon it was out of sight. Mary walked quickly down the track back to the house where Frank was sitting in the kitchen with a beer.

"I've seen it again" she said with excitement

"What" Said Frank?

"The orange light, it's just gone over again" she said.

"Come on outside and see if it's about" she said grabbing his arm. They went outside and stood looking around, but there was no sign of it. "It's probably some secret plane from the airbase up north, or something like that, I don't think it's your spacemen" He said smiling to himself. "I've made you something to eat" he said as he walked inside.

"I'll have it when I've had a shower" she replied quite sharply, as she didn't like Frank's sarcasm. After a few minutes Mary went inside and went upstairs, undressed and stood naked in the darkness looking out of the window into the blackness of the night asking herself questions. "What was it? Who is it? what are they doing?" then after a short while she walked slowly to the shower and switched it on to let it warm up, then with these thoughts in her head the warm shower bubbles flowed over her. Mary climbed into bed and lay quietly in the dark thinking of what she had seen when her phone pinged, it was a text message from Kath "Just heard from Alan and he'd love to come on Saturday"

"Great" she thought as she nodded off.

Frank woke Mary with a cup of tea. It was a lovely sunny morning. "Thanks" she said still trying to stir herself.

"I've decided we're having a few over on Saturday and I'll put dinner on for us all, Just us with Alan, Rob and Kath, you ok with that?"

"Yes Ok, be a nice change, I'll try not to be a miserable git" he said with a smirk and winked. The next few days were busy, Frank had a couple of cattle auctions to go to and Mary had the monthly paperwork to get ready for their accountant so they were both on the go. As Saturday drew near Mary was starting to put her mind on what to do for dinner for them all, she was feeling quite excited at entertaining for a change and getting her cookbooks out. The phone rang, it was Kath "Need any help".

"No I'm ok, on top of everything (she lied), looking forward to seeing you all" Mary said with a smile.

"How's Frank about us all turning up?"

"Oh he's fine, looking forward to it, see you later Kath" Mary hung up

"Now, what the hell am I going to cook? Maybe we should have just had a barbie" she thought! Saturday arrived and it was a lovely evening, quite warm with clear skies. Mary was well prepared and Frank had been a big help, much to Mary's surprise.

"It'll be good to see them all, looking forward to it" Frank said. Mary just looked at him, as if to say I hope you can stay awake? Mary was busy trying to bring her ideas for dinner together. She was confident but a little nervous as it had been a while since she entertained at home. She knew in her mind that the friends she had would not be critical as they would all just enjoy each other's company. For dinner she had decided on Bruschetta with goats' cheese and onion marmalade as a starter followed by a game casserole for mains, cheese and biscuits to finish. "Frank could sort the booze" she thought. Frank noticed a car coming down the track towards the house, "Kath and Rob are here". Kath hurried around and tidied the rest of the kitchen. She was happy that all was done and decided just to relax and enjoy the evening. "Hi guys "said Kath as she jumped out of the car waving two bottles of wine "Rob's got the hump as he was horny at tea time and I wouldn't let him play"

"Lucky Kath "Mary thought.

Rob walked up and Kissed Mary "Hi Hunni" Thanks for the invite, looking forward to it" he said as he handed her a lovely bunch of flowers, unaware that its bad etiquette to give the hostess flowers as its creating another job for her to do, like trimming them and putting them in a vase, when she was up to her eyes in cooking and meal prep. "Hi Rob, fancy a beer?" it was Frank, walking out of the kitchen with an arm full. "Cheers Frank, good to see you" Taking a beer from him. "What's this, I've not tried this one" Rob asked. It's Titanic

Iceberg from a Stoke on Trent Brewery, really nice. I get a few of theirs" Frank was enthusiastic about his ales. They went outside to sit on the veranda while the girls were laughing in the kitchen. A taxi came down the track and Monty ran down to greet it. Alan hopped out with a carrier bag in hand containing two bottles of wine, made a fuss of Monty and they both made their way to the house. Frank stood to greet him "Hello mate, good to see you"

"You too" said Alan "Any of those beers going spare?"

"Yes of course" said Frank taking the wine from him, come on in.

"Hi Al" the girls said in harmony like two pop singers "Good to see you" as they got back to the duties in hand and setting the table "Hi girls, something smells good" he said inspecting the cooker. "Hey hands off" Kath said playfully "It's nearly ready, go and sit down." The evening was a success, good food, good conversation and laughter. Mary looked around the table and all were chatting and thought how lucky she was to have such good friends. How easy this little group of people are together. After the meal they all went outside and sat around chilling with drinks and chatting. Mary asked Alan about the telescope and how it was coming on "Its ok, going well, we should be testing it properly next week so you can pop up for a look"

"What do you think about life out there?" Mary asked Alan.

"I think there could well be, but I've not seen anything. There are a lot of theories but nothing is proven"

"I really think there is" said Rob "Too many normal everyday people including pilots and military staff have seen odd things in the night sky which can't be explained, and in this unlimited cosmos we can't possibly the only ones about surely"

"Well my Mary thinks she's seen a spaceship, don't you Mary" Frank said with a smile "E.T's flown over our place looking for a phone".

"What's this then, tell us more" Rob asked showing interest.

"Well it's just that over a night or two I've seen an odd light in the sky, orange in colour, moving slowly and quietly through the sky. I couldn't see any detail but it was odd, and I definitely know it wasn't a plane" Mary said "Other people in the hills must have seen it"

"Only if they were looking up at the time, as most people in the evening are watching T.V" Frank said. "No Frank this was easy to see, it may have been small but it was bright" said Mary with conviction. Alan joined the conversation: " Well you know what you've seen Mary, no-one can take that from you, I've no reason to doubt you, keep your eyes open in case it comes back, mind you, what you can do about it? I don't know other than report it"

"How exciting Mary, men from Mars heading to your farm. I believe that there must be someone out there, we can't possibly be on our own in the universe and why should we think that we are the most intelligent. I bet there are far more advanced civilisations out there than us, what's to say they're not keeping an eye on us" Kath said, considering she could be quite the comedian, was quite serious while talking on this point. Alan looked at everyone: "I will admit folks that when you see what we do through the scopes it is hard to believe that we're alone, I mean there are billions of stars in our galaxy and billions of galaxies out there. However the distance between all these means they would have to have something special to travel in time to be able just to pop in now and again and look at us. Maybe you should all come and have a peek through the scope when it's ready, I think you'll be surprised" he smiled. "Well I think it's quite interesting and I hope I see it again" Mary said hopefully.

"I doubt you'll see it again Mary, most people who see something like this only see it once, enjoy the experience and move on" Alan said, taking a drink from his tin, "Any more of these in the fridge Frank, It's really nice"

"Rob come on its getting late, let's give Alan a lift back, I'll drive" Kath said as she felt Rob had had too much to drink.

"Goodnight all" said Frank as he stood with Mary to wave them off." Loved this evening and we'll do it again soon" Their car then made its way up the track to the road and out of sight. A few weeks went by and Mary and Frank were busy on the farm, the weather was good and the opportunity to get things done was too good. Mary had quite a lot of paperwork to do and Frank was busy buying and selling cattle plus adding to the other animal stock and ongoing repairs to the farm. Their social life had been quiet and they hadn't mixed with anyone much at all in this time. Mary popped over to Frank as he was in the yard; "Fancy lunch?"

"Ok thanks, a sandwich would be great" he said, looking at his grubby hands. Mary went into the kitchen just as the phone rang.

"Hello"

"Hi Mary its Alan"

"Hello, nice surprise"

"Just to let you know that the Observatory is not completely finished yet but the telescopes up and running and, if you like, you can both pop up one night and have a look. After that we could all pop down to the pub."

"Brilliant, over the next few nights if that's ok"

"Ok Mary, chat shortly" Mary put the phone down, "How exciting" she thought and danced over to the fridge for things for a sandwich for them both. "There you go" she said handing Frank his lunch and flask of tea.

"Alan's just called, we can go and have a look through the telescope one night if you fancy"

"Ok, might be interesting. I know you like the night sky but I'd like to see what they pay him obscene amount of money for"

"Is that all you can think about, Alan's salary? What about all the life out there, the never ending cosmos, E.T phoning home?"

"I'd have more interest if we could climb aboard a ship and go and have a look" Frank said as he sank his teeth into his butty. Mary just looked at him shaking her head "Boring git" she thought. After tea it was slowly becoming darker, but it was a lovely evening and Mary thought about walking up to the field to check on Shiloh. She was happy for him to stay out but wanted to check his feed and water. "I'll only be a few minutes Frank, Just going to check on the horse" she said as she left. It was quite a walk to the top field but it was the nicest of all their fields and Mary thought Shiloh had a better view from up there. The grass was tall enough for her to run her fingers through as she walked and Monty was sniffing the ground ahead as if he'd found something interesting to follow. Mary opened the gate, went through and closed it after her and made her way to the field shelter and the hay store to get the hay for his feed. Shiloh was nudging her playfully. "Will you get away mate" she said giving him a shove while she hung up the hay bag to a comfortable height for him to reach his evening snack. Fed and watered Mary then just had a little walk around the field with him and Monty, chatting to them both. As Mary turned around towards the hills she stood still, took a deep breath as there in the sky was the same orange light, moving slowly and silently towards her. It was lower than before and as it approached the orange glow subsided and she could see a triangular shape, dark in colour, maybe a dirty grey. She could see no detail, no windows or doors, but there were some dim blue and red lights around the perimeter. She quickly thought about the size and figured it was about 50ft along the straight sides. It seemed to pause as it went over her, as if the occupants were taking a look at her. Curiously, she didn't feel scared, only shocked at something so unusual. Instinct took over and she found herself waving at it. Shiloh jumped for a second as if startled and Mary looked at him to calm him, and then looked back at the craft but it had disappeared, gone in a split second. She stood there a while, astounded at what she had seen. "Who is it and how the hell did it do that?" she thought "What the fuck is it?" Mary ran down the hill from the field, through the gates and onto the house where Frank was sitting in the kitchen watching the television. "Frank you'll never guess what I've just seen."

"Where the hell have you been" he said quite loudly

"What"

"You heard, I've been all over the place looking for you" he said

"What's wrong with you, you know where I've been, and don't you dare raise your voice to me" She shouted back "I just popped up to feed Shiloh and came straight back".

"You've been gone three and a half hours for God's sake," he said.

"What, I can't have" she said looking at the clock, It was 10.30.

"You left here at 7.00 for a few minutes you said. I've been to the field and you weren't there. The horse was but no you, I've been frantic" Frank said quite upset. "But Frank, I went to Shiloh fed him and came straight back to you, it was 15 minute max" she said with a look of wonder.

"Three and a half hours Mary, believe it!" Frank said with anger in his voice.

"This is not possible" she thought. "What's going on? "

"Frank I have to tell you while I was there I saw the spaceship, it was a big grey thing, It came really close, I saw it" she tried to say convincingly. "Don't come that spaceship crap with me, this is going too far" he said while pulling the ring on a beer can. "I saw a spaceship" she said breathlessly with tears in her eyes. "Oh yeah, did the little green man say hello or did you nip into the woods with him for a quick fuck, because I bet you've been with someone" he said going red with temper. Mary said nothing and walked over to him and hit him so hard across the face that he dropped his beer and fell against the fridge. "Well that would have at least proved that there was one man on this farm that found me attractive" At that she walked out crying and made her way upstairs, stripped off, dropped all her clothes on the floor and climbed into bed. She lay there in the dark thinking about what had happened that night and how three and a half hours had just vanished. She lay for a minute then she got up, walked to the window and looked up into the black sky peppered with bright stars. "It's beautiful out there" she thought "I wonder who it was, where they're from, why are they here, although maybe it is something from the base." She thought about it for a while hoping that it would come back.

It didn't, well not that night........

Chapter 3

In the morning Mary woke, got out of bed and looked out of the window. It was a bright day. She walked naked to the shower and ran the water and watched as the room steamed up. Gently she climbed in and let the warm water wash over her, grabbed the sponge and shower gel and had a few moments of pampering herself with the bubbles. She was in no rush and was lost in thought. After a short while she dropped the sponge and stood under the water flow enjoying the warmth before returning to the bedroom to dress. When she walked downstairs Monty greeted her and she stooped down to give him a fuss. Frank was cooking breakfast for them both with the assumption that Mary would want some. Mary walked over and clicked the kettle on and grabbed a cup to make a coffee, for a while neither of them spoke. "Fancy something to eat, I've done bacon and eggs" Frank said dropping an egg on the floor."I'll have a bacon sandwich, thanks." Frank made her a sandwich and handed it to her. "Did you really see that thing last night?"

"Frank I'm serious it came right over the top, a big grey object"

"Honestly, is that what you saw, what about the orange one?"

"It was orange as it approached but it dimmed and I could see the shape, as clear as you're standing here, then it just…….. Disappeared……poof!"

"Call the police; see if it's something from the airbase further up north."

"They wouldn't believe me; they'd ask if I'd been drinking"

"Well, you had a couple of wines" he said jokingly, "Seriously Mary, If you saw it someone else must have too," Frank said in a caring way, wondering if it was what she said it was. "I don't know what to do now" she said flopping down on the sofa. Nothing was said about the argument they had last night. The day was as busy as usual when Frank noticed a police Jeep coming down the track from the main road and It pulled up outside the house. The door opened and out stepped PC Dave Stewart, the rural police officer. They knew Dave as he popped in now and again while on his rounds checking if all was well "Dave, what can I do for you?"

"Is Mary about Frank? She gave us a call this morning saying about seeing something strange last night. Did you get your wallet out or something? " he said smiling.

"Very funny" Just then Mary appeared wiping her hands.

"Hello, thanks for coming Dave"

"What can I do for you Mary, what's happened" he enquired. "Come with me and I'll show you" and she led the policeman up through the gates and onward up to the top field where Shiloh was grazing. "It happened here at dusk last night, I saw a UFO"

"Oh did you? And what did it look like?" PC Stewart said. "Look Dave I know what I saw, I was with my horse and it came over very slow, very low, dark grey colour, triangular shape, no windows, no sound,. I saw it I really did, it was here, about 50ft across"

"Ok Mary, I don't doubt that you saw something but we've had no other reports of anything strange going on last night, in the sky that is. Did you get a picture of it, had you got your phone with you by any chance, any evidence?"

"No, it took me totally by surprise. I watched it for a short time then it just disappeared, vanished......poof....she said, waving her arms in the air!"

"Frank said that it may have been something from the airbase, what do you think?" "I don't know Mary, could be I suppose, they can be a bit secretive about what they're up too. They don't have to tell us everything they do you know" Dave said trying to be supportive.

"Are you really sure about what you saw Mary?" Dave asked.

"Listen Dave, I'm very sure, it was as clear as I'm looking at you"

"Tell you what, I will check this out. I'll contact the base and make enquires there, if I get no joy I'll contact air traffic at Manchester to see if they can shed any light on it, is that ok for now"

"Thanks Dave, I'd appreciate it" she didn't say anything about the time loss.

They walked back to the car.

"I'll be in touch" said Dave as he got in his Jeep and pulled away.

A few days later Mary was preparing tea for them both when she heard a car pull up, it was Kath and Rob.

"Hiya folks, good to see you"

"We were in the area and thought we'd surprise you"

"Come on in, I'll get us a drink, Frank will be here shortly, will you stay for tea, It's a stew and I've done plenty, I'd like a chat"

"Love to Mary, we've no plans, that would be great, eh Rob"

"Lovely" said Rob as he helped himself to a wine bottle from the rack.

"Hi Guys" said Frank as he walked through the doors, what's up"

"Nothing at all, just fancied seeing our good friends, we were on an errand down the road and thought we'd stop by" said Kath with a smile. "Stopping for tea" he asked

"Try and stop us "Kath said giving him a hug. Mary was getting the glasses for the drink when Kath turned to her.

"What's up Mary, something exciting happened?"

"I've seen it again Kath" Mary said excitedly while pouring Kath's drink

"Oh Frank got it out then at last? "

"No, you twit; the spaceship. I've seen it close up as clear as you are standing here"

"When was this then" Kath said as she picked up her drink.
"The other night, I was with Shiloh up in the field. I saw the orange light and felt that it was getting closer and before I realised it had come very close to me and was hovering over the field. Not a sound came from it, no windows or doors that I could see just a dark grey shape sitting there as though it was watching me".

"Boy, you really need that shag."

"Oh stop it Kath, I'm really serious"

"What did you do then?"

"I waved at it."

"You waved at it, men from Mars and you just waved at it"
"Well it's funny because you'd think I'd be scared but when I thought about it after I wasn't, I felt an anticipation but also a sort of calmness. I looked at it for what seemed a while but was probably seconds, Shiloh stirred and I glanced at him and when I looked back it had gone, nowhere to be seen"

"And"

"And…..I came down and told Frank, following a little of his usual sarcasm he suggested I call the police"

"And did you?"

"Yes they were here earlier, Dave the officer says he'll look into it and come back to me so we'll have to wait and see" She thought for a while then followed on" I was wondering, why the light seemed to come this way a couple of times now, why this direction, why stop over me and also Kath something weird happened. I was only up there for a few minutes when this happened and I rushed down to tell Frank and he said that I'd been gone for three and a half hours, Kath he was frantic, saying he'd been to the field and I wasn't there, that's three and a half hours I can't account for, what's going on Kath?"

"Maybe they're going to whisk you away" Kath joked.

"Seriously Mary, it is strange. I wonder who it is? I'd love to see it myself, let me know what the police say. Now come on lighten up and lets join the boys or they'll drink everything". As they walked back in they passed Rob handing biscuits to an enthusiastic Monty. "You'll get my dog fat, Rob" Mary joked. The night went well, and Mary tried to put the experience behind her as everyone enjoyed the meal and lively chat and laughter which they always had when they got together. A few days went by and Mary and Frank were busy with their usual farm work and they had been to market selling some of their produce. They were actually travelling back from one market in the Jeep, Frank was driving and Mary was sitting quiet just letting her mind wander when she said to Frank: "Listen, times moving on and I don't feel like cooking. Fancy an Indian in the village?"

"Are we dressed for it" he said

"We may be in our Jeans but we're clean, let's go and don't spare the horses" she smiled. They pulled up outside "The Taste of Spice" in the village, switched the Jeep off and sat for a moment, it had been a long drive from the market. "Come on then, I'm peckish" Frank stated as he jumped out and shut his door. Mary watched him walking to the door for a moment before joining him as she felt so tired she didn't feel that she could move.

"Ahh…..Mr and Mrs Scott, How good to see you" Sanjay always remembered their names and gave them a nice welcome although they were not frequent visitors. "You follow me as I have a nice seat for you both" he said as he took them to a cosy corner seat. "Thank you Sanjay, you're a star" Mary said with a smile as she flopped into her seat. Frank sat down opposite and picked up his menu.

"Can I get you something to drink" Sanjay asked "A pint of lager" Frank replied.

"Make that two please" Mary added a she had worked up a thirst today.

"What's your fancy then?" she said as she perused the menu.

Frank and Mary were quiet while they looked through the choices. Sanjay returned with the drinks, condensation forming on the glass.

Mary ran her finger down the wet glass as she thought of the old film "Ice cold in Alex" in which John Mills did the same before drinking his down.

"What may I get you?" Sanjay enquired.

"I'll have the Chicken Naga Please" Frank said, handing in his menu. "And I'll have the Chicken Passanda, also we'll have pilau rice, 3 poppadum's with chutney to start and a peshwari nan, thanks" Mary handed him her menu. They both sat back and enjoyed a long drink. There didn't seem many people in the restaurant but it was early really, it was quite a nice atmosphere, very friendly. The meal arrived and they both sat quietly while enjoying their choices. Whilst they were eating a couple came to walk passed them, it was PC Dave Stewart with his wife Sue, quite a tall woman but very good looking with dark hair, she runs a beauticians in the town. "Hi Frank, Mary, didn't see you two come in, hope you enjoy it as much as we have"

"Hi Dave, good to see you, the foods good as usual" Said Frank wiping his mouth. "We're popping over to the Crown for one before home, fancy joining us when you're done here. Wouldn't mind a chat Mary about what's been happening up your way" Dave said. "Yes ok we'll see you over there," Mary said. "Ok see you in a bit" Dave said, Sue smiled and waved as they walked out. "I wonder what he's found out" Mary said" How exciting" When they finished they asked for the bill, Sanjay hurried over and placed it down with some complimentary chocolates. Mary picked it up and checked it, £32.00, she placed he card down and a few coins as a tip as they always did. Sanjay collected it, went away then came back with the card as Frank and Mary were already by the door. "Come on let's see what Dave has to say" Mary said while sliding her hand under Franks arm as they crossed the street. They reached the pub and pushed the door open. There were quite a few in but they spotted

Dave and Sue easily. "Hi Dave, Hi Sue" Frank said. "What can I get you folks?" Dave said holding his glass up so the staff could see it. "Two Carling Dave" Mary said "We've a thirst on after today trip to the market."

"Two Carlings, A Pedigree and a white wine spritzer please Joe" Dave shouted up to Joe the barman "How was the trading today?"

"Pretty good, we always do quite well, we breed good stock" Mary said giving Frank a high five.

"Have you found anything out Dave" Mary asked with a quizzical look.

"Well I did do some digging, but we have to be careful because the military can get a bit touchy and if I upset the wrong people it could hamper my promotion plans, Anyway I spoke to my colleagues in the office and bounced it off them, We obviously got the odd daft quip, and some of them said they'd spoken to people in the past who claimed to have seen things but couldn't prove anything. However they all said they had a belief that we're not alone as sightings of the unusual goes back hundreds of years. No-one said they had had any experience with this sort of enquiry round here though. I spoke to the Military at R.A.F Boulmer which as you may not know is an active air surveillance station base over the hills in Northumberland. They compile a recognised air picture, with radars monitoring the airspace around the UK and providing tactical control of the "Quick Reaction Alert" force, and asked if they were out on air manoeuvres or testing anything unusual on the night in question, and they deny everything. They state that all operations at the moment at RAF Spadeadam which is close to you are suspended for a few days due to runway work as they want to be able to land heavier aircraft in the future and to be honest I don't doubt them. If anything strange were to be picked up they are the ones who would find it, and if so they would scramble fighters from RAF Lossiemouth to check it out. "My friend at Air traffic control at Manchester tried to be helpful and checked if anything unusual had been reported and he came back with nothing to report. However

Mary when we first spoke about your experience I will admit I was a bit sceptical but I've got to be truthful, what happened to you really does interest me and I don't doubt you at all"

"Thanks Dave, I can't believe that it didn't register anywhere or no-one else saw it."

"Mary, maybe someone did see it but didn't show the interest in it that you did and passed it off as a plane. You say you've seen this UFO a number of times now?"

"Yes I have, at one time very close up."

"Were you not scared" asked Sue, having been listening closely.

"Surprisingly not Sue, if anything I had a feeling of calm, as if it was saying that it would not harm me, although I was surprised to see it of course"

"You will probably find that you never see it again but my advice is if you do try to get a picture" Dave said "And not a selfie of you with it in the background" They all laughed, then Frank cut in "My round I think" as he attracted the attention of Joe the barman. "Not seen you in the shop for a while Mary, why don't you treat yourself?" Sue said. "Oh I would love a break, get my hair done , a bit of pampering, seems like ages since I had the works" Mary said running her fingers through her hair "I'll make a point of having a weekend off and coming in"

"You do that, then me you and Kath can hit the town" she said smiling. Dave and Frank were talking when they were approached by George Fellows an older farmer whose farm was a lot further down the lane from Franks place and was double the size of Frank's. "Hello Frank' Dave you guys ok?"

"Hi George, can I get you one in as it's my shout?" Frank said

"No it's ok, I've got one on the bar over there, I wondered Frank If you can pop over to my place with your tractor, we've got a problem you may be able to help with"

"Course I can, what's up?"

"Well my missus was getting the sheep in the other day and she was down in the bottom field when she noticed something odd in the stream, it's an old car, there's no-one in it so I could do with another tractor to help to pull it out pull it out"

"I'll come round tomorrow if you like. Do you know anything about this, Dave?"

"No reports of anything have come in, but I'll have a look tomorrow George" Dave said looking thoughtful "I'll meet you there tomorrow Frank."

"Thanks boys" George said before returning to his pint.

"Strange" Frank said.

"Probably been stolen and not reported missing yet" Dave said taking a drink from his glass. Having stayed for more than they were going too they all said their goodbyes and made their way home. As Mary and Frank opened the door they could see Monty in his basket fast asleep on his back.

Mary went over and tickled his tummy and his tail started wagging. "Fancy a trip over to Old George's place with me tomorrow, there's a car in his stream that he wants pulling out and he needs our tractor" Frank asked Mary.

"Ok…..sounds interesting!" she said. The next morning Frank got the tractor started and was waiting by the back door for Mary to come out. As she did she ran to the tractor and hopped on. She was still tying her hair up as Frank slid it into gear and set off up the drive and down the lane with Monty running behind.

Chapter 4

It took about 15 Mins to reach George's as the tractor was powerful, but not very fast. Attached to the tractor were a number of heavy ropes that Frank felt would come in handy and when they arrived PC Dave Stewart was already there as they could see his Jeep. "Come in the house folks, kettles on" George shouted over the noise of the tractor. Frank switched it off and they made their way into the kitchen of the farmhouse and into the kitchen. It was typical of old farmhouses, very roomy with a huge table dominating the centre and an Aga coal fired cooker set in the huge chimney breast. The warmth in there was very evident as once these cookers were lit they generally did not let them go out, so they were usually on for 24hrs at a time. Monty settled by the warm cooker looking very happy. Sitting at the table was PC Stewart with a huge mug of tea and a plate of toast which George's wife Ethel playing Mother had insisted that he ate. Two more mugs of tea appeared for Frank and Mary followed by some toast. "Oh no we've had brekkie" Mary thought as the toast arrived, but when she saw it she changed her mind. The toast was good thick bread toasted to perfection covered with real butter, it looked divine, and she couldn't resist and it tasted gorgeous. She lost herself in her thoughts with the first piece as the men were talking about the car in the stream. "I'll guide you all down there, good to see the ropes Frank, thanks," George said.

"Have you had a look Dave?"

"Not yet Frank, thought I'd wait for you" he said tucking into more toast. Mary was reluctant to leave the lovely, traditional kitchen as she felt so comfortable. She had a little glance around as she was leaving. Their tractor plus Georges with Dave on board made their way across the fields. It seemed a long way to Frank's but George's farm was so much bigger than their own. Eventually they came to the stream. They jumped off the tractors and walked to the edge, the car was partially submerged under the water but the water was not too deep so getting in to attach the ropes should not be a problem. "How and why the hell has this ended up here" Frank said scratching his head. "It looks to me as if it's come from the lane up there on that hill, there's a small break in that hedge over there" Dave said pointing to an area that looked as though it had been pushed down but was starting to straighten itself out. "Once we get it out I'll do a check on the registration to try and reunite the owner, if they realise yet that it's missing" Dave said while pulling his wellies on. Frank was unloading the ropes and Mary was stretching them out from the tractors to the river. George was first in the water feeling about for the towing bracket at the front and frank went in at the back to try and locate one there. George and Frank were well prepared with heavy duty waders on so they were comfortable while carrying out this task. Dave stepped in the water trying to be helpful but sank up to his knees as his wellies filled with water, he just stood there...stuck. Everyone was laughing really hard. Eventually even Dave saw the funny side and broke into laughter as he struggled to get out onto the bank leaving his wellies deep under water, "Never mind Dave, you'll soon dry out" said Mary while in fits of laughter. Fortunately his shoes and socks were in the boot of his car so he could manage till they were back at the house. Frank and George found it a struggle to attach the ropes but eventually they succeeded and made their way to the bank and out of the stream. Ethel had made flasks of tea for them so they all had a drink and a break before attempting to pull the car out. "I don't know, if we have joyriders they're usually all the way over into town, if kids have left this here that means they have a major walk home. Also we've not had a missing car report for weeks, still let's get a registration number and see where that takes us" Dave said, still shaking water out of his uniform. Mary stood by Dave as the tractors burst into life and started to take the tension, she looked him up and down trying not to laugh at his situation. The tractors started to pull, both tractors were attached to the front of the car as the back of the car was deeper in the water. At first it was quite hard but slowly the stream started to give up its prize. The car started to slowly make its way up the bank and onto the field and as it did so the tractors made sure they had pulled it well clear before stopping. Water was pouring from every possible place on the car. It car was quite a new Ford Fiesta, red in colour and certainly not the sort that a joyrider would go for. Dave went over and opened the door, once again without thinking and he got another soaking, much to everyone's delight. Thankfully it confirmed that no-one was inside other than some soaking wet personal items, but nothing to identify the owner. Dave walked around and opened the boot only to find it empty. "Well, now we have a registration number I'll do a check. If you guys tow it up to the farmhouse I'll get the garage to come and collect it and take it to the station yard" Dave said. "Are the keys still in it Dave" said Mary; she was now sitting on the tractor with Frank. "Yes, but it's not going to start is it?"

"No Dave we realise that but if we're going to tow it we need someone to steer it"

But its soaking wet inside there" said Dave pointing at the seat.

"So are you, now get in" said Mary as everyone started laughing. Dave got in and felt the water held in the seat soak him even more "Bloody great, just bloody great" he thought as the tractors took the strain and started up the fields heading back to the farmhouse. Monty was running at their side with a big stick he'd found looking pleased with himself. The next few days were uneventful, both of them dealing with varying farming duties. Frank was tied up with the tractor for a while because he felt that the pulling on the car had caused issues and the rusty old thing appeared to be suffering a bit. Mary was busy moving fencing up on the top field to give Shiloh more room to run around, not that it needed doing but she was just happy to do so. She had attached a trailer to the quad bike and taken some bales of hay up with her to put in the store shed by his field shelter but while she was busy with the fence Shiloh found the hay. Mary spotted him from across the field "Oh no, the hay" she thought and ran up to stop him. "Come on boy, you'll need some of this for later, don't be greedy" She laughed to herself at how sneaky he'd been, but she loved him. "I'll tell you what" she said whispering into his ear" I'll come up in the morning and we'll go for a nice long run, just me and you and Monty can come too" she said, It was as though the horse understood because he lifted his head, neighed and kicked the floor with his hoof. "Ok boy, see you later" as she climbed onto the quad and slowly made her way back down the track. When she arrived back she was surprised to see Alan there, sitting on the porch with Frank and both had a beer in their hands. "Hello, what brings you here? How nice to see you. Have you come to stop Frank working and take him down the Crown?" she said with a smile. "Well you're partly right, I've come to take you both down the Crown but only when you've been with me to the observatory for a look at the telescope"

"Oh Alan that would be great, I've been meaning to talk to Frank about coming up but with one thing and another I keep forgetting" she said. Mary made her way into the kitchen to get herself a drink.

"It's not very dark yet Alan, would you like a quick bite with us beforehand" Mary said while washing her hands in the kitchen.

"What's the choice?"

"Yes or no "was the reply from Mary

"Well…..It's a yes then" Alan said casting a glance at Frank who was smiling. Mary rustled up something simple and quick, Chilli and Rice with crusty bread and a bottle of wine. They all sat, took their time and enjoyed the promptu meal before Frank and Mary went up to get changed while Alan played with Monty. After a short while they jumped in the jeep and followed Alan out of the farm and off for a twenty minute ride into the hills to the observatory. By now it was quite dark. When they arrived Mary and Frank jumped out of the jeep and looked up at the sky and were taken by the masses of stars which were visible from up here. They looked at the buildings and were impressed as the buildings were a lot bigger than they imagined. There were two flat roofed buildings which looked like offices and one which was circular with a domed roof, Frank figured out that this was were the main telescope was fitted. Alan called them into one of the office buildings. There were a couple of men in there they nodded as to say hello "Firstly this is where a lot of the research is sorted out. All of the work enquiries will be bought together in here and investigated before the scopes are put to work. Not sure how many people will be in here though" he said while Frank and Mary looked around, for a while whilst Alan spoke. "Come with me through here and look at the telescopes" Alan said as he opened another door and walked through into the circular building.

"Wow they're bigger than I thought said Frank, looking up at the structures. "Alan what actually is an observatory, I mean what goes on here?" Mary asked. "Well…..briefly …..It's a location used for observing terrestrial or celestial events, astronomy, climatology , metrological etc……Things that are useful to scientists in monitoring what's going on in space or in our atmosphere."

"Well who uses them mostly?" Frank asked. "Astronomers mostly, so much better than eyes, depending on the telescope. They can see colours or can collect light that our own eyes are unable to, such as radio, microwave, infrared, x-rays, etc."

"Hang on Alan, keep it simple, you're losing me," Mary said. "Well….its main purpose is to make objects in outer space appear bright, plenty of contrast and as large as possible. I suppose that defines its three main functions, light gathering, resolution and magnification. "

"How do they work" Mary asked.

"Well, simply put, these are called reflector telescopes so the image is formed when it hits the curved mirror, then magnified by a second mirror and sent to the eye piece for you to view. The smaller of the two is attached to the computers so in a minute we'll find you something to look at then you can look through the bigger one and then we'll get the little one to show us the same image on the screen."

Alan sat down at the computer and started typing. Frank and Mary saw the telescopes start to turn slowly and as they did so the large domed roof began to open to show the night sky. After a few moments the machinery stopped. "Now then I'm going to dim the lights in here and you can have a look through here." Alan stepped up and pointed at the eyepiece "Go on Mary, you first" Frank said. The lights dimmed and Mary stepped up and put her eye in the rubber eye cup of the viewing lens "Oh my god, that's brilliant" she said "What is it?" Alan stepped forward "That's our closest galaxy neighbour, the Andromeda galaxy. Its 2.5 million light years away from us. It looks the same as our own as it's a spiral galaxy."

"Frank look at this, it's brilliant" Mary said excitedly.

"Frank stepped up and put his eye on the viewer "Wow that's fantastic, so difficult to comprehend the size of it" he said.

"Now look on here" Alan said pointing at the large screen. "I programmed the smaller one to view the same thing and this is the image it's picked up, stunning eh." The image on the screen was outstanding, Frank and Mary couldn't believe the quality of the image they were looking at. As they were looking at the screen the door opened and one of the men came in. "Sorry to disturb you folks but it's getting late and we need to drop some wiring in here" he said politely. "Yes ok, well leave you to it" Alan replied. "Sorry Mary, I did think we'd have more time but we'll have to let them get on."

"It's ok Alan, really pleased we've been able to see what we did, absolutely amazing" Mary replied.

"So it's to the pub for a quickie then?" Frank suggested

"Sounds good" was the reply in harmony as they made their way out and off to the Crown. The next morning Frank and Mary were up early as usual and Frank was going through the paperwork as he decided he wanted to bring this up to scratch today. After a small breakfast Mary said she fancied taking Shiloh for a small run. "Why not" said Frank "It's a nice morning so spy your chance". Mary moved the breakfast things and tidied up, left it all neat and tidy for Frank. Mary and Monty walked up the track to the top field where Shiloh was. She could see that he was pleased to see her. She opened the gate and let herself in closing the gate behind her. She handed some hay to Shiloh to distract him whilst she put on his saddle, did up the straps and made sure he was comfortable. She put her foot in the stirrup and climbed on and settled in ready for a short ride. Mary made her way to the gate and opened it, she could easily reach the latch from where she sat, and pushing it open they walked out and turned right to walk up the track and around the perimeter of the farm. It was a lovely day, the sun was shining and she felt really good, free and enjoying the solitude which surrounded her. They walked steadily along the track for quite a while until she turned off to walk through some woodland which she always found so picturesque.

The smell of the pine trees always pleased her and as she walked through she came out in the meadow which was in the centre of the woodland and was quite open. The grass was quite unusual here and was quite long, coming up almost to Shiloh's knees. Not that it bothered Shiloh, of course, he was enjoying himself as Mary could tell. Mary was lost in her thoughts when she realised that the grass had become unusually short "Funny" she thought "Where's the grass gone?" She sat up on Shiloh looking around and noticed that she was in an area a bit like a small football pitch. The area was about 60 to 70 feet around and the grass wasn't short, it was flattened. She could see the edge and the grass was still high. "How odd" she thought, "Who's done this, there are no kids up here who would want to play football, most of them are in the village or town." She jumped off Shiloh give him a break, but also to have a look around the area. She noticed a huge log sitting in the long grass so walked up and sat down to enjoy the quiet. From where she was she could see the flattened grass and was casually staring at it when she realised the grass looked as though it had been caused by a whirlwind as it seemed flattened in a circular motion. She sat looking at it for a while watching Shiloh nibble at the longer grass. Then she decided it was time to move on and climbed onto Shiloh. "Here Monty, lets go" she shouted. Monty came out of the long grass with a stick in his mouth. "Come on Shiloh, let's go" giving him a very gentle kick. As she was walking through the trees she realised "Oh my God….. It's a crop circle" she turned back, rode up and had another look. "It is, it's a bloody crop circle, I don't believe it!" she sat mesmerised at what she was looking at.

Chapter 5

Mary rode Shiloh back to the field with Monty running behind and as she got to the gate she reached down and lifted the latch. Shiloh walked in followed by Monty. Mary jumped down and took off his saddle to put away. She checked he was fed and watered before making her way back to the farmhouse. Frank was sitting in the kitchen with a brew and a sandwich "Hi, fancy a cuppa" he said. "Thanks, yes I will, Frank I've been out on Shiloh up to the meadow and would you believe it there's a crop circle up there" she said excitedly. "Really, are you sure no-ones just doing something up there?"

"But who, we're the closest to that and there's no sign of building or anything like that, there's really not enough kids around here who would want to do that. Anyway it's huge" she said picking up the cup of tea he had made for her. "I know" she thought and put her cup down and picked up the phone and pressed the buttons. "Hi this is Mary Scott up at

Gregory's farm, can I speak to PC Stewart please?" there was a pause.......

"Hi Mary, what's up?"

"Can you pop over here when you're free, I need to show you something."

"Of course, it'll be about an hour, is that ok?"

"See you then" she said putting her phone down and picking up her cup. Soon Mary heard the sound of Dave's jeep pulling up outside and Monty jumped up to go and greet his visitor. "Hi Dave, thanks for coming" Mary said as she walked out to meet him. "No probs" he said while engrossed in playing with Monty, then when he'd done "Right.......what's up" he said, giving Mary his full attention. "Hop on the quad bike behind me Dave, I want to take you to see something."

"I'm intrigued" said Dave as he climbed aboard. They took off up the track creating dust as they went, Monty running behind them excitedly with a stick in his mouth. After a while they reached the pine trees and rode through the long grass into the clearing and then Mary stopped the bike and stepped off. Dave brushed the dust out of his hair, straightened it then got off and joined Mary.

"Well……..what do you think" she said, looking around.

"Nice place for a picnic" he said, not sure of what he should be looking at.

"Look around Dave, It's a crop circle."

"Is it, are you sure?" he said looking a bit closer at his surroundings "Look Dave, It's a perfect circle of about 60ft, look how the grass is pushed down, not one blade is broken just pushed flat and in a way that a whirlwind has done it in a circular pattern," Mary said while pointing this out.

"Oh yes, I can see what you mean, It's perfect."

"Look Dave it must be that UFO, it's landed and made this for some reason" she said excitedly. "Mary, I believe that you saw something, you know I do, but there's not one bit of proof, we've not seen anything creating this. What can I do, I can't do anything can I? If it lands and you stand next to it, ask them if they'll wait then give me a call and I'll nip over" he said sarcastically, "Now would you run me back please?" Mary realised he was right while riding back and began feeling guilty for wasting his time and when they arrived back she gave him a hug, thanked him for coming over and watched him drive off. Mary walked to the porch and up the steps then took a seat with Monty at her side. She sat for while reflecting on things that had happened to her recently. "I don't think anyone believes me with all this, I'm not going to mention anything else, I know it's happened to me and that's all that matters" at that she stood and went inside "C'mon fella, tea time" and Monty followed with tail wagging. The next few days were uneventful. Frank had sorted the tractor which they were both pleased about. Although old, they both were fond of that tractor. The farm was looking good, tidy and well cared for. It was a working farm but they both had a quality that they didn't want it looking scruffy around the place and had pride in it. This particular morning Mary was engrossed in her work now and had put the past experiences behind her. "Mary we need to decide what we're going to do with the small field," Frank said which came as a surprise to Mary as she hadn't really given that field much thought. It was only small and they'd just let it lay fallow. There were three men with metal detectors who had shown more interest in it than Mary and Frank. They did have permission and used to just turn up now and again; nice men, Ron, Tony and Joe. They had found bits and pieces but nothing of real interest. It made Mary smile when she saw them on a sunny day sitting with their sandwiches. She thought they were like the men in "Last of the Summer Wine."

"Maybe you're right, I'll pop and have a look and see if I can get inspiration with meditation thoughts" she said smiling "Look, never mind the hocus pocus, just come up with some decent suggestions" Frank said shaking his head. Just then the sound of a jeep got their attention as it came down the driveway. Mary made her way around the side of the house to see PC Dave Stewart pulling up. He switched off his engine and got out of the jeep and started fussing Monty. "Hi Dave, good to see you, what's up" Mary said with wonder in her voice. "I've got a bit of news you may be interested in regarding the car in the ditch"

"Oh…go on?"

"Well we did a check on the registration and we found the address of the owners, and we found that it was an address in the Midlands. Local police went around but found they were away on a break. This meant we had to leave it for a while till they arrived home"

"Oh dear, well at least you know who owns it though" Mary replied "Well, we had a bit of good luck this morning when Geoff from the garage in town called us"

"And?"

"A man and a woman turned up a couple of days ago and asked him if he could help as they had been in an accident, gave him directions and wanted him to go and fetch the car. Now, knowing that we had recovered it and taken it to the pound Geoff was quick to give us a call as he felt that the couple appeared nervous. He was good enough to give us the address where they are staying." We invited them down to the station to give us a statement, made them comfortable and they told us what happened. "What had happened to them then? " Mary said looking interested. "Well, they're an elderly couple and they're booked in to a hotel not too far away as this is where they're taking their break, travelling around looking at the scenery around here. It appears that one evening recently they were travelling back to their hotel when they took a wrong turn and the road brought them onto the lane up above George Fellows farm. Now by this time it was getting quite dark and they were a little unsure where they were."

"Ok come on Dave, get to the point" Mary said. Dave looked at her before continuing "Well....It appears that while on that lane as they went around the bend they were faced with a big orange bright light flying straight at them. They say that they've never seen anything like it. They said it was huge and they felt it was going to hit them and at that point they lost control of the car and it went down the hill and into the ditch. They were unhurt and made their way back to the road where a lady stopped and gave them a lift to town. They say they've only just come forward on this as they have been so scared by the incident. When I asked why they hadn't called us they said they didn't think anyone would believe them".

"Dave don't you see, It's true what I've told you, we've seen a UFO," Mary said. "You have to believe me now."

"Well, I will admit Mary I would have looked at their story differently had I not heard of your experiences. I've no reason to charge them with anything as no damage was done to George's property and I'm pretty sure they were not drunk. They've been told where the car is being held and they are going to arrange to have it collected and taken to a garage locally. They said that they felt the holiday was spoiled and have now caught the train home"

"How amazing, I'm so glad they're safe though" Mary said

"Well it seems to confirm your story Mary, but you do realise that even though the three of you have seen this there is still no proof and even if there was there's nothing that anyone could do about it, so enjoy the memory of your events hunni," Dave said as he opened the jeep door. "Must go now Mary, see you two soon for a beer. "Thanks Dave, thanks for letting me know that news," she said and waved as he started to drive off. Mary ran round to Frank and spent some time telling him about Dave's visit. Frank found it very interesting and sat and listened. They spoke for quite a while before getting back to their chores, Mary remembering about going to have a look at the little field. Mary started walking down to where it was, the air was quite still and it was a lovely warm day. Monty trotted down behind her enjoying some new smells as they didn't come down this way very often. Mary approached the field and came to the gate, opened the big, rusty latch and swung the gate open. As she walked across she felt that the field had a rough, rustic charm about it with the wild flowers and tall grasses, adding an air of mystery. "Maybe we could offer it to the village school for a small fee so they can practice their gardening skills, or grow veg. "she thought. "It's too small for horses really, I think Shiloh would feel trapped in there. Just then from nowhere a great gust of wind almost blew Mary off her feet. Grass was waving around, leaves were blown up in the air, like a small tornado. As quick as it arrived it disappeared and all calmed down "Where the hell did that come from she said to herself, brushing her fingers through her hair. Monty was unconcerned; he'd found a nice stick to chomp on. She looked around but all had gone back to normal. "Strange" she thought. Mary walked back to the gate, Monty followed with his stick. Once he had passed through she closed the gate behind them both. "We'll have to give this some thought, it's a shame if we can't put it to some use" she thought while leaning on the gate. After a little while she started walking back to the house and trying to think of ideas for the field. "I'll put it to the gang next time they're all here, they're always full of bright ideas" She thought. When she got back to the farm Frank was in with the cows." You are right Frank, we should find a use for that field, it's a shame that it's just sitting there"

"I've thought that for a while, but what could we do with it that would make money" he said thoughtfully.

"What about if we ploughed it up then planted vegetables?" she said "Good idea Mary, we could sell them in bulk to the shops in the village or put a sign up on the lane and offer them to the public. Mary thought for a while, "Or, why not put bee hives in there? People are paying good money for honey. Local honey is supposed to be better for you because of its protective health qualities; you know I like the thought of that." She smiled to herself. "Mary if you fancy that it's ok with me, in fact we could do both, the fields big enough"

"Ok, I'll check it out. What do you fancy for tea Frank? "

"Surprise me "he said walking in amongst the cows. "Great" she thought "He's so helpful." Mary went into the house and into the kitchen to check the freezer, then while she was thinking about what to have she poured a wine and threw a biscuit to Monty. "I know what we'll do, I'll fire up the barbie" she thought. Mary pulled her phone from her Jeans and called Kath "Hi it's me. Are you two free for an hour this teatime, as I thought I'd fire up the barbie."

"Yes, as it happens we'll be down your way at about 5ish, is that ok "Kath asked.

"Just right matey, see you then" she said putting the phone back in her jeans.

"Right.....to the butchers" She said to herself. Mary jumped into the jeep followed by Monty and he settled on the seat beside her looking out of the window. The jeep burst into life and Mary drove off into the village. She was lucky as there was a parking space right outside the butchers as she pulled up. She jumped from the jeep. "Stay there boy" she said to

Monty as she shut the door. Mary walked into the shop. "Hi Stan" she said with a smile.

"Hello Mary, how's things on the farm"

"Great thanks, few more plans in place so I'll keep you informed"

"Sounds exciting, what can I get you hunni" Stan said wiping his hands on his apron. "I'm just going to fire up the barbie so I'd like four small steaks, some sausage and some pork chops. That way there's a choice for them" while Stan prepared her order Mary looked around the shop and found it very appealing. Stan always had a good range of produce on show. "There you go Mary, I'll put it on your bill, sort it out later you go and enjoy yourself" he said to her. "Thanks Stan, you're a sweetie" "And here" he said as an afterthought "We can't forget Monty, here's a big knuckle bone, it won't splinter and it's full of marrow"

"Oh thank you Stan, he'll love it" she said as she left the shop. She jumped into the jeep and shut the door "Have I got a treat for you Mont" she said to him as she could sense the bone. When she got back she started to prepare everything for tea. She was only going to keep it simple, a mixture of salad with dressings and they could choose what meat they wanted to eat and she could freeze the rest. It's the company that counts she thought. "Hiya, we having a barbie then" Frank asked as he was wiping his hands. "Yes, Kath and Rob are coming just for a quick hour and a bite, they'll be here about five o clock"

"Ok, I've done in the barn, I'll nip up and have a quick shower" then he left and went upstairs. A short time later when Mary had finished preparing the food she put the coals on and lit the barbie. "I'll let that sort itself out while I have a shower" she thought. Mary made her way upstairs to their room and started to undress. She undid the clasps of her dungarees and let them fall to the floor, stepped out of them and then took off her t-shirt. She was in her bra and pants and made her way to the bathroom only to find Frank was still in the shower, the room full of steam and the radio on.

"Oh I thought you'd done" she said as she started to walk out "I won't be long, nearly done" he said without looking her way. She stood in the doorway for a moment before walking back in, she unclipped her bra and let it fall to the floor and then took off her pants before getting in the shower with him, and she looked him up and down and thought he had a lovely body. For a moment she looked down and thought it looked like he was pleased to see her as she started to lather her lovely youthful body. "I'm done now, I'll give you some room" he said as he stepped out and onto the mat and grabbing a towel off the rail. "See you in a min" he said as he went to the bedroom. "What is wrong with that man" she thought as she carried on washing. Mary finished her shower and dressed in a t shirt and jeans before making her way downstairs to find that Rob and Kath had already arrived. Frank was chatting to them while bringing things out onto the table on the porch. It was a lovely evening, quite still and comfortably warm "Just nice for a barbie" Mary thought as she stepped outside. "Hi folks" Mary said while making her way to the barbie to check if it was ok. She lifted the lid to plenty of smoke but when that cleared she saw that it was ready. "How are you both?" she said looking at Kath who was dressed in a wide brimmed hat and a lovely and easy to wear summer frock. "Great, we've booked a holiday, was spur of the moment but we decided that you only live once" Kath said excitedly. "Where you off to? "Frank said while putting a sausage or two on the grill "The Cook Isles in the Pacific. It's lovely there by the looks of the brochures. We fly out in two weeks."

"What's your fancy on here?" Mary said pointing to the food.

"We'll have a couple of those steaks Mary, with the chips and salad"

Frank put them on the barbie with the steaks for him and Mary.

"Kath, do me a favour, would you get me and Frank a drink, he'll no doubt have a beer, there's cold ones in the fridge and I'll have a G&T with ice, cheers," Mary said while sorting the salad on the table and putting the cutlery out.

"On its way" said Kath as she stepped into the kitchen. Frank and Rob were by the grill. It had settled down and a very light breeze was blowing any smoke downwind away from them. Mary walked over to see how things were progressing and chat to the lads. Suddenly from nowhere a strong breeze came in blowing over the farm, it seemed like a small tornado, as it came over the field it seemed to gather strength and as it approached they could see that it was blowing things over, part of one fence went as it moved in their direction, barrels were rolling across the yard. "Quick Frank grab the food" Mary shouted. Frank and Rob tried to grab the food but it was too late as before they knew it the wind was on them, the barbie was blown yards away with the food scatted everywhere. The tables and chairs on the porch were blown out into the yard with the food going to ruin. Rob shouted "Frank help me to get the hose, the coals have set fire to the long grass." Mary screamed "OH Frank, be quick the grass is on fire." Frank and Rob grabbed the powerful hose that was used to wash out the barns and before long the flames were out. Kath stepped out of the house with the tray of drinks only to have it blown out of her hands and her hat went bouncing over the yard. She was fighting with her dress as it was being blown over her head. Monty was having fun chasing his ball which was being blown along. Then all of a sudden it stopped, as quickly as it had arrived it had gone. They all stood quietly looking at each other. "What the hell was that" Rob said dusting himself off. "I can't believe that just happened," Frank said in disbelief. "I mean a normal whirlwind would have carried on over the fields,   I would have thought but that just stopped dead," Rob said while looking to the sky. They all looked around at the carnage and the smoking grass "Well…..you two really know how to throw a party" Kath said looking around. "Best get tidied up," Rob said as he set off to retrieve the barbie and all its bits. Mary and Kath were putting the table and chairs back on the porch "I just can't believe it, look at the mess" Frank said "What the hell was it?" After a short while they had tidied up and the place seemed back to normal, however all the food was ruined?

"Frank, Mary come on jump in the car me and Kath will treat you to tea at the Crown, come on Mont you can come too"

"I need a pint after that Rob" They all jumped into the car and off they went. As they walked in the pub Joe looked them all up and down "What's happened to you lot then, been having fun" he said as he leaned on the bar. "It was that strong wind that came over earlier, like a tornado, blew the farm to pieces" Frank said. "No-one else in here has mentioned it at all, must have been just at your place, now what you having" he said putting a pint glass in his hand. "Give me a pedigree and half of lager for Mary, what's your fancy Rob?"

"Peddy and a G&T for Kath, ice and a slice" rob replied "The girls have got a table in the corner and I've got the menus. They got the drinks and went to sit down with the girls to relax after their adventure earlier at the farm. Monty was curled up beside the table being enjoying fussed by passing customers. "I can't believe what happened earlier" Frank said taking a drink from his glass "What a waste of good grub"

"Never mind hunni, put it down to experience, your cooking's not that good anyway," Mary said and they all had a good laugh then settled down to order their meals. The early evening went well as the food was always good in the Crown. Nothing fancy just good homemade pub grub but it was always popular with the locals. As they sat there Alan walked in with one off his work colleagues and saw them. "Hiya, how's things, blimey you look as though you've been busy."

"It was that damn storm that came over, did it affect you lot up in the hills" Kath asked. "What storm, it's been lovely all day with fab views, we've been sitting outside for a meeting this evening with the weather boys, and they've been fine tuning their kit. "You mean you didn't see anything" Mary said. "Nothing unusual, no it's been lovely," Alan said "Anyway, excuse me and I'll catch you later" he said as he started to walk away. They all turned to carry on with their conversation but after a moment Alan came back "We did have a funny moment earlier but nothing to do with weather, well we don't think so anyway The weather boys have a small radar which can pick up low cloud movement so they can see what's coming in which may obstruct any visual viewing or create atmospherics which can play tricks on the kit. Well they were setting this up and they picked up an object coming in towards the direction of the observatory and we watched it on the screen. As you can't see detail they thought it was a small plane so as it got closer almost on top of us we stepped out to have a look at what was approaching us and we had a clear sky with nothing in view, not a sausage. We looked again at the screen and yes, there it was right next to us but once again we went outside and nothing to be seen. It would have passed near to you probably. One of the boys has stayed up there as obviously something's wrong with the kit, he said again before joining his colleague by the bar. "How odd, anyway, more importantly, more drinks anyone" Frank said standing up "Ok" was the enthusiastic reply from all. Frank smiled and walked to the bar. Later that evening when they got home Frank popped the kettle on and was getting the cups out with the coffee.

"Oh Frank, I've just thought about Shiloh. I'm off to see as he's OK," Mary said grabbing her little jacket as it can be a bit fresh up in the top field. For speed she jumped on the quad bike and set off with Monty running alongside.

Chapter 6

Mary arrived at the field and switched of the bike. She could see Shiloh all calm and relaxed chewing on some hay, but he did seem pleased to see her as he started walking towards her "Hello boy, are you ok matey?" she said rubbing his nose.

As she was standing there she looked around and noticed that everything was just as she left it last time she was here, nothing out of place "Odd" she thought " You would have thought that wind would have caught this area too but it hasn't, how strange".

"Come on, let's get your coat on in case it goes cool tonight" and she moved to her little store shed where she keeps these things. Just then she stood for a moment realising that the wind was starting again and it was building with force. "Oh no, not again "she thought, only this time it was far enough away from her not to cause her any harm and it was over the next field which was empty so it couldn't do any damage. As she looked she realised that this was no ordinary wind as it was like a stationary tornado, a standing swirling wind obvious by the dust it was picking up, and she stood watching it. And then as she stared, she started to shake, she couldn't believe what she was seeing. The wind began to stop as an object began to appear. It was the spaceship. It seemed to appear out of nowhere and just sat there about 10 feet above the field in total silence. She didn't feel in any real danger as a sense of calm swept over her and she started to relax and look hard at this object. It was the same one, grey in colour with no visible doors or windows. She walked a little closer to it looking in amazement at this sight to behold. She looked and could see nothing that it could be standing on "How is this happening? "She thought. "Who is it I wonder? Where are they from?" She felt as though she heard a voice in her head telling her not to be afraid. "Is that me making this up?" At that a window appeared in the craft so she automatically stepped back, she could see that the craft was lit inside but rather dim. Then she saw a figure come to the window, it looked like a normal man. "Don't be afraid" she heard in her head again, "Is it me doing this?" she thought. She stepped forward again to get a closer look but the light inside made the figure seem more of a silhouette so she couldn't see detail. "I thought aliens would be different to us "She thought. "We're not all the same" the voice in her head said. "What's happening, no-one is going to believe this," she thought. Herself and the figure stood looking at each other for what seemed a while when the person in the craft raised his right arm as if he was attempting a wave. Mary did the same but slowly. "I will return" the voice in her head said "I'll be here" she found herself saying. And at that the craft shot into the sky at the blink of the eye. Never before had Mary seen anything like it, and she just stood there looking up, lost in her thoughts when she felt a push in her back and she screamed. It was Shiloh nudging her, she smiled and stroked his nose while looking again at the sky. "No way am I discussing this with anyone, they all think I'm cracking up" she said to herself. "Come on mate, where's your coat" she said to him and he followed her back to the shed. Mary found herself being very slow now. It seemed ages before she had Shiloh's coat on and his hay bags filled for the evening. Once this was sorted she walked slowly to the gate opened it and walked out, almost forgetting to shut it after her. She climbed on the quad bike and sat for a while just gazing at the night sky before starting for home. While riding back she was trying to get her head around what she had seen" I don't believe it, I just don't believe it. Did I really see that, has that happened to me? I can't believe it." The quad bike came to rest by the back door of the farmhouse, Mary stepped off, stood there for a moment and looked up at the sky again in wonder. She walked through the backdoor and ignored Monty who was in his basket wagging his tail at being pleased to see her. She went into the kitchen and clicked the kettle on and just leaned on the worktop. Frank walked in "Hi, everything ok up there" he said

"Yes fine" she replied in a thoughtful way.

"Shiloh ok" he asked

"Everything's ok, just leave me alone Frank," she snapped.

"Wow, hang on girl, I only asked."

"Yes and I only replied, I'm off to bed, leave me alone" as she left the room abruptly. Frank stood for a minute thinking at what he'd done wrong but decided to leave it and let her cool down. "What the hell can have happened in the field that's made her like that?" he wondered. Mary slammed the bedroom door and sat on the bed thinking about what she had seen. "I can't believe it," she thought. "The wind at the barbie must have been the craft, I bet it was that craft that made the crop circle. This I am definitely keeping to myself." She undressed slowly and got into bed. The light was off and the curtains open so she could easily see the night sky and she just lay there thinking about the evenings events before she dozed off to sleep. When she woke the next morning she realised that she had slept in quite late, Frank had got up and gone to work on the farm without disturbing her. She lay there for a while and realised that Frank had left her a mug of tea but as she reached for it could tell by now it was only warm, must have been there for a while. After a while she threw the covers back realising she was naked as she hadn't even bothered to put on her nightwear, and stepped out of bed and felt a bit faint. She got up and walked to the bathroom to splash some water onto her face to try to waken herself up, then grabbing a dressing gown from the back of the bathroom door she walked onto the landing and looked out of the window. She could see Monty rolling on his back playfully in the dust of the yard, this made her smile. Mary stood there for a short time before going down stairs to the kitchen and clicking the kettle back on, noticed it was still warm from the previous brew that Frank had made. Then she picked up a slice of bread and popped it in the toaster. While it was warming up she stood by the worktop with her arms folded lost in her thoughts. It made her jump when the toast popped out and the kettle switched off just after. Then with her small breakfast she sat at the kitchen table quietly looking at the post which Frank had brought in. "Nothing exciting here" she thought, throwing it to one side. While sitting there she could not get out of her mind the previous night's events, it was driving her daft. "Don't mention this to anyone" She kept telling herself "They won't believe you, I don't believe it myself". Frank walked in "Oh hi, are you ok?" he said "Yes thanks" she replied as she bit into her toast. "You don't seem yourself Mary." "Frank just leave it, put it down to women's problems," she said trying to distract him away from the real issue. "Oh…..Ok, take it easy today then if you like, we're pretty much on top of everything now" he said as he walked out of the door. "I wonder when he'll be back" thinking of her visitor. "I wonder if I'll catch him, could be anytime, what does he want here, are we going to be safe?" the thoughts were rapidly running through her mind. While she was sitting thinking about things her concentration was broken by the sound of a lorry approaching. "Who's this "she thought, casually standing up to have a look through the window. "Oh my god it's John for the milk, I bet Franks forgot too" Mary rushed upstairs and got her shorts and a top on quickly before running down to greet him. "Hi John, sorry , I think we both forgot that you were due, can you bear with me while I find Frank and we get prepared for you, won't be long, help yourself to anything in the kitchen" She shouted as she ran out. Mary ran around to the back of the barns where Frank was once again under the bonnet of the tractor. "Frank, have you forgotten, Johns here for the milk" she said breathing heavy after running. "You're kidding" he said banging his head on the bonnet in surprise. "He's early this time. I didn't think he was due for another few days."

"Well he's here now eating our kitchen out if I know John," Mary said "Ok on my way" as he left the tractor and made his way around the house and into the kitchen.

"Hi John, how's things" Frank said as he entered the kitchen. "Oh you know Frank, I'm upright and breathing, always a blessing."

"John I won't be long and I'll have everything ready, give me 10 mins" Frank said before leaving again. "You caught us unaware John, sorry" Mary said "What can I get you while you're waiting?"

"Oh you're ok Mary don't worry, I'm ok with this brew, I've finished it now so I'll go and help Frank."

"Thanks John, you're a good one" Mary said, starting to relax again. It wasn't a bad thing John turning up and surprising them both, it shook Mary out of here sullen period and she appeared to come back to her normal self, forgetting for a while the events of a few days ago. Mary left them both to it and thought it was about time she got busy. She thought about Shiloh and decided to pop up and see to his feed and as it was a nice morning she decided it might be good to take him for a run. "Come on Monty let's go see Shylo" Monty jumped up wagging his tail as he loved going for walks. They left the house and started up the path towards the top field. The track was quite dusty as they hadn't really had any rain for a while, and the grass was looking a little parched although the rural setting was looking lovely. Monty ran ahead having spotted a rabbit and hoped to catch it although there was no chance as the rabbit was far quicker. When she arrived she decided that she would walk Shiloh down to the meadow so she put on his head collar and lead him through the gate. The three of them took a steady walk down the paths which lead to the meadow and when they got there

Mary let go of Shiloh and let him wander in and chew the grass. Mary looked at the circle of grass that was flat but noticed that now it was beginning to get back to normal "I'll miss that crop circle" she thought. After a while she made her way back up the path to put Shiloh back and headed home. The next day Mary was getting her shopping list together "Need anything from town Frank?" she shouted as Frank was outside. "No I'm fine thanks" he replied "Ok, won't be long" she said as she grabbed the keys to the Jeep and left the house. The drive to town was uneventful and it wasn't long before she arrived and found a good parking spot. It was a nice day and she was enjoying pottering around the shops getting the groceries and other bits and pieces. She was in no hurry and decided to pop in for a coffee. On the way to the coffee shop she took a shortcut through an alleyway that she had not been down for a long time and she came across some little cute shops that had opened. "I wonder how long these have been here? "She thought as she slowly made her way down browsing into the shop windows. As she walked down she came across a quaint little second hand bookshop that she'd not known about and she made her way in through the little doorway. As she opened the door the bell tinged to alert the owner of a customer, and she made her way in. "Hello there," a voice said while being hidden by some books. "Hello, mind if I have a look around?" Mary said. "Help yourself" was the reply from an invisible man. It was a lovely little shop with little nooks and crannies to explore. Mary had no real need to go in but just fancied a look around. As she was looking a face appeared next to her "Hello, I'm Mike, It's my little shop and I hope you like it and find what you want" he said. "I'm not after anything particular, just browsing."

"Ok, If you need any help just shout," he said before disappearing. Mary was quite taken with him. Mike was well dressed, she thought him to be about mid-forties and very good looking. "Wow, where's he been hiding" she thought to herself with a smile. After a while he reappeared "Anything caught your eye" he enquired. "Yes, you did" she thought before replying "No not really, however do you have any books on UFOs?"

"Yes, over here" he said making his way to the area "You don't look to me a person that's interested in that topic."

"Well, it is a new interest and I just wondered what you have." She didn't want to give anything away."

"That's all I have at the moment, but I'm sure more will come" he said enthusiastically. "Ok I'll have a look, thanks" Mary started to look through the choices not knowing which was best. While she was looking she found herself thinking about Mike. Was he single, married, did he have kids, she tried to put him out of her mind and carry on searching. "What am I thinking?" she said to herself. After a while she settled on a couple, one was on sightings of UFOs and the other was people who had been abducted by aliens. "I'll take these two please" she said looking for her purse. "Thanks, that's £ 6.00 for the two please, hope you enjoy them, it's an interesting subject, and I've been interested in them for years but never seen anything though. Hopefully one day the truth will come out" he said handing them to her in a brown bag. "Thanks, I'll let you know what I think, see you again maybe" She said with a smile before leaving the shop. Mary, pleased with her purchase, made her way down the alley way and on to the coffee shop, opened the door and found a seat. "Can I help you?" said the waitress.

"A regular latte please" Mary said. "Ok, just be a moment" said the waitress as she tidied the table before disappearing. Mary got out her books that she had just purchased, one was a paperback on alien abductions and the other was quite a big book with a collection of photos that had been taken of UFOs by people all over the world. She started to flick through the book and was amazed that so many people had seen these crafts. Prior to this she hadn't really given UFOs any thought at all. The coffee arrived. "Thank you" Mary said in appreciation, the waitress smiled. As Mary flicked through the book she stopped on one page. "That's it, that's the one I've seen." She was amazed, someone had photographed one similar to the one she had seen and she felt rather excited by this. She picked up the smaller book and read the back cover and found that this related to people who felt that they had been abducted by aliens. "Should be interesting" she thought. She opened the bigger book again to the page which she recognised. "I did see it, I know I did" she had this compulsion to tell someone straight away. She drank her coffee and paid, bid her goodbye and left the coffee shop to make her way back up the alley way to the bookshop. As she arrived she found that Mike had shut the shop to get a sandwich but was just coming back and unlocking the door. "Hello again" he said with a smile. "Hi, have you got a minute as I've something to show you?" Mary enquired "Of course, come in. I'm just going to have a sandwich and I always shut the shop for half hour while I do this so if you don't mind being locked in with me I'll make us both a brew while you show me what it is." Mike said putting his things down, locking the door and clicking the kettle on. "Yes ok, that'll be nice" Mary said while making herself comfy in the kitchen of the shop. Mike made a couple of coffees. "Sugar in yours" he asked.

"No thanks, just milk" Mary replied. "Now tell me, what is it you want to show me." he asked. "Well as you appear interested in UFOs I wanted to show you this." She took the bigger book from her bag and opened the page that she wanted. "I've seen this UFO over my farm in the hills just recently, that's what's made me want to get some books on them."

"Really, how fantastic, I'm impressed, how did it feel to see it" he asked

"Strange, you would think I would have been scared but I felt a sense of calm all over me. I just stood there looking at it for what seemed ages but it was probably just a few minutes really, and then it just disappeared, vanished into thin air." She was telling him this with enthusiasm because Mary felt that just for once she had found someone who really believed her. "Wow that's amazing, I'm quite jealous, I wish I could see one." Mary could see that Mike was genuinely interested "What happened then?" he asked.

"Well the police have been looking into it but come up with nothing really, other than finding a holiday couple who had a car crash caused by a big bright light in the sky. They were ok though, just a bit shook up," she said while drinking her coffee.

"How cool is this. Wow why can't I be lucky enough for this to happen to me, please keep me informed if it happens again as I think this is great" he said offering her a sandwich.

"No thanks, anyway I'm off, just wanted to tell of my experience" she said standing up and getting ready to go.

"Ok, I'll let you out, its time I opened again anyway to cope with the imaginary rush of customers" he said with a smile "But do come again."

"Yes, I will, thanks I've enjoyed the chat" Mary said with a smile as she left the shop.

Mary walked up the alleyway and out into the street. As she walked back to her Jeep she was thinking about the impromptu meeting with Mike and how she enjoyed it and how good she felt that someone believed in her. The thought helped to put a spring in her step as she approached her car.

Chapter 7

Mary made her way home looking forward to being able to read her books with a glass of wine. As she pulled into the driveway she saw Monty running up with his tail wagging to greet her. "Hiya Mont, come on let's get you a treat" she said rubbing his head. Monty knew the word treat and he ran into the kitchen in anticipation. The rest of the day rolled on with Frank busy outside with the farming duties and Mary dealing with some paperwork, post and answering the phone while thinking about her experiences but before she knew it Frank popped his head around the door. "What we having for tea?" he asked "Oh shit, is it that time already, leave it with me I'll have a think and I'll rustle something up," she said as she put her glasses on top of her head and looked thoughtful. Mary went to the freezer, opened the door and had a search through the draws before finding what she wanted for tea - stir fry. It didn't take long to prepare tea and they were soon sitting down to eat, Frank opened a bottle of wine and although it was a quick meal both Mary and frank said how much they enjoyed it. Afterwards Mary tidied up and washed the dishes and then made her way to the sofa with a glass of wine to make a start on her book "Alien Abductions". The evening went by very quickly as Mary was engrossed in her new boo She picked up the wine and went to pour another glass only to realise that she had finished the bottle, then she realised just how long she had been reading. It was 2am and she was well over halfway through her book. She had been reading about Betty and Barney hill who were abducted in Sept 1961 and lost two days and Travis Walton who was abducted in 1975 and was missing for 5 days. Mary was fascinated by this, she had never really had any interest in UFOs or known anything about this subject until recent events occurred. She realised that these people didn't know what actually happened to them until they had been hypnotised and the stories came out in detail. But one thing was clear; Mary realised that the loss of three and a half hours must have been down to being abducted herself. She put the book down and sank further into the sofa trying to take all this in. After a while she fell asleep where she said

"Hey, wakey wakey sleepy head." It was Frank standing over her with a cup of tea. It was morning and she was still on the sofa. "Morning hun, thanks for the tea" she said drowsily wiping the sleep from her eyes. Having drank her tea Mary decided she needed to stir herself as there was work to do so she got up and made her way to the bedroom to change. First on the list when ready was up to the field to feed Shiloh. The walk up was quite brisk and Mary was smiling as Monty was having fun chasing the birds. Mary was lost in her thoughts and the time went by before she made her way back." Come on Mont, let's get some lunch ready," Mary said rubbing his head. Monty knew the word lunch and when he heard this he made his way to the gate, chasing the birds on the way. Lunch for them all came and went and Mary busied herself all afternoon with various chores, all small but non the less important to the smooth running of the farm. It was a nice evening and when they'd finished Mary suggested that when she'd fed the horse they have a drink on the veranda. Frank nodded in agreement and then she made her way out. "Come on Mont, walkies" she shouted wondering where he was. He soon caught her up and they walked in the twilight up the path to the field gate, opened it and went in. Mary smiled as Shiloh was running around the field throwing his back legs in the air, he seemed to be really enjoying himself, and even Monty was standing watching him. Mary made her way to the store and got out some hay and feed for his tea. Once this was done Mary took a moment to tidy up around the shelter. It was a lovely starry night, no moon and the sky was black, Mary loved it like this. "C'mon Mont let's get back." Monty had ran down the field chasing a rabbit then turned to make his way up to Mary. As she turned to the gate she screamed. There hovering over the field silently was the ship. It shocked her at first but she started to calm down. It was about eight feet off the ground, the blue and red lights flickering dimly in the evening light. "How did that get there so quietly?" Mary thought as she stood and watched it. Nothing happened for a while, it just sat there, silent, dirty grey in colour with no sign of life. It seemed a while but eventually the window appeared and then a few minutes later the figure of the man was there. Mary heard in her head. "Greetings" and he lifted his hand up in a type of wave "Hello" she thought, then she said "Can't we talk properly, you know, with speech, I'd like to know more about you" then she waited for a reply………and waited. After a while the man walked away from the window "What's he doing now?" she thought and she stood and waited. A doorway opened on the underside of the ship and very slowly a ramp came out and touched the floor. A moment or two went by and then the man appeared walking down the ramp and out towards Mary. Mary could feel herself shaking. He stood in front of her about ten feet away. Mary looked him up and down. He was easily six foot tall, blond shoulder length hair and a perfect male body and he wore a blue tight fitting one piece suit. "He's gorgeous," she thought. "Hello" she said and waited to see if there was a response. After a moment he spoke. "Hello" partly raising his hand. "What do they call you?" she asked "My name is Sol" was his reply. "

"My name is Mary, I'm so pleased to meet you. W here are you from?" Sol paused as if he was thinking of what to say.

"We are from a place very far from here, across the galaxy" he said. "You speak our language very well" Mary said enquiringly "It has taken time for us to perfect your voice and speech pattern, telepathy is a universal language of communication so wherever we go in the cosmos beings are able to communicate with each other this way. Humanity on your planet is very young and has a lot to learn. You are still so far behind in many things" he managed to say this very well, Mary was impressed as to how easy he seemed to master it. "So where are you actually from?" she asked knowing full well she probably wouldn't understand the answer. "We are from the distant star system that you know as Alpha Centauri, a star system that is inaccessible to yourselves and will be for many years to come as you have only recently acquired the technology to reach your Moon." Sol replied in a calming voice. It appeared to Mary that the ease of speaking was coming very quickly to Sol. "How did you get here then if it's so far away?" Mary enquired "We have the technology to make space travel very easy. What would take you hundreds of your years to travel a distance in space we can do in a few of your hours." he said. "I've never seen a spaceship before, I feel really honoured" Mary replied feeling that she did not know what to say. "Would you like to see inside, you will be very safe" Sol asked. Mary hesitated before saying "Yes please, I'd like that" at which Sol turned and walked back towards the ship and made his way up the ramp. Mary followed and hesitantly walked up the ramp behind him and made her way through the doorway into what seemed a small corridor but she could see a small room ahead which she walked towards. The lighting was quite dim and an unusual colour she thought. As she entered the room she looked around and saw that all the surfaces looked like polished steel and spotlessly clean with a couple of seats of polished steel which reminded her of barstools. There were no windows to be seen and she wondered where these were. "This is where we control our craft" Sol said pointing to the panels. "There are not many controls considering how far you have to travel" she said while walking around looking at everything. "We have technology far more advanced than you could ever imagine. Just then a woman appeared, she looked very similar to Sol, similar stature, blond hair and blue eyes, a beautiful female and wearing the same blue suit as Sol. She stopped and looked at Mary without saying anything. "This is Taki, we operate this craft together" and at that Taki nodded to Mary before disappearing again. "Follow me" Sol said as he walked through another small doorway and into a space where Mary could see a number of small rooms which appeared to have ultra-modern beds in them. "These are our relaxation areas. We need to rest too," Sol said. " Sol turned to Mary "You must leave now as we have to go, I will see you safely out" as he walked back through the craft and to the entrance. "One question before I go, why you keep coming back to me when there are so many other people to look at?" she asked. Sol looked at her and thought for a moment. "You don't realise it but I have observed you for a while before you even saw us. I have watched you in your daily life from a distance and I realised you were good for me and decided you were what I wanted and needed so I let myself be seen but only by you and no-one else" he replied. "I suppose I should feel flattered" she said as she walked down the ramp and to a safe distance from the craft.

Sol didn't answer but looked up at the sky for a moment then looked back at Mary. "I must leave now but I will be back" then turned and walked back into the craft. Mary waited and after a short time the craft moved away quite slowly at first but as it lifted into the sky it gathered speed and shot away at an unimaginable rate. Mary stood for a moment taking in what she had seen. "Ok, see you later" she said quietly.

Chapter 8

When Mary arrived back Frank was fast asleep, she wanted to wake him and tell him what had happened but she knew he would probably make fun so she left him alone. The next day Mary and Frank went to the cattle auction as Frank felt that they could accommodate some more sheep which would help with a better lamb production. There were a lot of people there and the bidding was brisk. Frank was successful with a purchase and was quite happy with himself, meanwhile Mary had secured herself another half dozen chickens so she was chuffed too. "Fancy a coffee Mary?" Frank asked. "Certainly would and I'll have a burger as well please" she said as they walked to the burger van. "Hi Mary, Frank good to see you" It was George Fellows from the next farm. "Hi George good to see you, how's Ethel" Mary enquired "Oh she's ok, likes it when I'm here and out of her hair." He laughed as he said it. "Did you get anything yet, has anything taken your fancy?" he asked. "Yes we got some sheep and some chickens to add to the stock. Quite happy with them" Frank said. "Well good luck to you both, If you need anything you know where we are," George said as he walked away giving a wave. "Thanks George "Mary said watching him go. The auction came to a close and Mary and Frank drove home quite happy with their new stock. "With these new sheep we should hopefully do well with the lambs next year," Frank said with enthusiasm. "Well that's great, I hope so. I think I'm going to start putting eggs by the gate with an honesty box for passers-by, we'll be producing more than we need soon. I've just had a thought, what about a farm shop? We could sell dressed lamb, eggs, vegetables and other stuff, It would give us a good reason to get the other field operational," Mary said with a big smile as though she had just seen the whole new future of the farm. As they approached the town they were both on a high. "Let's go to the pub for one" Mary said "Good idea, I like the sound of that," Frank replied. When they arrived they were happy to see that Kath and Rob were there. "Hi folks how are you" Mary said giving them both a hug. "Hi Mary Hi Frank, what you having" Rob said getting his wallet out. "Mine's a

Pedigree" Said Frank "Mine's a white wine please Rob" Mary added. The lads started talking about sport as Mary turned to Kath. "Kath I've something to tell you" Mary said quietly. "Oh go on then, what's happened?"

"I've met the spaceman"

"You've what?"

"I've met him Kath, he landed, got out and we talked, not for long mind but we chatted. He's tall, strong, long blond hair with blue eyes and his name is Sol and he has a partner in the ship called Taki. Kath he's gorgeous" Mary said while obviously thinking of him. "So he's not a weirdo like you see in the Sci-Fi movies then?"

"No not at all, he seems just like us. He invited me on board his craft and he showed me around, it was great, I felt really safe. We chatted about this and that then he said he had to go but he'd be back again and then he just took off and disappeared" Mary said thoughtfully "Sounds like all my old dates, they took off and disappeared," Kath said taking a drink. "I couldn't understand why he keeps coming back to me, what is it about me that he finds he wants to keep coming back, so I asked him. He said he'd been watching me for a while and decided I was right for him and he wanted and needed me?" Mary said with wonder in her voice. Mary took a drink and looked around the pub, Kath watched her with a look of worry on her face but said nothing. The next hour went well with a couple more drinks before they all said their goodnights and made their way home. The next couple of days were busy as Mary and Frank were moving fences, planning expansion on the fields and making more room for the new stock. Both were quite happy with how things were working out and feeling optimistic for the future. However, while working Sol was not far from Mary's mind at any time.

One morning Mary decided that they needed supplies. "Frank I should go to town, we're running really low on food stuffs, and do you need anything as I'll have to get some things in?" Mary said to Frank while he was eating his breakfast. "No I'm ok, check the beer levels if you like?" he said "Ok I'll do that and I'll see you later" Mary replied as she walked out of the kitchen and made her way to the bedroom to change. It was a lovely morning so Mary chose a light summer style dress as she was always in jeans lately and she wanted to be comfortable and a little feminine for a change.

She made her way downstairs and grabbed the keys to the jeep "See you a bit later, phone me if you need anything" she shouted through to the kitchen before walking down the hall and making her way out of the front door and off to the Jeep. She smiled at the thought of being dressed as a lady and driving an old Jeep "Quite a contrast" she thought. Mary arrived at the town and in her usual way found a parking space quite easily. She jumped out of the Jeep and made her way to the butchers "Hi Stan, how's things" she asked enthusiastically. "Hello Mary, nice to see you, I'm ok and how is your Frank?" He said while wiping his hands on his apron.

"Oh he's ok, I've left him working hard" Mary said before going on to give Stan quite a large order to stock the freezer up. Stan looked after her on price as he had lambs in the spring and they saw to it that he was looked after in return. Mary found herself quite busy on this trip as she had a lot of things to get, other groceries and a few bits and bobs and she found that this took up most of the morning but she was enjoying her time to herself. Mary made her way across the town having done her errands and made her way to the coffee shop where she hoped to have a little time to herself to catch up on her reading as she had taken one of her books with her. The more she read about her new found passion the more she found it totally engrossing. She walked down the small quaint side street to the shop, opened the door and went in. There were not many in and Mary found herself a nice corner seat where she could sit with no one to disturb her other than the waitress. "What can I get you?" said the girl "I'll have a large Americano coffee with warm milk please" Mary said with a smile. "Certainly" said the waitress as she disappeared behind the counter. Mary opened her bag and pulled out her book, she then sat back and started to read. She was still amazed about how many people were convinced that they too had been abducted, she never realised that this was such a common issue worldwide. "All of these people can't be making this up, surely." She thought as she flicked a page over, then her coffee arrived "Thanks" she said and the waitress smiled as she placed it neatly on the table. Time went by and page after page was turned then the bell of the door went which caused her to look up for a moment, It was Mike from the bookshop. Mary waved as Mike saw her and came over "Hi Mary, what brings you here today" he said "I just had a few bits to do in town and thought I'd have a little time undisturbed to read my book over a coffee" she replied "Oh I best leave you alone then, enjoy" he said as he started to walk away "Don't go, come and join me, we can talk UFOs" she felt that she did not want him to go and hoped he would stay. "Are you sure?" he asked "Of course" She replied pulling a chair out for him. The waitress appeared. "Yes Sir" she asked "Two Americano's please"

"Certainly, coming right up" she said as she walked away. "I may as well freshen yours up as well Mary" Mike said looking into her eyes. "Thanks" she said wondering what he was thinking as he looked at her. "What are you doing here Mike, who's looking after the shop." "I normally close a little earlier today as it gives me chance to catch up on a few things too, I'm just on my way back from the bank, I need to pop back to the shop for an hour but I'll keep the door locked and It'll allow me a little time to catch up. "The coffees were not long in arriving and Mary and Mike spent quite a while enthusiastically chatting about Mary's experience and the books she was reading "You know Mike I really did see a UFO, it was big, about 50 feet wide, triangular in shape and the occupant waved at me" she said with conviction in her voice, " The man got out of the craft and walked towards me, and do you know I wasn't scared. I had a calm feeling that came over me. We stood looking at each other for a while before I said hello and told him my name. He told me his name, It's Sol. He took me inside the craft, it was so interesting. We chatted for a short while before he said he had to go, but he did say he'd be back." Mike looked at her "So he speaks English? Mary I don't doubt you, why would I, what did he look like?" he asked grabbing her hand across the table, she let he fingers wrap around his. "Like men here really, he was tall and very good looking, he had a figure of a sportsman, very athletic with long blond hair and blue eyes, Mike I really saw this" Mike looked at her before speaking "I've had a chap who's brought some more books in and I'm sure there's some more on this subject in amongst them, fancy a look" he said looking her in the eyes "Ok, drink up, let's go" she said with enthusiasm. They left the coffee shop and made their way to Mike's bookshop and as they arrived Mike unlocked the door and let Mary in closing the door behind him. "Come through here" he said leading her into a more comfortable back room which had comfy chairs and a sofa. "Some of my customers come in here and chill with a read, I don't mind as they are regulars and do buy off me eventually, the books are there in that big box, you have a look and I'll get us a drink, fancy a gin and tonic as I've a drop left." Mary thought about it for a moment "Oh go on then"

Why not she thought, getting down on her knees to rummage through the box. She was enjoying herself pulling the books out and hunting for the ones she hoped would be in there when Mike appeared at her side with two Gins.

"Cheers "Mary said taking one from him and taking a sip

"Cheers Mary, have you found anything that Interests you" he asked

"Not yet, still searching.

There must be something interesting in here" She said

"Oh I think there is "he said looking at her" She turned towards him then realised he meant her and at that she felt herself blush. Mike reached over and touched her cheek before moving in and kissing her. Mary was taken aback and slightly shocked but as his tongue searched her mouth she gave in, dropped the book she had and put her arms around him pulling him in tight. Mike helped her up and pushed her back onto the sofa and was almost on top of her, Marys buttons on her dress were under strain at this and the two top ones popped open. Mike noticed this and while they were hungrily kissing each other he reached down and undid the rest of them opening the front of her dress and showing her small pretty bra which was holding back her ample breasts. He stopped kissing her and moved his mouth to her open neck kissing it gently as her pushed the dress off her shoulder. Mary was in a mixed state by now, she was enjoying every moment but knew it was wrong, it shouldn't be happening but she hadn't had passion like this for a long time and parts of her body were telling her she was really excited. Just then it happened Ting Ting, the little doorbell of the shop sprang to life "Oh God, I forgot to lock the door" Mike said as he jumped up and started to rearrange his clothes. "Are you there Mike" a man's voice shouted from the shop "Yes, just give me a moment and I'll be with you" he said trying to compose himself. Mary just lay there for a moment, her dress open and her breasts on show and feeling quite exhausted at the amount of passion that had gone into those few minutes, as she sat up "Oh god what am

I doing" she thought although she realised that she now felt rather horny. Mike reappeared to find Mary dressed and arranging her make up. Don't go yet" he said "Mike I must, this is wrong" she said as she grabbed her bags and made her way out towards the door. "Look Mike, let me think about this, I'll see you again in the coffee shop one day, just let me go Mike as I feel all mixed up" then she opened the door and left to make her way back home. On the way it gave her time to calm down and compose herself but she couldn't stop thinking about what had happened. In her mind she wanted it to go all the way, she wanted to feel the passion that she had been missing. As Mary pulled into the farm and pulled up by the house Frank came out "I was wondering where you were, have you enjoyed you trip out" he asked? "Oh yes, more than you could imagine" she said as she winked at him and smiled while pulling her bags out of the Jeep. "Oh hell, I hope I've buttoned my dress up right" she thought. "What's your fancy for tea" she asked

"Surprise me" he said wiping his dirty hands on his rag "I'll finish in the barn and be with you in a bit" he said as he walked off. "I'll surprise you alright" she thought "I'll tell you what I've just been doing in the bookshop" at that she went inside to prepare some tea. After tea Mary went up to check on Shiloh and sort his feed for the evening, it was a nice clear night and Mary took a moment to gaze up to the sky, "He said he'll be back, I wonder when" she thought before setting off back home. When she arrived back at the house Frank was at the desk with paperwork scattered about " I thought I'd have a go at this as you always seem to get saddled with it" Frank said to Mary "Ok thanks" she smiled to herself as Frank looked as though he'd lost the plot with it all. "If you don't mind then I'm going to bed with my book, see you in a bit" she said as she walked up the stairs. When she got upstairs she slowly got undressed in the dark with the moonlight coming in through the windows. As her clothes dropped to the floor she was thinking that she found it exciting that Mike had found her so attractive and how she enjoyed feeling the passion. She walked to the big window in the bedroom and stood naked in the moonlight, see was happy doing this and that no one could see her. As she stood there her thoughts were still with Mike and that passionate session with him and with this thought she let her fingers wander over her body very gently. She felt her nipples and they were beginning to stand up, this felt good and she cupped her breasts in both hands and began to wish Mike had done this, her right hand let go and started to stroke the side of her body all down the right side from her breast to her thigh, teasing herself as she kept touching her breast as her hand came up. Slowly she let her hand drop down and her fingers were just touching the top of her thigh. She loved the feeling. Her fingers made their way to the inside of her leg which were slightly apart before moving slowly upwards to her groin and sliding into the small valley between her legs "Oh God that feels good" she thought, squeezing her left breast really hard, Just then her fingers found their target, she let out a gasp of delight as he stood by the window enjoying the moment. She let go of her breast and grabbed the wall for support as she was reaching her crescendo "Oh my God "she said to herself as she was at the point of no return she thought "Oh Mike " and she slumped against the wall exhausted but with her hand still between her legs and thinking of Mike. She stood there for a minute or two, getting herself together and relaxing. A little while later Mary appeared downstairs "I've made you a G&T, it's there on the table," Frank said seeming quite pleased with himself. "Cheers, coming to sit outside for a while?" Mary asked "Yes ok, I'll just finish up here, fancy some cheese and biscuits?" he asked. "Yes thanks" Mary replied. And as they sat outside on the lovely evening Mary could think of nothing but Sol and when he would be back and of her encounter with Mike and if it would happen again. The next morning Frank and Mary had their respective tasks to deal with when they heard a car on the driveway, It was Kath. Mary dropped her tools and walked over to where she'd parked and found Monty already there giving Kath a good welcome. "Hi Kath, good to see you" Mary said "You too hun, I was around so I thought I'd drop by to see how you're doing?" Kath said."Come on in and I'll put the kettle on, come on Mont you can come too" Mary said giving him a rub. Monty ran ahead and into the house as he knew he would be getting a treat. "What's been happening with our man from Mars?" Kath asked as Mary was getting the cups out and clicking the kettle on. "No more than I've told you already, why do you ask?" Mary replied while throwing a biscuit to Monty and thinking that she'd not seen Kath this serious in a long time. "I'm worried about you Mary, something's not right here. Firstly I don't doubt what has happened to you, you're my friend, I trust you implicitly and you're a very intelligent woman, I don't know how I would react to these thing happening, but why is it happening to you in this way? Most people who have seen a UFO only see it once in a lifetime and yours is becoming a friend of the family. "There has to be a good reason why he's picked you and quite frankly Mary It worries me as these people don't travel across the cosmos for a little interplanetary chit chat, there has to be a damn good reason" Kath said as she looked at Mary who was deep in thought. The kettle clicked off and Kath walked over to complete the coffee making as she knew where everything was. Mary sat down by the table and put her head in her hands in thought. Kath finished the coffee and put the cups on the table then turned to reach for the biscuit box and sat down. "Mary I'll say again that I don't feel that this is going to end well at all, I've an awful feeling about this mate," she said opening the box and passing a biscuit to Monty then taking one for herself to dunk in her tea but as she did so the biscuit snapped and fell into her cup, she rolled her eyes in disappointment. "You'll get my dog fat" Mary said. "Have you told Frank about all this?" Kath asked. "No I haven't, I feel that he'd just ridicule me. Sol has said to me that no one else will see him so you're really the only one I can talk too, oh and I have told Mike as he's really into UFOs" Mary said without thinking. "Oh yes, and who is Mike when he's at home?"

"Oh I've not mentioned him have I He has a small bookshop in town, I got to know him while shopping for books on this subject and he told me how interested he was and wanted me to keep him up to speed with what happens He makes me feel sane with all this." Mary sat up and had a drink of her coffee. "There's something else as well" she said thinking about her tryst with Mike but realised what she was saying and stopped "Oh it doesn't matter".

"I know you're right Kath, why me. I've told you before, I asked him why me and he said he'd been watching me for a while and decided that he wanted and needed me....What for ? I told him it wasn't the most romantic proposal I'd had," Mary said while playing with her coffee cup "Don't say anything to anyone Kath, let's just see what happens," Mary pleaded. "It's ok, your secret's safe with me but understand I'm not happy about this and I'm worried what the outcome is going to be. On that note I'm going, I've to meet Rob down the pub later for lunch. Let's get together again soon and ring me if you need me," Kath said as she was leaving the house. "Bye" she said. Mary sat for a while just thinking about what Kath had been saying before pouring another coffee and gazing out of the window. After a while she got herself together and carried on with her jobs around the farm but still thinking about the problems to come and how Kath was showing so much concern for her.

Chapter 9

Later that evening while Mary was preparing tea Frank came in and switched the kettle on. "Fancy a coffee," he asked "Yes, ok thanks" Mary replied. Frank made the drinks and sat down by the kitchen table. "Are you ok Mary" he asked "Yes I'm fine, why do you ask?"

"Well I don't know really, you just seem a bit off just lately, not your usual self" Frank said as he'd recently noticed something about Mary which made him wonder. "I'm sorry if you think that, I'm ok I suppose I've some things on my mind but nothing you should worry about, you know how you feel sometimes" Mary said while grabbing some plates. "Well if you're sure you're ok, but do talk to me if you're worried about anything" Frank said not sure if he believed her. "I will don't worry" Mary replied thinking to herself "If he only knew." After tea Mary walked slowly up to the top field with Monty to see to Shiloh and give him his tea and as usual Monty chased after a rabbit knowing full well he would not catch it. Mary was running her fingers through the long grass which lined the track they were walking. It was a lovely night, the stars were bright and it was quite warm. They arrived at the gate and Mary lifted the rusty latch and pushed the gate open and made her way in followed by Monty before closing the gate behind her. Shiloh heard them coming and ran towards them both. "Hiya boy, come on let's get you fed" she said as Shiloh followed her to the hay store. Mary filled his hay bag and hung it up and he soon got stuck into that while she put some feed into his bowl on the floor. Shiloh seemed content with what he had and Mary walked across the field and sat on an old seat enjoying just doing nothing and gazing at the night sky. "I wonder where they are now, will they be back tonight I wonder? What is it he wants from me? He says he wants me and needs me but what for? He can't love me as we've only just met. What's going on, hope he's back soon." She realised she was beginning to miss him. "Come on Monty let's get back before we're missed, at that she got up made sure Shiloh was safe before making her way back to the house. Frank was sitting on the porch. "Hi I'll get you a drink, what's your fancy?" he asked. "Mmm....I think

I'll have a large red please" she said as Frank walked into the house and she settled herself into one of the chairs, "Should I tell Frank what's been happening, how would he react?" she thought. Just then Frank appeared with Mary's drink and passed it to her, Mary took the drink and gave him a smile before settling back in the chair and thinking about Sol. The following day started as any other, when Mary woke she found that Frank was already up and out but he'd left a mug of tea on her bedside table, she smiled. "I'd best get ready and pop to the bank first thing, I'll have a quick check if we need anything while I'm out" She thought while sitting up and drinking her tea noticing Monty's black face looking up at her as if to say are you getting up today. Mary got up and got herself ready and made her way downstairs. Here Monty, let's get you your breakfast," she said as she gave him some food. "I think I'll make Frank something before I leave." she thought, or else he won't eat till lunch". "Frank I've made you a hot breakfast, it's in the oven" she shouted to him across the yard. He waved and gave her a thumbs-up. Mary hopped in the Jeep and headed for town to pay in the banking. It was a lovely sunny morning and she noticed how nice the town looked at this time of year when the sun was out. She parked the Jeep and made her way to the bank. There were not many in but the obligatory queue had to be there and Mary stood patiently and waited as she was in no real hurry. Her turn came and she went to the cashier and paid in her money, got her receipt and turned to leave when she heard a voice call her name "Hiya Mary" it was Mike in the queue. "Hi Mike, I'll wait for you up here "as she pointed to seats at the back of the bank and walked up and took a seat and waited. Eventually Mike appeared "Hi Mary, good to see you, I've been wondering about you, how's things" he asked "I'm fine thanks, life's good" she replied feeling a little embarrassed about their last meeting. "Can I get you a coffee around the corner as I'd like to hear what's been happening with your spaceman" he asked, Mary thought for a minute "OK Mike that would be good" she replied as they walked out and made their way to the coffee shop. Mary sat down as Mike asked what she would like and ordered for them both. "Anything exciting to tell me?" he asked Mary as he sat next to her. "Nothing more Mike, Sol, said he would be back, but I don't know when. He didn't say. The thing is Mike I'm beginning to miss him, I think. My friend has been asking me about this as I did confide in her as I have you. She seems to think this isn't going to end well, but he may not even come back, who knows, but I have been thinking what he could possibly want with me, why does he seem to find me of interest" Mary said with a thoughtful expression. "Mary we don't know and I agree with your friend as this does sound strange and I would be very careful," Mike said. "Yes, Mike but I can't explain the feeling of safety and security that I feel when I'm in his company, it's as though he has something like a switch that just relaxes me."

"Maybe he has Mary, however I do find this exciting though, are you going to try and take some pictures?"

"Mike I'd never thought of it, I'll keep my phone with me in the future just in case" she said. Mary and Mike chatted for a while before Mary said she needed to go and got up to leave.

"Keep me informed Mary, I 'm really interested in what's happening and pop in the shop if you're passing"

"Yes I will next time I'm in town" Mary said offering him her cheek to kiss, which he did and said goodbye. Mary made her way home and as she was driving back she thought about her encounter with Mike in the shop last time; she thought how she in reality she enjoyed it although she knew it was wrong. Maybe I will stop by she thought with a smile on her face. Mary arrived back a little later than expected and decided it was too late for lunch but decided to do an early tea, Frank was OK with this as he was still comfortable from the hearty breakfast she left him earlier. She opened a bottle of wine and poured herself a glass before sitting down on the porch and now her thoughts were with Mike. "This is wrong" she thought. "I've got Sol who says he wants and needs me and I've got Mike who I know likes me and what's more I like him, but I still love Frank." What the hell's going on in my life?" The next day Mary was making a note of the jobs she had to do today, nothing major but enough to keep her busy when Frank walked in "George has a problem on his farm and he needs another pair of hands so I've told him I'll pop over. I'll text you later and let you know how we're getting on" before kissing her as he was leaving. "Ok no worries, see you later" she said with a smile. Mary liked George and Ethel and wouldn't want them struggling. Mary decided that first of all it was Shiloh that needed feeding so she set off with Monty in toe up the track to the top field. She felt really happy as she was walking up and realised how lucky they were to have this lifestyle and as she approached the gate she was even happier as Shiloh was enjoying himself rolling on his back in the grass and this made her laugh. She opened the gate and went in, Shiloh spotted her and got up to walk towards her happy to see her as usual. "Hiya mate," she said while rubbing his nose "Let's get you fed" she said making her way to the hay store and opening the door. Mary filled Shiloh's hay net and hung it on the hook at the side of the field shelter and put some feed in his tray on the floor. He seemed happy at this and tucked in. Mary sat on the seat in the field and watched Shiloh feeding. Mary loved this horse but felt she was not riding him enough just lately. "I must make an effort to ride more," she thought. Just then a strange feeling came over her, and she recognised this feeling and sure enough she was right. Very slowly in the adjacent field Sol's craft began to appear as if from nowhere until it was a solid shape. Mary felt a sense of excitement and walked slowly towards it before stopping a few feet away. Nothing happened for a few minute then the hatch opened and the ramp came out followed a minute or two later by Sol who walked down and turned to walk towards Mary. Mary watched as the ramp of the ship went back inside and the hatch closed, then the ship started to disappear again "What's going on "she thought. Sol was near to her now. "Hello Mary."

"Hello Sol, where's your ship gone?" she enquired

"It's still there but hidden from view for a while. I have a little time for conversation if you wish." He said to her "Of course, come and sit over here with me" Mary said leading him to the seat in the field, they both sat down. "I wondered if and when you would be back" she said to him.

"I will be a visitor here for some time as I have tasks which are allocated to me. We are here in number but spread across the planet."

"You mean there are lots of you, more spaceships?" she said excitedly.

"Yes Mary, many of us, but very rarely will they been seen. Each one has a specific purpose."

"What's yours Sol?" Mary asked.

"I can't discuss that Mary, but it is important for our regeneration" he said almost smiling as he said it.

"Are you all planning an invasion to take us over?" "No Mary, nothing like that, you're watching too many of your movies," Sol replied.

"How do you know of our movies?" Mary said with a puzzled look "Our people have been monitoring your radio and television signals with interest ever since they were very first broadcast long ago However we as a race have been aware of life on this planet for thousands of your years and have been monitoring your development and actions ever since"

"Why, for what reason, why does it matter to you?"

"It matters a great deal, we need civilisation on this planet to take care of the eco system and not damage the planet in any way. There are resources on this planet which we use and will continue to use and we will not allow these to be compromised in any way. If we felt that things were getting out of control then we would have to step in and take control, and that is something we will not do lightly. Your civilisation could not cope if we stepped in" Mary thought for a minute "What sort of things do you take from here and why?"

"There are numerous things which are of use to us in our world, but if I was to tell you I don't think you would like it," he said. Mary was now quite taken by how good and easy he was speaking to her, she felt it was like being spoken to by any other human being and felt very comfortable talking to him. "Mary I must leave now but will attempt to have more time with you next time" Sol said as he got up to walk away. "So you will be back then" Mary said feeling quite sad that he had to go. "Yes Mary, I will be back as I need more time with you" Sol said as he walked off towards his craft which was now beginning to come back into view. When fully in view the hatch opened and the ramp came out. Sol walked up the ramp without looking back, the ramp retracted and the hatch closed, then there was a pause and eventually the craft lifted off and seemed to just disappear into nowhere. Mary just sat for a while feeling a sense of loss at him going away again. "How interesting, I should jot all this down in a diary, it might make a good book" she thought. Slowly she got from her seat to make her way back to the house, as she made her way to the gate all the things he had said were going through her mind. She went through the gate, locked it and made her way home. When she arrived back she went to the kitchen and undid a bottle of wine. She had things to do but at this time she didn't feel like doing anything other than sitting in the sun with a drink and thinking about what had happened that morning. Mary made her way outside and sat on the porch, two glasses of wine went down very quickly and she was now on her third while trying to make sense of everything. The rest of the morning went by and as the afternoon drew on Mary decided she should think about preparing tea. Just then Frank texted her: "Back in 30 mins" the text read. "Best get a wiggle on" she thought. Frank arrived back and came into the kitchen "Something smells good," he said.

"Don't get excited; it's only a chicken salad," she said

"Have you had a drink hun, if so where's mine?" he said smiling at her

"Open a bottle Frank, I'll lay the table outside and we'll eat there" she said trying to act normal but still thinking about Sol. "How did it go at George's?"

"Oh ok, he was very appreciative of the help, I wonder if he's getting a bit too old for the farming business you know. It's heavy work for an older man." "I know but that's all he knows, take that away and what's he got?" Mary replied. After tea Mary sat down in front of the TV and went to sleep and Frank started a little paperwork.

Chapter 10

Next morning having seen to Shiloh, Mary was hoping she could slip away as she was anxious to tell Mike about what had happened but she had no excuse to go to town and she felt that she hadn't really helped Frank as much as she should over the last couple of days. Mary decided the best thing was to get a grip and get some work done so she got dressed in her working clothes and got stuck in with the feeds for the sheep and the chickens. Once she had decided on this she found herself working really hard all day. "Hey, what's got into you today, you've hardly had a break" Frank said handing her a cold lager "I don't know hunni, I suppose I've not been much help over the last couple of days and feeling a bit guilty"

"You're fine, don't worry. We're on top of everything so you've nothing to worry about" Frank said to her to make her feel better. Then he added "Look Mary, we took this on for a better, easier, stress free way of life compared to what we were doing in London. We have to work at it I know but we have to enjoy it in whatever way we can as well. Some days the duties may be things I can deal with and visa versa and some days we'll work together. Just relax babe, I know something's wrong with you I can tell, well just relax and chill," Frank said with genuine compassion in his voice. "Ok Frank, I think things have got on top of me lately for some reason, I'll try," she said then having thought for a minute she said: "Frank would you mind if I pop to town tomorrow just for some 'me' time, just for a couple of hours?" and waited for his answer. "Yeah no probs, if it makes you feel better it's fine with me" came the reply. "Great" Mary thought "Just great. When morning came Mary decided on a nice summer dress as it looked like it was heading for another warm day. She got ready and made her way downstairs to the kitchen and made Frank some sandwiches for lunch and left them on the table with some cake for later when he was ready then made her way to the Jeep and set off for town.Mary drove into town at a leisurely pace as there really was no rush as she enjoyed the time to reflect on the last few days and was keen to tell Mike all about it.

When Mary arrived she parked the jeep and switched it off then she got out and locked it and walked down towards the shops. Mary found herself in the little lane where Mike's bookshop was and was quite excited in telling him of the recent encounter with Sol. "I wish I could talk to Frank without fear of ridicule. It's so good that Mike's so interested in this and believes me, at least I feel comfortable talking to him" she thought. The little bell of the shop door tinkled as she opened it and walked in, "Hi Mike, how's things?"

"Hiya Mary, good to see you. It's quiet here now, busy morning but I think the readers of the town have gone home" he said smiling. Mary thought how nice he looked, dressed casual but smart. "Fancy a coffee?" he said dropping the latch on the door and putting the closed sign on

"Yes that would be good.

"Ok come through to the back" he said leading the way

"I've seen Sol again, although it was brief" she said while standing by the sink while Mike made the coffee.

"Really, what happened, what did he say?"

"Well he was saying that he was one of many that were visiting and each of them had their own particular purpose for being here, he didn't say quite how many were visiting but I had the impression it was a lot. I wonder what they're doing here." Mary said "Mary, don't you think that you should report this, after all this is no game is it" Mike said trying to think sensibly while putting the coffee in the cups

"Yes Mike you're right but who would believe me, I have no proof, I can't even tell my husband for fear of ridicule" she said looking a little lost. Mike turned to her and took hold of her hands "Look Mary I think that your friend is right to worry about you safety, no-one wants any harm to come to you," he said with conviction. He looked at Mary and she looked at him and he bent forward to kiss her. Mary felt herself go weak, she responded by putting her arms around Mike and pulling him closer as she enjoyed the passionate kiss. "Come through to the flat" Mike said and walked through a little door which leads into his living area which was cosy. Mike turned and took hold of Mary and kissed her again while undoing her dress and she unbuttoning his shirt. Before long they were in bed making love and Mary felt loved and wanted, she was experiencing some thing she'd not had in a while and was throwing herself in with enthusiasm. After a while they were both lying in each other's arms, Mary felt safe and contented, and exhausted and she had thought about this moment for a while and now it had happened…..

"What now, where do we go from here?" she thought "I love Frank but why can't Frank and I be like this," Mike turned to her. "I'll just be a moment" he said as he got out of bed and walked toward the kitchen. Mary looked at him and now noticed just how good his body was "Wow… look at him" she thought. A few minutes later Mike returned with the coffee, "I had to boil the kettle again" he said as he put them down and got back into bed. "Mary you are gorgeous as he leaned over and kissed her with another lovely kiss, then started to kiss her neck "Oh god Mike do it again" she said pulling him on top, Mary was lost again in the bliss of lovemaking. Eventually the time came for Mary to leave "Mary I want to see you again soon" Mike said putting his arms around her. "I want to see you again too Mike but we both know it's wrong, I like the way I can talk to you, you make me feel wanted but I know I'm doing wrong. I feel mixed up with everything at the moment" Mary said sounding concerned but still putting her arms around him and holding him tight "I've so enjoyed this visit Mike, I really have but I must go now. I'll be in touch later" She said as she kissed him and left the shop. Mary walked slowly back to her jeep, while she knew what she had done was wrong she could not help but feel good. She had wanted to make love to Mike as she did find him attractive and she'd enjoyed every minute "Oh God that was good, I wouldn't mind doing that again soon though. What am I thinking? Stop it Mary, you love Frank, this was a one off" she found herself saying under her breath. Mary got into her Jeep and made her way home and was thinking about tea and what to have. The next couple of days went quite normally and both of them were busy with the jobs. Mary happened to pop into the kitchen and the phone was ringing, she picked it up. "Hello" she said "Hi hunni how you doing?" It was Kath. "Oh I'm ok, listen I've been wondering about tea, fancy popping over and I'll do some chilli" Mary said quite enthusiastically "Yes ok, what time?" Kath asked "Oh about five should be ok" Mary replied "Great, see you then hun" Kath said and hung up. Mary and Frank finished the jobs and were tidying up when Mary said "You finish what you're doing and I'll go and sort the chilli for tea. I'll pop some beers in the fridge for you and Rob" Mary said. Mary made her way to the house and started preparing tea, it didn't take long as Mary only wanted to do something simple for them all and it didn't seem long before Kath and Rob appeared, armed with bottles as usual. "Hiya folks" Kath shouted as they walked in. "Hi Kath, Hi Rob good to see you both" Mary said giving them both a kiss. "Rob do you mind sorting your drinks while I finish laying the table, Frank will be in shortly"

"No probs" rob replied as he hunted for the corkscrew and went onto the porch.

"How are things" Kath quietly asked Mary

"Much the same, nothing exciting's happened over the last couple of days" she replied "Have you seen Sol?" Kath asked "No not for a few days, I am thinking he's due, I don't know why but I get this feeling inside, difficult to describe but it happens. I do know they won't show up if there are other people about though" Mary said while leaning on the table looking thoughtful. "Be careful Mary, I'm worried about all this, something's not right to me" Kath said quietly. "Kath I do wonder about it all you know I do. What is it that he's after, still never mind that now let's get the boys in and eat" Mary said with a smile. The four of them sat down in a relaxed manner and ate their meal with lots of chat and laughter; after all they all get on so well and the evening goes very well and appeared to them to go very quickly. Eventually it was time for Kath and Rob to leave. "Thanks for a great evening you guys, we always enjoy coming here" Kath said. "You know you're always welcome here, see you later, bye Kath, Bye Rob" Mary said "Bye Frank see you soon"

Rob shouted as he went to his car. Mary and Frank tided the kitchen and put the dishes away then Frank said he was going for a shower "I'll have one after you, give me a shout when you're done" Mary said as she poured herself another wine "Okey dokey" he said as he walked off. Mary took her glass and sat outside for a while looking at the stars while her hand stroked Monty as he was sitting at her side. Eventually she heard Frank shout her to say he was done with the shower. "Come on Mont, let's go as it's getting late" Mary said giving his head a rub as she got up to go inside. Mary locked up and made her way upstairs to the bathroom and undressed and jumped into the shower, it was lovely, just what she needed after a hard day and busy evening with friends. Having dried herself off she dressed in pyjamas, made her way to bed, settled down and made herself comfortable "It was good tonight , I really enjoyed it" Frank said "Me too, they are good company those two, they do make us laugh" Mary replied as Frank turned to her and put his arm around her " Are you tired" He said as he undid the buttons on her top and started kissing her neck "Well…. not really I suppose" she said to him but in her mind she thought "What's got into him tonight". Frank and Mary made love, Mary enjoyed it as she had not had passion with Frank for a long time but on reflection it was more exciting with Mike although she knew it was wrong and that made it more exciting, she knew that. However Mary lay in Frank's arms and she felt a sense of satisfaction and security and knowing that this is as it should be, then they went to sleep locked cosily together.

Chapter 11

Next morning Mary was walking up to see to Shiloh and was thinking that she would take him for a quick ride around the perimeter of the farm. As she approached the field two fighter Jets flew down the valley and she had a wonderful view of them. Shiloh was pleased to see her and he seemed excited to see Mary sorting the tack out sensing he was going for a walk. Once he was ready they set off with Monty at their side and after a while they came to the glade where she first saw the crop circle which was now grown back to normal, but it didn't stop Mary dismounting and sitting for a while and enjoying her thoughts of Sol, wondering where he was now, why they come here and his interest in her. After a while Mary jumped back onto Shiloh and carried on with her ride eventually making her way back to the field and making Shiloh comfortable and seeing to his feed before making her way back to the farm and her chores. "Frank do you fancy a buttie and a brew" Mary shouted across the yard "Yes ok, I'll come over in a minute" he replied. They had both had a busy few hours and Mary had let food go out of her mind. She made a simple ham salad sandwich and a cup of tea to last them till they ate later "Great, thanks for that "Frank said as he sat down to eat. "Fancy popping for an Indian later" Mary asked "Why not, then we could pop in the Crown for one" Frank replied. So they did, after they had finished for the day they showered and changed and made their way to the Indian restaurant and as usual Sanjay was on duty. "Good evening Mr and Mrs Scott, how good to see you again" he said enthusiastically. "Hi Sanjay, good to see you too" Frank replied. "I have a lovely table for you over here" and he lead them to a cosy table in the corner where they settled themselves down and perused the menu. "Would you like to order drinks?" Sanjay asked. "I'll have a lager please Sanjay" said Frank "Me too, I've a thirst on" said Mary. There were not many in tonight and Mary and frank were discussing the day and what's needed for the future in the way of stock, plans for expansion later on and jobs that needed doing in priority. Following their meal made their way to the Crown for a drink or two and as they walked in they found it quite full as they made their way to the bar. Jody the barmaid came over. "Hi Frank what's your fancy?" she asked "A pint for me and a white wine for Mary" he replied. As usual Kath and Rob were there and some old familiar faces and as Mary looked around she saw Burnley Paul with his wife Sharon, so called because he was from Burnley and as there were others named Paul who got in there Burnley became his nickname. Paul was sitting with Bob and his wife Denise, Bob was an ex miner from Whitehaven a few miles down the road on the coast but chose to move up to the village nearer their family. He sometimes worked behind the bar and he concocted his own cocktail and called it Sexy Bob" the locals said they liked it to keep him amused. Mary smiled at the thought of that, and then there was Dave Stewart with his wife too. What a nice crowd tonight she thought as she looked around. Frank appeared with the drinks. "There you go hun" he said passing her a glass of wine "Thanks, not much room is there" she said making conversation and as she said this Dave Stewart and his wife made their way to them: "Hi Mary, Hi Frank good to see you" said Sue , Dave's wife "Hiya folks, we've just been for an Indian and thought we'd pop in for one" Mary said while taking a quick drink "You know Sue you and Dave should pop over to ours next time we have a get together with the others, the more the merrier" Mary said "Sounds good, we may even get to see your UFO." Dave said smiling "Dave you never know" Mary said playfully punching his shoulder. "Seriously though have you seen anything since" He asked "No not really" Mary lied realising that if she spilled all no-one would believe her. "Well next time if you do try to get a picture, a selfie" Dave said as he turned to talk to Frank. "Take no notice of him Mary, he thinks he has a sense of humour." "Oh its ok Sue, the problem is that unless people see these things for themselves they will not believe anything anyone says. If someone had come to me with this story I think I would have been doubtful myself. Anyway putting that aside I'll sort another get together soon and I'll call you two over if you're free"

"Great I'll look forward to it" Sue replied. The evening went well and they all mixed and had a chat and a laugh but before long it was time to go and Frank and Mary said their goodbyes and made their way home. As the Jeep pulled into the drive Mary said "Fancy a nightcap on the veranda? " Frank thought for a minute "Yeah why not, you sit yourself down and I'll get us something" and he got out of the Jeep and made his way inside to make the drinks, as he did so he let Monty out and he bounded over to Mary who was now settling down in her seat. "I wonder when he'll be back?" she thought, just as Frank appeared with the drinks. "Here you go, what a nice night its been, the impromptu ones are the best" he said taking a drink from his glass "I've really enjoyed it, we have nice friends don't we?" Mary said. "The best" Frank replied. They chatted for a while and then Frank turned to Mary and said "I'm off up now, fancy coming with me" and winked at her. She looked at him and smiled, then said" What's up with you all of a sudden, are you on something" as she finished her drink and got up "Well don't look a gift horse in the mouth " she thought as she finished her drink and followed him upstairs. The weather over the next couple of days turned quite nasty which gave them a problem with the cows and the sheep and Shiloh spent some time in his stable. "Livestock's so much easier to deal with when the sun's out "Mary thought as she made her way to the chickens through the mud and then smiled as she saw Frank fall over in the wet having being pushed by a cow. However the bad spell didn't last long and the sun was soon out again and it was back to shorts and t-shirt weather which obviously pleased them both. This particular morning the phone rang "Hello, Mary speaking, If you're double glazing we've got it and we've the best deal on power in the North" she said jokingly "Oh hello Mary, It's George, Is Frank about? he asked "Hiya George, hold on I'll get him" she replied as she put the phone down and went to find Frank who made his way to the phone. "Hi George, what's up" He asked. "I'm sorry to put on you Frank but we've got a problem with a hay delivery, there is loads of it and it's proving a bit hard for me and my mate and we could do with another pair of hands. Any chance you could lend a hand?" he asked. "Yes, of course but George do you mind if I just finish off here and I'll pop over in about an hour" he said "Oh thanks so much Frank, see you then," George replied then put the phone down. Frank finished off what he was doing and decided to pop over to George's "See you in a while hunni, George needs a bit of help, I'll call you when we're done" he said as he grabbed his jacket and made his way out to the Jeep "Ok, give me a call if I can help" Mary added as she watched him walk off. Mary made her way to the barn to deal with her jobs and the tasks ahead for the day which kept her busy until lunchtime when she realised she needed to see to Shiloh so she made her way up to the field to see to his feed. As she arrived she was pleased to see Shiloh as he was as pleased to see her and they both made a fuss of each other. Mary made him his feed and a snack and Shiloh seemed very happy. While Mary was watching him she started to have a feeling, a feeling she knew all too well , a feeling that told her that Sol was due to visit. Not long after she saw the light appearing over the hills. When she saw this she developed a warm feeling, a feeling that she was greeting a loved one or someone special, but really in her mind she was…..it was Sol! Mary watched as the craft came into view and slowly came down and landed in the field adjacent to where Shiloh stood and watched. Mary stood and watched as this slowly came down and was brought to a stop. After a few moments the door of the craft opened and Sol appeared in the doorway, hesitated for a moment before walking down the ramp. Mary watched him as he approached her" Hello Mary, I've been looking forward to seeing you "Sol said as he got close to her. "

"I feel the same Sol, I was becoming to wonder when you would be back, it seems a while since I saw you last"

"Mary, we have many duties here on your planet, I get to come here as often as I can as I do want to see you, I have passed by many times but I have to pick my time when you are alone to visit. No one will see us at that time as we have the technology to remain unseen to your people." Sol seemed quite sincere "I'm alone now for a while, so you're quite safe" Mary said

"Mary, would you like to come aboard our craft for a while"

"Yes I would, thank you." Mary said as she walked forward with Sol and stepped onto the ramp and walked into the craft. She remembered how clean it was, spotless, very shiny steelwork throughout. They walked into what was obviously the control area of the craft but found it sparse of controls, very limited and with no windows which she could see. "Would you like to have a trip in this craft" and then looked at her with his lovely blue eyes "Yes I would" Mary replied as she looked up at his athletic figure towering over her. Just then an opening like a window appeared in the craft and she realised that they had already taken off and were in space. Mary couldn't believe that they had taken off and she had not felt the craft move. She moved towards the window and looked out at the most beautiful sight of her life, Earth from space, something she had ever only seen on the movies "I don't believe it, I don't believe it, how wonderful is this" she thought "This is spectacular Sol, I could never in my life imagined what this would be like, thank you"

"Mary I want to show you something" and as he said this he moved to the control panel and pressed a few buttons. At this Mary noticed through the window that the craft began to turn and as it did so hundreds of other craft similar to the one they were in came into view "Oh my God Sol, what's happening, there's so many of you" she asked with a sense of excitement. "Mary, our race have visiting here for many years and we are able to sit here in space undetected while carrying out our missions. Each one of the craft that you see has a different mission to accomplish and this has been going on for thousands of your years." "What is your mission?" Mary asked

"You asked me this before Mary and I can't tell you, you wouldn't understand, but trust me no harm will come to you" Sol said "Come with me and I will offer you some of our refreshment" and at this Sol walked out of the control room into a short corridor which led to a casual room, a room which was obviously there for relaxation during journeys as it had comfortable seating, dim lighting and a bed. Mary found it very comfortable and felt quite at home in there. Sol stood by a small machine and pressed a button and some liquid came out into a small cup, one for each of them.

"You'll like this Mary, it's nothing more than a fruit drink as I've said before we are quite similar in many ways as we have to drink too" he said as he passed her a cup.

Sol stood close to Mary as he put the cup to his lips and had a sip, Mary watched and gazed into his lovely blue eyes then had a drink herself and found it really nice. Mary felt really comfortable in Sol's company, because of his good looks and the low lighting she could forget that she was in the company of an alien. She put down her drink and reached up to put her arms around Sol and as she did so he leaned forward and kissed her.They stayed in that position for a moment before Mary had the compulsion to break away for a moment and stepped away. She looked at him and then started to undo her blouse and let it fall away then slowly she took off her bra and then let her shorts fall to the floor. Sol looked her up and down before removing his uniform suit, before long they were both naked in bed. Mary watched as the wall of the craft started to open like a window as she realised they were going to make love to the light of the stars "This is wonderful" she thought.

Mary pulled the strange sheet up to cover her breasts and realised that it was a type of metallic sheet but felt very comfortable on the skin. Sol and Mary began to embrace and Mary began to enjoy the passion of what she considered a real man, firm, muscular and confident. At the point where they started to make love Mary started to feel strange, her head became light and filled with colours, then she felt as if she was floating in the air, she could feel great ecstasy, a feeling so great she had never experienced before and she realised that she could not feel Sol in her arms. Eventually the feeling of elation was reached at a fever pitch and she sensed an orgasm like never before although she felt she was alone floating in a sea of colour. Gradually Mary felt herself calming down and could see the colours slowly fading away and sensed she was sinking back into the bed, when she settled she opened her eyes to find Sol at her side "Sol, What was that, I've never experienced anything like that before, that was really something else," She asked. "We produce young a lot different where we come from, normally it is a lot different than what you just experienced, however I did feel that I wanted to experience a little of your primitive way of copulation which is why we are here in this bed, what you experienced was a part of my spirit entering you, a part of my soul as we became one for that moment. Did you find it pleasurable?" he asked.

"I most certainly did." she said trying to regain her breath and composure. After a while Sol got up and dressed. "You should dress and meet me in the control room" he said as he walked out a few moments later Mary appeared at his side in the control room. " I thought you may like a little trip to see this, something you won't see every day" at that Sol started to move the craft away from the others and Mary was so excited though she could not feel the craft move at all and within seconds they were by the Moon. "Oh my God Sol this is wonderful, how amazing Oh my God it looks so beautiful" Mary was finding it hard to believe what she was seeing "All that effort our spacemen made to get here and we were here in the blink of an eye. It doesn't seem real, thank you Sol for this wonderful experience" Mary said while giving him a hug. "Mary I need to return you now, but we may do this again at a future date," Sol said to her "I hope so Sol, I hope so" Mary looked at him and felt she was falling in love, but realised this shouldn't happen The craft made its way around the Moon and as it did so Earth appeared from the horizon "Oh Sol look at that, it's wonderful, Oh my God it's wonderful. Wish I had my camera" Mary stood in the field and watched as the craft slowly disappeared from sight and slowly turned and walked to her little seat where she wanted to sit and digest what had just happened "I just don't believe it, I don't believe it, that was wonderful. I wonder when he'll be back" she thought. After sitting for a while Mary made her way home and found Monty sitting on the porch in the sun "Come on mate let's get some tea ready for later" and made a fuss of him before going inside. While Mary planned what to have later she was away with her thoughts. "What's going on in my life? It's been so long since anyone showed any interest in me, then all of a sudden I have three of them on the go What am I going to do?" she thought as she pulled some pork chops from the freezer "Pork chop, beans and cheese, that'll do for tonight "she thought then she opened a bottle of wine and sat out on the porch with Monty and decided she needed a drink. A little while later frank appeared driving down the track and as he pulled up Monty went to meet him with tail wagging. Frank jumped out of the Jeep and gave him a fuss as he walked to the porch "Oh I see, started without me then" he said smiling at Mary "Have you had a tough day?"

"No not really, bit boring I suppose" she said thinking to herself "He would never believe me with this episode, best say nowt I think."

"What's for tea or are we out again" Frank asked

"I've done pork chops Frank" she replied

"Ok, I'll shower first, won't be long"

"Ok, I'll get tea on the go" Mary said raising herself out of her chair and making her way to the kitchen. Weeks later Mary woke at about six one morning and lay there thinking and was aware that there had been no sign of Sol for a while, and she did think that she wouldn't see him again. She had a feeling that the fun was over and resigned herself to that fact "I've had an experience of a lifetime which I will treasure and never forget" she thought. As she got up she felt a little off colour "I don't feel right, wonder if I ate something funny last night" she thought as she made her way downstairs to find Frank already there. "I've done some breakfast hunni, sit yourself down" he said feeling proud of himself. "Frank I don't feel well, I don't think I could eat a thing, I don't know what's wrong. Must have had something funny last night" She said and at that she had to run to the toilet to be sick. "I'll call the Doctors when they open at 8.00 and try to get in this morning, I'm of back to bed for now" she said. "Ok I'll come and check on you later" Frank said as he sat down to eat. Mary did call the doctors and she did manage to get in that morning. She sat reading a magazine in the waiting room for quite a while before she say he name called on the illuminated sign and made her way to the Doctors office "Hello Mary, what can we do for you" the Doctor asked. "I just feel right off colour this orning, I think I may have had something funny to eat last night" she said to him

"Ok, firstly I'm going to ask you to put a sample of urine in this bottle and we'll test for infection" Mary made her way to the toilet to do what was asked, passed it to the nurse then went back to his room where the doctor gave her a full check over with blood pressure, temperature, weight etc then after a short while the nurse appeared with a piece of paper for the doctor, who looked at it and placed it down on his desk. "Well Mary we've gone through everything you've said and we've given you a full check over and the conclusion is this; you're pregnant, about 6 weeks, congratulations!" The Doctor said with a little excitement in his voice.

"Oh my God, are you sure?" Mary said with an element of shock in her voice

"Quite sure dear, I hope its good news for you?" the doctor replied.

"Well, yes of course it's just that I never expected it, I mean we did say that in the future we would like kids but we were hoping to plan it a bit better than this, wow.....I wonder how Frank will react" Mary said quietly.

"Good, leave it with me and I'll get you booked in for an ultrasound scan, you'll be notified by letter of you appointment, it'll be about two weeks, well goodbye Mary, see you again soon" the doctor said opening the door for Mary.

Chapter 12

Mary had a mixture of emotions on the way home: "Me a Mother? I can't believe it. Will I get it right, will I be able to do it, and oh my God this is scary" she was thinking all sorts of things to herself as she pulled onto the track which leads to the farm. As the Jeep pulled up Monty came bounding over with his tail wagging. Mary opened the Jeep door, stepped out and gave him a fuss "Hiya boy, come on in I need a drink" she said to him as he ran by her side to the house. Mary went into the kitchen and poured herself a drink the sat down to take in what the doctor had said to her. "I know there's no turning the clock back now but am I ready for this "she thought "And how's the best way to tell Frank?" A little later Mary was preparing sandwiches for Franks lunch when he appeared in the kitchen "Hiya, how did you get on at the doctors, do you feel better?" he asked "Yes and no" She replied "But we'll chat about it later, there's a sandwich for you here, how's your morning been?" Mary added casually. "Thanks for the butty, Quite productive this morning, I seem to have achieved success with a lot of those little odd jobs that you think I'll do that later, well I've done them all" he said with satisfaction in his voice. Frank ate his lunch with speed as he was still anxious to get back to work, Mary could see this so did not want to start a conversation about babies now, she knew it was the wrong time. Mary decided to wait till they were having dinner later. Frank finished lunch and set off back to his jobs leaving Mary to tidy up which she did at a steady pace with her thoughts on becoming a mother. Later that evening Mary had prepared a nice meal as a surprise for Frank, fillet steak. She knew he liked this as a treat now and again and she had put a bottle of champagne in the fridge to celebrate with. The evening meal went well with easy flowing conversation when Frank went silent for a minute. "What's up Frank, something bothering you" Mary asked "Well not really other than I can see a distance in you again today and I feel that you're keeping something from me" he replied. Mary rose from her seat and made her way to his side of the table and pulled out a chair next to him and sat down and took his hand in hers. "Well Frank, there is something wrong and because of this I won't be able to help as much on the farm for a while".

"Oh God Mary, what's wrong hunni, what did the doctor say, is it serious?" he said with slight panic in his voice. At this Mary was enjoying seeing him get worked up

"Yes Frank it's serious" she said smiling in her mind "Oh Mary what is it" he asked

"I'm pregnant Frank, we're having a baby" Mary said with tears in her eyes.

"What, really, are you serious" Frank asked excitedly. "Yes Frank, you're going to be a dad" Mary said smiling. "Oh hunni that's fantastic, I'm so pleased. Me and you as mum and dad, how great is that?" he said as he gave her a hug and a kiss.

They spent the rest of the evening chatting about the future, what about this, and what about that, what name shall we call it if it's a boy or a girl. The evening went by very quickly and before they knew it, it was bed time. Mary by this time was feeling very tired as the emotion of the day had taken its toll on her and she was ready to turn in. The next morning

Mary was on the phone to Kath to invite her for tea "Hiya Kath are you two about later if so fancy popping over for a bowl of chilli "Yes love too, how about 4 ish?" Kath asked "That will be great, see you then" Mary said with a smile. Frank finished early and was showered and changed as he was as excited about telling Rob and Kath as Mary was. Tea was almost ready when they heard Rob's car pull up outside the house. Mary and Frank went out to meet them with Monty by their side "Hiya" Mary called out as they got out of their car with bottles in hand "Hiya Mary, hiya Frank" Rob called back as they walked to the house "Good to see you, tea's almost done, Rob you know where the bottle opener is" Mary said "I'm already on to it "Frank said waving it in the air. "There you go Rob" he said passing it over "What you having Mary" Frank asked "I'll start with a Gin I think" Mary said "You'll start with a gin, Blimey are you on a session" Kath asked "You could say that" Mary replied "Come on everyone foods ready" and Mary placed a large pot of chilli down onto the table "Help yourselves to rice folks" said Frank putting a plate of hot garlic bread down next to the rice "How's the farm going, still thoughts on expanding" Rob asked as he started his meal "Well funnily enough we planning quite an expansion later this year" Frank replied "Well it goes without doubt mate with expansion goes expense, now any expansion that hasn't been planned can be a major drain on your cash." Rob said seriously then to a bite of his garlic bread. Mary and Frank found Rob's statement really funny and laughed hysterically, Rob looked in disbelief as he couldn't understand the funny side "So what's so funny" he asked "Well, let me put it this way, we are having expansion and it wasn't planned" Mary said. "Well Mary be careful, best start budgeting" Rob said "we're pregnant" Mary said with a glow on her face. "Wow how fantastic, I'm so pleased for you, "Kath said as she jumped up and went to Mary to give her a hug "Well you had me there Mary, great news, best of luck to you all." Rob said smiling. Frank got up and went to the cupboard and pull out two bottles of Brut Champagne and four glasses "Right folks, before Mary ives up drinking, let's have a celebration" he said looking very proud as he popped a cork and started to pour. While Mary was still trying to get used to the idea of being pregnant she received an appointment to the hospital for an ultrasound scan. This is a normal procedure for women having a baby. When the day came Mary went and asked Kath to go with her which she did as Frank was busy with the lambing. "Come on Mary lets go" Kath said as she'd arrived happy to offer to drive Mary to the hospital. "Ok ready let's go" Mary said grabbing her jacket and bag. On the way there they were chatting. "How do you feel, I must say you don't seem very happy about this pregnancy" said Kath "Nervous mate" came the reply from Mary. "Oh everything will be fine, don't worry" Kath said "I know it will and I do find the whole thing exciting, but Kath I do have a problem with all this and it's bothering me more than you can imagine," Mary said thinking she may have said too much. "Why what's wrong, tell me" Kath said. "I can't yet Kath, I've things going on in my mind but when I've sorted it we'll talk it through, I promise." They pulled into the hospital car park by the sign for the maternity unit. There were a few in the waiting area but it didn't bother Mary and Kath as they were happy chatting about various topics and using the time as another opportunity for a catch up. The nurse appeared and called "Mrs Scott?" and looked around. "I'm here" said Mary and the nurse came over. "Hello, I'm Sue one of the nurses, we won't be long before you're in as we're running well on time this morning, we'll call you shortly" the nurse said as she walked away. The doctor that day was a Mr Menon, an Indian man but born in America and served in the American Airforce as a doctor becoming highly decorated and reaching the rank of Major. On retirement from the forces he came to England to specialise and was now Head of Maternity at the Hospital in Carlisle. It wasn't long before the nurse came and called Mary and escorted her through to a changing room. "Can you slip out of your Jeans and pop this gown on please, then just come out to us" the nurse asked, "Yes ok" Mary replied undoing her buttons. A few minutes later she appeared in the customary backless hospital gown. Good morning Mary, I'm Dr Menon. As you know we're going to give you an ultrasound scan which won't take long and this will give us a guide to how the pregnancy is going. You won't feel anything other than the cold gel on your tum. Your husband can come in to watch if he wishes" he said. "Thanks but I'm with my friend as Frank's dealing with the lambing" she replied. "Ok now I'll leave you with the nurse and I'll speak to you at another time, nice to meet you" he said in a nice calming voice, then he left the room. "Let's help you onto the couch Mary "said the nurse as Mary started to get onto the couch and made herself comfortable. The nurse lifted Mary's gown and then applied gel onto Mary's belly making her squirm with the cold. "Sorry Mary that always surprises people "she said as she started the scan. The nurse had a monitor in front of her while scanning and usually this would be turned so that the patient could also see what's happening but on this occasion the nurse kept the screen turned towards her as she was not sure what she was looking at although all the vital signs for the baby were good. "Is it ok?" asked Mary. "Mary all the vital signs are as they should be, no problems at all and your baby has a very strong heartbeat. I just can't get a clear picture so the kit must be throwing a wobbler this morning, are you ok just to wait a moment?" asked the nurse "Yeah I'm ok, quite comfy" came the reply from Mary. The nurse left the room and walked down the corridor to Mr Menon's office, knocked and went in. "Hi Sue, something wrong" asked Mr Menon. "I'm not sure, I've done the scan and the vital signs are really good but it's just the picture I'm getting, I've not seen anything like this and I'm wondering if the kit's faulty. Can you come and have a look?" Sue asked "Ok two minutes and I'll be there" the Dr replied. Sue made her way back to the room "Hiya, have you nodded off while waiting" Sue asked "No but I feel very relaxed" Mary said "The doctor is coming to have a look at what's wrong with the kit he won't be a minute" Sue said. Just then the door opened and in walked Dr Menon "Right let's have a look, Dr Menon started the scan again, Mary your baby has a very strong heartbeat and the other vital signs and very good, no problems there. We are just getting a very poor picture on the screen and I feel that this is our problem which I can only apologise for" he then turned to Sue with a look that told her something was wrong. Dr Menon pressed the print button on the machine and Sue noticed that Mr Menon slipped the photo away into his pocket but she knew it was not for her to say anything at this time. "Mary we are happy that at this early stage everything is as it should be, unfortunately we're having printing problems so there will be a little delay on you having your souvenir of your visit, but we'll make sure you get one next time. Now I'm going to arrange another visit for you so we will be in touch as my secretary will drop you a line with your next appointment. Enjoy the rest of your day" at that he left the room. "Come on Mary let's get you dressed" sue said while helping Mary off the couch. Mary made her way to the changing room and got dressed then made her way out side to where Kath was waiting. "Hiya hunni, was it OK?" Kath asked "Yes it's a very healthy baby the doctor says." Mary replied smiling as they walked out of the Hospital. "Sex" Kath asked "No, you're not my type" Mary replied smiling "No twit I mean the baby" Kath said. "They didn't ask but I told them I don't want to know 'til it arrives," Mary said. Mary and Kath got into the car and set off for home. "Firstly do you fancy a bit of retail therapy followed by a wine Mary?" Kath asked "Kath you know me so well" Mary said and off they set. Meanwhile back in the hospital Sue was tidying the room as Mary was the last patient of the morning and when she finished she made her way to Dr Menon's room, knocked and entered. Mr Menon was sitting looking at the photo from the scan "Is there something wrong Dr" Sue asked "There could be Sue, there could be something very wrong. I need to speak to someone rather urgently. Sue nothing must be discussed outside this room, Is that clear, I trust you and you must trust me and if you come across Mrs Scott again before our next appointment as far as you're concerned everything is normal, OK? When I know more I will talk to you but not until I've done some research" he said "Yes of course" Sue said. The doctor knew he could trust Sue as they had a very close relationship and intended to marry when the time was right. "See you later hunni" she said to him on leaving the room "How interesting, wonder what's up" She thought as she walked down the corridor. Mr Menon sat at his desk with the photo in his hand deep in thought as his military past came flooding back to him. He reached in his pocket and pulled out his mobile phone and dialled a number and waited for a connection before speaking "RAF Mildenhall, can I be put through to Colonel Jeff Stewart please" he said and was then put on hold Eventually a woman answered and said "hello, Colonel Stewarts secretary can I help you?" The doctor thought for a moment "Hello, this is retired Major Victor Menon and I need to speak to the colonel over a matter of national security," he said. "Just one moment sir and I'll try to locate him" she replied before putting him on hold for what seemed an age. The phone clicked "Hi Vic, it's been a long time to what do I owe this pleasure?" he asked in a relaxed way "Jeff it's not pleasure I'm afraid, can I take you back to 1976 at groom lake and the Nordics" he said. "I remember" said Jeff "Well they're back, and it looks like they're on a breeding run, we need to arrange a meeting urgently," Victor said "How do you know this Vic, have you proof?" Jeff said "Yes, we have an impregnated patient who came to see us this morning, it appears its just 6 weeks" Victor said "Is the patient aware of who the father actually is

"Jeff asked "I don't think so, she arrived with her friend for a scan, the husband was not present as they are farmers and he's lambing. We should get the team together straight away" Victor said "I'll call you back in a short while, I need to make some calls, stay where you are by your phone" Jeff ordered.

Chapter 13

Mary and Kath arrived at the town. "Right, firstly let's pop and have a wine then we'll wander to the shops" Kath said "Sounds good to me" Mary said as they made their way to the wine bar. They opened the door and went in and Mary spotted a cosy table in the corner. "I'll get the table while you order the drinks" Mary said making her way over. Kath came back with a bottle of Pinot Grigio in a cooler and two glasses "There you go, a little celebration for your scan" Kath said undoing the wine. Mary just looked at her as she poured the wine "What's up, didn't you want wine" Kath asked looking concerned. "Yes its fine, Just what the doctor ordered "Mary said quietly. Kath looked at her "What is wrong with you, you're up one minute and down the next, what's troubling you? Don't you want this baby?" Kath asked. "Yes of course I do, it's what I've always wanted but…." Mary paused "But what "Kath asked "What's the matter" she added "Kath…..I'm not sure who the father is, Kath listen to me, I don't know who the bloody father is!"

Kath looked at her in amazement and disbelief "WHAT are you saying Mary, surely it's Franks" she said "Well there's a good chance it is......and..... There's a chance it isn't" Mary said seeming relieved that she's told someone. "Well who the hell else have you been bonking then?" Kath asked while taking a drink from her glass. "Well it could be Sol's" Mary said. "You mean you've bonked the spaceman as well, an orbital orgasm" Kath was surprised by this "Oh Kath it was so nice, he took me for a trip to the stars in his ship, I saw earth from space. The wall of the bedroom went translucent and it was as if there was no wall between us and the stars, it was beautiful, so beautiful, in a way I've never known before, so different from here on earth. He made love to me so well and made me feel so important and I didn't want it to stop. When he brought me back to earth I felt that I didn't want him to leave, it was like being in love all over again. He did say that I was important to him and he would be back again, can't wait for next time" Mary said having a good drink from her glass. Kath looked at her quite shocked. "I know you've not been getting it Mary but having the two of them is a bit much. Well which do you think is the dad" Kath said "I'm not actually sure if it was either of them" Mary said with a feeling of dread about telling Kath the next bit. "Oh right………Hang on what do you mean by that, you're not sure if it's either of them" Kath looked startled "Well who the hell's is it then Mary"

"Remember me telling you about Mike the bookshop owner, well It could be Mike's" Mary said wondering what her answer would be. "Jesus, You've had him as well, you've had the three of them, are you now some sort of nymphomaniac, have you had the butcher, the baker and the candlestick maker as well, Oh Mary what are you doing," Kath said with total disbelief. "Well Kath, it all seemed to happen very close together and each time seemed the right time" Mary said sounding as if she was getting upset by now. "Oh Mary what are you going to do hunni, what a mess." The phone rang in Dr Victor Menon's office and he picked it up "Hello" he said, it was the Colonel "Vic can you get to RAF Spadeadam by 10.00 in the morning" he asked "Yes I can why?" Victor asked

"Bring your evidence and a plane will pick you up and bring you here. I'm getting to old team together, you're coming out of retirement for this one Vic" Jeff said and just hung up before Victor could answer. Mary started to cry "I don't know what to do Kath, I'm going to have to think this through long and hard. Frank' really excited as he wants to be a dad but we were going to wait a bit longer. In my mind it's Franks but in reality I'm not sure," she said. "Well not much you can do about that now you've just got to go with it and look forward to being a mum" Kath said taking a drink of her wine. The girls chatted for a while before steadily making their way back to the farm where Kath dropped Mary off and made her own way home to Rob.

Chapter 14

The next morning Victor Menon arrived at the gate of R.A.F Spadeadam and the Guard stepped out and stopped his car by the gate "Can I help you, sir?" said the Guard. "You certainly can Corporal, I'm Major Victor Menon retired and I've been told to report here to meet a flight which will take me to R.A.F Mildenhall to see Colonel Stewart," Victor explained. "I see sir, could you please just wait one moment while I check?" the corporal replied. "Certainly" said Victor as the Corporal made his way inside the Guardhouse. A few moments later the guard appeared. "Very well sir, you are expected, if you drive up to the main hanger ahead of you and park in the bays someone will meet you and take you to your aircraft which is here and waiting" said the guard as his colleague raised the barrier. "Thank you "said Victor as he drove off. It didn't seem long before Victor was airborne and on his way, his mind in a whirl at the thought of dealing with the Nordics again. The small executive jet soon arrived at R.A.F Mildenhall and Victor was met by a car which took him to the main offices. As he arrived he was met by Colonel Jeff Stewart "Hi Vic, Good to see you, have you brought your evidence?" Jeff asked. "Yes of course, safely in my case" Vic replied. The men made their way through the office building to a room which was already occupied by a number of military top brass Army, Navy and Royal Air Force and some people in black suits, about 6 in all. Victor was introduced to them but was not told who he was meeting. "Sorry Vic, need to know basis" Jeff said. When they were all comfortable Jeff spoke "Do you have the photo Vic, can we see it?" Jeff asked. Victor produced it from his case and handed it to him and Jeff looked at it in silence for a moment. "Gentlemen we have our proof, they're back" he said handing the photograph to one of the men in suits who examined it and then passed it around to the others who showed great interest in it. "How sure are you of this, the image looks a bit strange to me, how can you can tell?" said one of the top brass. "It was 1976, we had a lot of experience with these at Groom Lake in Nevada, there's no mistaking that this is an alien foetus, a hybrid, and gentlemen we have to get hold of it before the Nordics. We can't let this one slip by and be sure they will be back for it" Colonel Stewart said in earnest. "And how do you propose we do that, I'm sure the mother would be put out to say the least if we just took her baby from her," said one of the suits. "We'll come to that later, for the time being Victor can you let the mother think everything is ok and running well?" Jeff asked "Yes I can, we know that we have a few months before any of us can do anything with the foetus, even the Nordics. I have a photo of a normal one which I can show the patient next time to put her mind at rest while we put a plan in place" Victor replied "Very good, in the mean time I want Tornados from R.A.F Lossiemouth scrambled to patrol the North of England and Scotland on a daily basis to look for and report anything unusual until this is over. Can someone deal with that immediately?" The Colonel asked. "I'll get onto it now" said one of the officers. "Vic, we'll fly you back up north right now, you must keep us informed of the progress of the foetus. As soon as we can we'll take it out and get it to NASA and they're chomping at the bit for this one, how we do it we'll work out later. For now thank you gentlemen" Colonel Stewart said as he stood up and bid goodbye to them all. "Come on Vic I'll escort you to your ride" he said. As they arrived at the Jet the Colonel turned to Victor "Thanks Vic for being so prompt in contacting us. We want a result with this one before the Nordics come back for it, it's important as you know" Jeff said "I know, I'll stay on top of it and keep you informed" Victor replied as he climbed aboard the Jet and closed the door. The bells rang at R.A.F Lossiemouth and the tanoy came to life. "Scramble Eagle flight, Scramble Eagle flight" A voice ordered. The flight crews had the aircraft ready in minutes and the two pilots were hurrying across the tarmac to their respective jets and climbed the ladders to get in and strapped up. Once in they made their way to the end of the runway and were given immediate clearance to take off, which they did at great speed. "Eagle 1 to tower, Eagle 1 to tower" said the pilot "Tower to Eagle 1, we read you" came the reply "Where are we going and what are we looking for?" said the pilot. "Coastline of Scotland and around the lakes, especially the hills around Carlisle report anything unusual, stay up there to your maximum, all we know is that we're expecting something, what that is we're not told, sorry" said the controller. "Eagle 1 to tower, thanks and out, Eagle 2 hope you packed your lunch as we're out for a while "said the pilot "Roger Eagle 2"came the reply. Mary and Frank had just finished tea and Frank was doing the dishes. "I won't be long, just going up to feed Shiloh" she said. "Ok see you in a bit, but take it easy hunni" Frank said. "Come on Monty you can keep me company" she said and at that Monty jumped up excited at the walk. It was a lovely evening and Mary took her time walking up and as she did so two jet fighters flew low over the hills "Wow…see that Mont, I wonder what they're doing , impressive" she thought.

"Eagle two to Eagle one, come in skipper" the radio crackled "Eagle one, go ahead" the pilot who was known as Bonehead (his nickname) replied. "What are we looking for, I mean the squadron have these sorties all day long for a week now but what should we look for, over?" the second pilot was known as Prince (nickname) due to coming from good stock himself.

"Bonehead I don't know, no one will say, I have asked and they say there could be a threat but they're not giving any more details other than we're to keep an eye on the radar and report anything strange". The boys who were flying yesterday were asking the same and the reply was just keep your eyes open for anything unusual, over" Prince said to him. "Well we best just enjoy the views then, over" replied Bonehead as they carried on their sortie. Victor Menon was on his rounds at the hospital when the phone rang in his office. "Hello, Mr Menon's office" Mr Menon's secretary answered in a polite voice "Good morning, This is Colonel Stewart and I need to speak to Mr Menon straight away please" he asked. "Mr Menon is on his ward rounds as we speak , however if you hold I will page him" His secretary had been made aware that the Colonel would call at some time and had been told to get Mr Menon straight away "Menon here" he said picking up the phone. "It's the Colonel for you Mr Menon, I'll put him through to you now" she said "Hi Jeff, what can I do for you?" he asked. "Vic we've been doing some research from here. With the information you gave us on your patient we've had a copy of her notes sent down to us, we're in a position to get anything we want when it comes to national security as you know. Now from this we have found a match with one of our young military female offices within N.A.S.A who is willing to carry the foetus to term so it's vital that we get the timing right. We'll get the team and the volunteer from the states to fly over and have them in position at the hospital in readiness, I'll get onto our colleagues in the NHS to set us up a secure unit in your hospital for this purpose, once the operation is complete we will transfer them to Groom lake on area 51. While setting the unit up is carried out, people are bound to ask you what it's for so obviously mums the word, make something up and keep me informed of the progress of the foetus Vic" he then hung up without waiting for any answer.

When Mary arrived at the top field she lifted the latch on the farm gate and as she did so she noticed Shiloh walking up towards her. "Hello boy, no more riding for a while I'm afraid as I'm having a baby and I want to be careful, you don't mind do you?" She said to him while rubbing his nose. "Come on let's get you fed" and she made her way to the store to load his hay nets and feed bowl for the evening. She smiled when she looked around and found Shiloh bending his head down and rubbing noses with Monty as they did seem to get on really well with each other. When she was happy that Shiloh was ok Mary said goodnight to him and her and Monty took a steady stroll back down the track to the farm. A few days went by and all was normal on the farm, the usual chores to attend to, John the tanker driver came for the milk, Frank went to the cattle auction.

Mary made a trip or two into town but decided not to go and see Mike in the bookshop as she was still feeling mixed up about the pregnancy, but met up for coffee with Kath and tried to answer all the questions that she threw at her. Sol was firmly in Mary's mind during all this time as she'd not seen him for a while and she was beginning to wonder if he really was coming back. Mary was now sitting in the kitchen having a coffee and finding all the attention from Frank very strange, she'd never known him so attentive, she wasn't used to it and at times found it a little overpowering but was trying to be patient as she knew how excited he was about being a Dad "What if it isn't his" she thought "What if its Sol's, will it look alien when it arrives, and then there's Mike, what will he say or should I even tell him. It will destroy Frank, our marriage, the farm, everything we have worked for will go. If it's not Franks I'll just have to act as if it is his, but how will I live with myself, while the baby's growing up? I'll be wondering who it's going to look like when it's an adult. Oh fuck this just terrible, what have I done, what have I done? This is something I should be enjoying not worrying about like this" Mary's mind was in turmoil as she drank her coffee and wondered what to do next. Mary was outside on this lovely sunny morning feeding the chickens when she heard a car coming down the track, making her way round the house she saw it was the post van just pulling up outside the house, the door opened and out stepped the postie." Morning, more bills for us "Mary said with a smile "I don't think so this morning, I think you've got away with it today.

There's a small parcel and one letter" he said as he passed them to her. "Thanks very much postie, drive careful" Mary said as he got back in his van and pulled away and made his way down the track. Mary looked at the parcel and saw it was for Frank then looked at the letter and saw it was for her, she opened it and found it was an appointment for another ultrasound at the hospital in a weeks' time "Oh great, wonder if Kath want's to come again if Franks going to be busy, we'll see" she thought as she put the letter back in the envelope and walked into the house. Colonel Stewart's phone rang. "Hello Colonel Stewart's office" His Secretary said in an official voice. "Oh hello, this is Major Menon, may I speak to the Colonel please? " he asked "Certainly if he is free, hold on please while I check" she replied, a few moments went by then the familiar voice of Jeff Stewart came on "Hi Vic, what's new" he asked " Jeff I've booked my patient in for a scan next week, I could have done it sooner but I don't want to raise suspicion that something's wrong" Jeff thought for a minute "Yes I see your point, good idea, also we don't want her getting distressed as this could affect the foetus and we don't want that" Victor then added "Jeff I've got a good photograph of a foetus that I will show her to lead her to believing all is well. It's about the right size for the time so there's no worry of anyone picking fault with it and it should put her mind at rest for the time being" he said. "That's great, operations are under way to get the team and special equipment over from the states so we can set it up early to be ready for a quick transfer when the times right, I'll let you know when it's here and we've had a word with our contacts within the NHS, they will be quietly in touch with you to give you the room that you want at the hospital, they will give you anything you ask for so we need somewhere that's accessible from outside as we don't want to many prying eyes on our kit going in and people asking too many questions, also as you know the unit has to be made into as sterile unit as possible and I'm sorry to state the obvious to you Vic, I'm thinking aloud now" he said "I understand Jeff, I'll look forward to meeting your contacts and I'll keep you informed of any changes with our patient no matter how small" Victor said. "Thanks Vic, chat later" at that Jeff hung up the phone. Sue, Victor's girlfriend and also the nurse was standing in the doorway of Victor's office "What's wrong Vic, can't you tell me?" she asked. Victor looked at her for a minute "Have you finished your shift" he asked "Yes, why?" she replied "Come on then let's go for a drink and we'll chat" he said grabbing his jacket and switching his light off. Vic and Sue made their way to a little quiet pub not far from the hospital and Sue found a little table in the corner away from anyone else while Vic ordered the drinks. There were not many in this night and it was easy to talk to each other without being overheard. Vic came back to the table and put the drinks down "Cheers Sue" he said "Cheers, what's going on Vic?" she asked "We have a problem with a patient, Mrs Mary Scott, the one who was in recently with the unusual scan"

"Yes I remember her well, what was so wrong with that scan, why couldn't I see the baby properly, why the cloak and dagger mystery?" Sue asked "Well, Sue you were looking at a baby, but not one from this earth."

"I don't understand what you're talking." about Vic."

"Sue, the baby is alien, the father is an extra-terrestrial being, a spaceman in simple terms."

"You're having me on, go to the bar and get some crisps" She said taking a drink from her glass "Sue listen, when I was in the Air Force in the 70's I was based at Area 51 in Nevada. We had aliens there, they are real. There is a race of alien which we called Nordics because of their appearance. This race visited earth and started to impregnate young healthy women with their sperm, seed whatever they call it and let the foetus grow to a particular size before coming back for it a few months later, they were producing hybrids using earth women as hosts." Sue was listening with astonishment. "We on the base were trying to intercept a host when we found one and retrieve a foetus before the aliens came back for it but each time we were beaten to it. We have the chance now but this is going to be one big military operation. We need this foetus and we have to make every effort to beat the alien to it, they will be monitoring the patient and they will be back. We are setting up a secure theatre unit at the hospital and when the time is right we will take the patient there and remove the foetus and that will then be sent back to the States to the area 51 where they have secure facilities where it will be nurtured and then brought up. Sue I'm telling you this but I shouldn't, you must remain in my confidence, you will be a part of this, a part of history in the making, do you understand" he asked "Oh my God I don't know what to say, I can't believe it, yes I will do anything you want Vic, this is amazing, when will you try to retrieve the foetus?" she asked. "It will be at 3 months, I'm going to need you as my right hand, the yanks will be joining us with some R.A.F people but that will be a little later on, right now we have to convince Mrs Scott that her baby is fine and the pregnancy is going well, we need to be good actors now Sue" he said rubbing her hand and taking a drink from his glass.

Chapter 15

Mary was at home and the phone rang, it was Kath "Hiya, listen I know you have an appointment tomorrow for your scan, is Frank coming with you?" she asked "I don't think so Kath as we're busy here and I'm not much help at the moment, would you like to come?" Mary enquired hoping she would say yes "Of course I will, I'll come and pick you up, what time are we due there hunni" she asked "Be here for 10 and that will give us plenty of time" Mary replied "Ok see you then" she said and hung up. The next morning Kath was on time and pulled up outside the house where Mary was already waiting on the veranda. Mary go into the car and off they went "How are you feeling" Kath asked "A bit nervous, I don't know why, perhaps it's a feeling of dread that they may say somethings wrong" Mary said while looking at the scenery through the window "Oh don't worry I'm sure everything will be fine Mary, I think it's really exciting, we'll be Uncle Rob and Aunty Kath" and they both laughed at that. Mary loved Kath as a friend as she really knew how to lift her feelings when they were together. Conversation flowed and it wasn't long before they found themselves at the hospital and they parked the car and started to walk over to the maternity unit. Suddenly Mary started to feel strange and Kath spotted this. "Mary what's wrong, you don't look good at all? "Kath was concerned but Mary knew exactly what the feeling was but didn't want to tell Kath. "I went a bit faint I think Kath, I don't know why but I think I'm ok now, let's just sit for a moment on this bench" Mary said as she flopped down. "He's here, I know that feeling, but why here" she thought "Are you ok Mary" Kath asked.

"Yes I'm ok, come on lets go" she replied and off they set towards the door of the maternity unit. Mary and Kath walked in and checked in at reception and were asked to take a seat on the blue chairs and wait to be called. Sue, Mr Menon's nurse was by reception and was aware of Mary booking in for her scan. The door in Mr Menon's office and Sue stood in the doorway "What is it Sue" he asked "It's Mrs Scott, she's in reception now for her scan" Sue said. "Ok, as far as your concerned all is as it should be, treat her normally but don't let her see the monitor, I'll come in to you" he said rubbing his chin. Sue made her way out to reception. "Mrs Scot, would you come this way please?" Mary got up and passed her bags to Kath who was going to wait on the seats and made her way into the room. "Hello Mrs Scott, good to see you again, now if you would change into the gown and lay on the bed for me and we'll make a start" Sue said in a relaxed manner. Mary got changed and made herself comfortable on the bed. "Now I'm going to start the scan and as you remember it's going to be a bit cold when I first touch you" Sue said "It's ok, no worries" Mary replied and just then Mr Menon appeared. "Hello Mary, are you ok?" he asked in a jovial manner. "Yes thanks doctor, how's the scan looking" Mary asked "Well, looking at the vital signs all is well, a very strong baby Mary and I've no concerns at all, I'll print a photo off for you as a souvenir and you can see your little one. Are you wanting to know the sex or are you going to wait for the surprise, I would if I were you" and as he said this he pressed the print button on the machine and as the photo came out he exchanged it for one in his pocket "No I think we'll wait for the surprise thank you" she said "There you are, if you'd like to get changed and comfortable Mary and here is your photo" he said passing it to here. "Mary looked at it and started to shed a tear of happiness as she got changed. "I'll get my secretary to book you another appointment for a few weeks' time and you'll get the letter in the post, good day to you" and he walked out. Mary made her way out to where Kath was sitting and showed her the photo "Look Kath, my little one, how exciting" she said "Oh Mary it's great, do you know what it is?" Kath asked

"No, they would tell us but we want it to be a surprise, so I'll tell you when it arrives" at that she grabbed Kath's arm and they walked out. Victor picked up the phone and dialled. "Hello, Colonel Stewart please" he asked "Colonel Stewart's office may I help you?" his secretary asked "Hello its Major Menon" he said "Ah just one moment Major I'll put you through" she said "Hello Vic what's happening" he asked "Hi Jeff, Just to let you know that the patient has just been for her scan and it went very well. She has the alternative picture which will keep her sweet for a while and I'll arrange another scan for about three weeks as by that time we'll be getting close" he said "Well done Vic, keep me informed. The wheels are in motion to get our specialist team over to you and I've just organised accommodation for them at RAF Spadeadam. We're arranging for some discrete on the ground surveillance in here home area to keep an eye on things. Speak soon Vic" he said then hung up. "Fancy stopping off for coffee" Kath asked. "Yes ok, why not" They made their way home stopping at the favourite coffee shop and settled themselves down. A few minutes later the waitress arrived and took their order. "Mary you've not said but anymore thoughts on who the father really is?" Kath asked "Oh Kath I've thought about this so much, I'm not sure and how will I find out. What if I say nothing and it comes out looking like an alien, at least Frank and Mike look alike, What have I done Kath?" she said. They sat chatting for a while and had another couple of coffees before returning home. The ride home was nice and steady and Mary and Kath were still talking over the possibilities of this pregnancy and what the future may hold and soon they were coming down the main road ready to turn into the lane which leads to the farm. As they did so Mary happened to notice a black van with blacked out windows parked in the lay by but put no importance on to it. Then they turned into the lane. As they arrived back Frank was sitting on the steps to the house with a coffee "Hiya girls, how's it gone?" He asked "Great, I've a photo to show you" Mary said "I'm getting off Mary, see you later" Kath said "Ok, thanks for today Mary shouted as Kath pulled away. Just then two fighter jets flew over quite low "Wow look at those, they're about quite a lot just lately, must be training for something," Frank said while looking up. "Look at this Frank, our little baby" she said with excitement in her voice as she pulled the photo out "Wow…..how fantastic" Frank said while looking at it "I can't believe it, I can't believe it" he said with a tear in his eye. After a minute of looking at the photo Frank turned to Mary "Hey we need to start thinking about the nursery, which upstairs room do you think would make the best one?" he asked "How about the room overlooking the meadow, that's a nice one for a nursery" she said "Yeah great, I'll get on to it, shall we nip to town later for the decor stuff as I'd like to get started" he asked "Yes ok, let's do it" she replied "Oh I so hope this baby's yours" She thought. The next day Mary was making a list of things she needed from town, she was a little overdue with her shopping. Frank walked into the kitchen and started washing his hands "I'm popping to town to get some shopping hunni, is there anything you need as I'll get it for you" She asked "Not that I can think of, wine, beer the essentials maybe"

"If I've to stop drinking so much so can you" she said smiling "Don't be cruel"

"Ok, see you later, I may call Kath to see if she wants to meet me so don't worry. I have my phone if there's any problem"

"Ok hun, see you later" At that Mary made her way to the Jeep and set off up the track and out of the gate. As she turned onto the main road she spotted the black van, it was still in the same spot and she realised that from where the van was whoever was in it could look down onto the farm, although the farm is far enough away they wouldn't be able to see much from that distance she thought. "Van 1 come in" the radio came to life "Control to van 1"

"Van 1 receiving, go ahead"

"What's the situation up there"

"We're in position with a good view of the farm however we will have to alternate positions as not to arouse suspicion"

"Any activity so far?"

"Nothing unusual, typical comings and goings and the subject has just driven off, but nothing strange to report"

"Ok, we have van 2 about a mile away from you on the other side of the farm. You will be relieved at intervals, keep your eyes open. The visitors we are expecting can come in under cover so keep checking those radars and record what you see."

"Yes sir"

"I'm sorry to tell you what you already class as the obvious so I apologise, but I can't emphasise enough how important this operation is fellas"

"Its ok sir, we understand"

"Thanks, control out." Mary arrived in town, parked her Jeep and made her way to the shops. As she was walking her thoughts turned to Mike: "I've not seen Mike for a while, I'd better go and see him" and she made her way over the road and down the narrow street to the bookshop and went in. "Hi Mike, are you ok" she asked "Hi Mary, good to see you. I've been wondering when I would see you again" he came from behind his counter and they gave each other a hug. "It's good to see you too Mike, can we talk, there's something I need to say"

"Yes of course, go through and pop the kettle on while I finish putting this change away and I'll drop the latch on the door" Mary made her way through, popped the kettle on and got the cups out. She made herself comfortable on the sofa and a moment later Mike appeared. "Hiya, Coffee" he asked

"Yes, thanks"

"You seem a bit bothered, what's wrong?" Mike made the drinks and put a coffee on the table at Mary's side then sat down next to her. "Mike, I've been thinking, I can't see you again its wrong, so wrong."

"Well not the news I expected to hear, can I change your mind somehow?

"No Mike I've made my mind up."

"What's bought about this change of heart, you seemed to enjoy our meetings as much as I did, have I upset you in some way"

"Mike when we met I was attracted to you big time. Then when we got together I really enjoyed something I'd not had for a while and I was looking forward to the next time but then I realised that it was so wrong. I do love my husband although we've been through a funny patch. I do still love him and I've no intention of leaving him. I can't lead you on Mike, me and you are not going to happen."

"Mary I'm sad at this as you've lit up my life by coming into it, I think about you so much when you're not around"

"I have enjoyed us too but it's over from now Mike, please let it be".

"Well I'll have to get used to it I suppose, but if you change your mind I'm here"

"Mike I'm having a baby, it's got to end, and end right now"

"A baby, could it be mine?"

"Definitely not Mike, It's Franks, I know it is I've worked it out" she knew she was lying but she wanted to put Mike's mind at ease. "Wow…..so congratulations are in order then, I'm pleased for you Mary I really am. I will miss you."

"I will miss you too Mike, It's been good but, please try to understand."

"Oh I do baby. Let me know what happens with your spaceship though won't you?"

"I will, I promise, and now I must go as I've shopping to do"

"Ok Mary, good luck with everything and lots of love to you."

"Goodbye Mike" she kissed him and left the shop. "Thank goodness that went well, I was dreading telling Mike but it had to be done" she thought to herself as she walked away.

Chapter 16

The weeks were passing by and all was going well. The farm was doing well and Frank had found someone to give him a hand as and when he needed it which took the pressure off Mary. Mary and Frank were getting more excited about the baby and Frank had already got the room ready to be used as the nursery. Mary was really pleased with the décor as it was nice and neutral in colour with lots of soft toys scattered around, she felt so proud and was so looking forward to the future. The more time that went by the more convinced Mary was that the baby was Frank's. There seemed to be a more constant stream of visitors to the farm these days and Mary was finding less time for herself, she didn't mind as she knew it was the caring community around and she appreciated it immensely. She knew she would be quite alone if they still lived in the city. A regular visitor was George's wife Ethel who turned up each day with something she'd cooked for them, either an apple pie, cottage pie or similar. Mary was always pleased to see her though as she knew how much pleasure Ethel was getting from looking after her. One morning Mary was feeling that she needed a break and decided to pop to town, the local supermarket delivered most of the groceries for them but they were short of a few small things. Mary drove up the track and out onto the lane, after a few moments she reached the junction of the main road and waited for a chance to pull out. Then she noticed the black van, it was still in the same position at the point where they could look down on the farm "That's strange, I wonder why that's still there" she thought. When Mary arrived in town she made a phone call. "Hi Kath, I'm in town, are you about?"

"Yes hunni I sure am, I'm in the bank, fancy coffee?"

"Yes, shall I meet you in about 30 mins? I've just a few things to pick up then I'll be with you"

"Ok Mary, see you in a bit." Mary felt comfortable when she was alone with Kath. Although she was a regular visitor to the house Mary couldn't talk to her the same about her problems as when they were alone. They both dealt with the errands then met up in the coffee shop for their usual catch up. "Hi Kath, have you ordered?"

"No I was waiting for you, how you feeling"

"Apart from feeling fat I feel a little relieved as I went to see Mike at the bookshop round the corner just recently"

"Oh Mary you're not still at it with him are you?"

"Don't be silly, I've been around to tell him that it's off and I won't be calling again and the friendship has to end as I'm having a baby. He was a bit surprised but relieved when I told him it wasn't his"

"But you don't know that do you?" Kath said.

"No, I don't but at least it's one man out of the equation for now. "The waitress came over and requested their order "I'll have an Americano please with milk" Mary said

"So will I," Mary added.

"Thank you ladies" the waitress said as she hurried off. "I must say your bump's looking quite noticeable now hunni."

"Yes, I'm finding it difficult to move as easily and to find clothes that fit" Mary said laughing. "How are you feeling in general?"

"I feel scared Kath, a funny mixture of excitement and fear. I sometimes wondered what it felt like to be pregnant and now I know, although I've added my own worries to it I know."

"Have you seen Sol?"

"No I've not, funny how he's not been for a while now, I wonder why."

"Maybe his job here on earth is done and he's achieved his goal. With that he's been sent home."

"Kath you should have seen it out there in space. There were hundreds of craft just like Sol's all floating about, far enough out that we can't detect them. Sol told me that each craft had its own agenda here on earth, its own job to do and his race had been around for thousands of years"

"I think you should start to put him out of your mind now Mary, you're starting a new chapter in your life and you're off to a new start"

"Yes I know, it's funny really with so many people popping around the farm now I haven't really thought about Sol as much at all. If he has gone I'm glad, I have enjoyed the experience but I would be glad thinking it was over and done with. Having these men around is stopping me sleeping properly."

"Of course it is, that's how you got pregnant" Kath said smiling.

"Oh cut it out you know what I mean." Just then the coffees arrived and the waitress put them down on the table. The girls spent time chatting about the pregnancy and other things in general and before long it became time to go. Mary settled the bill and her and Kath hugged before saying their goodbyes and going their separate ways. Mary felt good as she walked back to the Jeep and was looking forward to seeing Frank again. The jeep came down the main road and approached the turning for the lane and turned down to make her way to the farm "Hold on a minute, I didn't see the van. Must have got it started again and gone home" she thought and carried on her way home. Mary pulled up outside the house to the noise of RAF aircraft flying low overhead and she looked up and watched them for a minute till they disappeared. Frank walked up to meet her "Hiya, are you ok?"

"Yes I'm fine thanks, there seems to be a lot of activity in the air just lately."

"I know, as I've said before it must be a training period from the base up north. Come on I'll start tea for us. Come and put your feet up" Frank said taking her bags off her and helping her into the house. A little later as Mary was feeling a bit brighter and she decided to have a slow walk up to Shiloh and sort his feed out. She was comfortable with this as it wasn't too exerting and she knew she would take her time. "Come on Mont you can come and keep me company" she said rubbing his head. They started off for a steady walk in the lovely evening breeze. Mary did her usual and ran her fingers through the long grass. Eventually they arrived and it was evident to Mary that Shiloh was pleased to see her as he came over quickly. "Hiya mate, come on let's get you fed" she said getting his hay net and his feed bowl and filling them both up and putting them in the shelter for him. Mary then sat down on the bench to enjoy a few moments of the lovely view from up on the top field. After a short while of relaxing and looking around Mary's eye's focused on the hills behind the farm, they were about a quarter of a mile away but you could see traffic occasionally going along the little road which ran alongside. As she looked she realised that there was a black van parked there, too far away to see any detail but she felt that it was the same black van that was by the main road earlier. "I wonder what they're doing, I might mention this to Dave if I see him," she thought. The phone rang in Victor Menon's office. "Hello Dr Menon's office, may

I help you" his secretary said politely "Hello, It's Colonel Stewart, could I speak to Mr Menon please?"

"Just one moment sir, I'll put you through."

"Mr Menon I've Colonel Stewart for you" she said switching the call through

"Hi Jeff, what can I do for you"

"Vic how are we for time, are we getting close now?" he sounded concerned "I've checked her notes Jeff and we have two weeks, this will bring us to the earliest point where the foetus can be swopped over which is three months. Once it has it's vital that the new host is put into critical care as soon as possible. I will be booking her another appointment later today for nearer the time," Victor informed him. "The team have arrived from the States and are here at Mildenhall, they will fly up to you in the next couple of days. Have our contacts been in touch with me regarding the room and are happy with what they've found, have they spoke to you?"

"No not yet Jeff"

"I'll call them now, speak later." Soon there was a visitor to Mr Menon's office and he introduced himself. "Mr Menon, I've been sent by Jeff Stewart to discuss some maintenance to a room for your needs"

"Ah yes we've just been talking about you."

"Sorry we're a little late in speaking to you but we have been here for a couple of days and we've found an area of rooms which we feel fits the bill. Would you come with me please and have a look?" he asked? Victor noticed that although this man was dressed in overalls he had a very authoritive tone and stature which suggested he was more than he seemed, so Victor decided not to ask too many questions at this time. They made their way across the hospital to an area which was close enough to the rear entrance of the hospital but was in a very quiet spot. It had easy access to the entrance of the rooms and should not attract too much attention from passers-by. Victor was led inside by the man and invited to look around at what work they had already done and was taken aback by their efficiency. "It's marvellous what you've done already, I'm impressed" he said to the mystery man. "The specialist technical equipment is arriving from the states shortly, next couple of days so we'll have everything ready to put that straight into place then it will be ready. As soon as this operation is completed this room will be stripped bare, nothing will be left behind, no-one will know we've been here. Now if you'll forgive me Mr Menon we must press on" and at that Victor felt that he had been politely dismissed and left. Over the next few days a couple of plain Lorries turned up at the hospital with the specialist equipment needed and Victor was invited in to watch everything being put together. This was done in as sterile conditions as they could possibly get as no chances were being taken on the safety of the foetus. Victor was amazed as there was equipment here that he had never seen in his whole career "How technology had moved on since I was in the military" he thought.

Chapter 17

The morning post arrived and Mary was opening everything to see what needed dealing with straight away and what could wait when she came across a letter from the hospital and found it was a request to attend an appointment with Mr Menon in one week's time "They are being very thorough, I've not known many people to have this attention through a pregnancy" she thought and put the letter to one side. Frank appeared and put the kettle on. "Frank I fancy a drink, what about nipping down for an early doors" she said to him knowing her wouldn't refuse "Sounds great, I'll give you a shout when I've finished later and we'll get off, I've not much to do today anyway, see you in a bit" he said taking his mug of tea with him "I'll make my own then" she thought as she flopped a teabag in her mug. The day went by and eventually Mary and Frank were on their way to the pub with Monty on the back seat. When they arrived at the main road Mary noticed the black van parked there again "Frank have you noticed that black van, it's been parked there for a few days now, I wonder what they're doing there. And there's one parked on the back lane behind the farm" she said. "I've not noticed really, maybe one of those road side censuses to monitor traffic flow in an area" he replied "mm.....maybe, but they're making me nervous as they can see down on the farm from both locations."

"Ah don't worry, I'm sure there's a good reason for them." There were not many in the pub, it was comfortable and Monty could wander around getting treats off people. It was a dog friendly pub as most country pubs are. "Hi Frank, hi Mary, how are you coping?" Joe the landlord asked ."I'm fine Joe thanks, a long way to go yet though."

"Shall we eat while we're here hun?" Frank asked. "Yes why not, there's a table over there, will you bring the menus?"

"Of course, go and get comfy" Frank arrived with the drinks and they were looking at the menus when Dave Stewart the police officer walked in as he was of duty and ordered a beer.

"Dave, could I have a word?" Mary asked.

"Of course, hiya folks what's up?"

"Dave it may be nothing but there's two black vans with blacked out windows, one is on the main road by the farm and one is on the lane behind the farm. They've been there for a few days now and I'm getting the jitters wondering if they're watching the farm. Can you have a look if you're passing by please?"

"Will do, I'll make a point of it tomorrow, leave it with me."

"Thanks, I appreciate it" she said as he moved away to the bar. Frank and Mary had a nice couple of hours eating and drinking but gave their goodbyes and made for home, Mary was getting tired earlier in the evenings now and was always glad to get on the sofa with her feet up. A few days later Mary was sitting with a coffee going through all the paperwork trying to take some work off Frank when she heard a car pull up. It was Dave Stewart. "Hi Dave what brings you here, come in and I'll make you a brew," she said.

"It's ok Mary I can't stop, it's about the black vans you spoke of. I did stop by on one of them and just made some basic enquiries, I didn't mention you at all. The occupants showed us military ID but wouldn't answer any questions. They directed us to the RAF at Spadeadam, It turns out they are government vehicles and there's a large exercise going on at the moment which the vans are involved in so there's no need to worry, see you soon in the pub no doubt," he said as he started the car. "Thanks Dave, you've put my mind at ease" she waved as he drove off. Little did she know that she was the object of their interest?

"Well there has been a lot of activity around here just lately, I wonder if it's anything to do with Sol, can't be, he's not been around for a while now?" she thought about it as she walked back inside .The day went by and the jobs were done so Mary started to prepare tea and put a pie in the oven. She walked outside to find Frank who was working in the barn "Hi, I've put tea in and I'm popping up to feed Shiloh, Won' be long then I'll finish tea for us" she said.

"Ok, see you in a bit" Frank said without looking up. Mary walked up at her usual pace, nice and steady with Monty at her side. She noticed that it seemed to be getting a little darker these evenings and a lovely sunset with a lovely red sky was beginning to happen, but it was still quite warm. Mary fed Shylo with his hay and his feed then sat down to enjoy a few moments on her bench. Mary started to feel a little off colour and at first thought it was to do with being pregnant but then it dawned on her, It's the feeling she got whenever Sol was in the vicinity. "He's here, he's coming back," she thought "What is he doing here?" She waited patiently scanning the sky for the light. She could feel the familiar breeze that accompanied his ship and was searching for a visible sign that he was about. Then she saw that it had already landed but had been kept invisible, or cloaked, as Sol called it, but came into view just long enough for Sol to step out before disappearing again. "Hello Mary" he said as he walked towards her.

"Hello Sol, I thought you had left for good, you've been gone for a while."

"Yes I have, we have other tasks to attend to while we're here. Very soon we will be moving out of your orbit and will be gone for some time."

"I would like you to come on board and take a trip with me."

"No Sol, I had hoped that you had gone for good. I don't want to be alone with you, it's wrong"

"I notice that you are now with child" he said looking at her tummy.

"Yes that's right, I don't want any harm to come to it, Frank and I are looking forward to being parents so this is why I no longer want anything to do with you" Mary gave no indication to her thought of who the father could be. "No harm would come to you or your baby Mary, we are a race that care for our young and ensure their safety too. "Why Sol, I'm sure you don't really want me do you, you have such a beautiful assistant so you won't want a pregnant Earth girl surely."

"I told you when we met Mary that I wanted you and needed you, well that still applies."

"Go away Sol, leave me alone to enjoy my family or the military will see you as they are watching the area." "We are aware of your forces and their primitive equipment, they will not pick us up at all and have no idea we are here now."

"Go now Sol."

"Very well Mary, so be it. But you are making it difficult for me to complete my tasks" and he turned back to his craft which started to appear again and the door opened. "Just what tasks are they that I'm making difficult" she called out but he ignored her and disappeared into his craft which disappeared again before taking off. "What's he on about, what problem could possibly cause him" she thought as she started to walk back to the farmhouse. After tea Mary spent the rest of the evening thinking about what Sol had said and it troubled her. Try as she might she could think of nothing that she could do that would cause a problem to Sol and hoped that she never would see him again. Mary went to bed that night perturbed, she lay there thinking about what Sol had said but couldn't understand it then eventually dropped off to sleep. A day or two later the phone rang and Mary picked it up to find it was Kath. "Hiya hunni, do you want me to pick you up for your scan?" she asked.

"Thanks Kath that would be great if you don't mind, but it's not for a couple of days yet"

"Yes I know but I just want to be prepared and ready for you, what time's your appointment?"

"It's 11.00am"

"Ok, I'll be there for 10.00, have the kettle on."

"Will do, see you then" and Mary put the phone down and sat there for a while reflecting on how her future was changing. Frank came into the kitchen "You'll never believe it, the generator round the back we use for power washing the kit has run out of fuel and we have none. I'll have to nip into town to pick some up, might just pop in for a quick one while I'm there if you don't mind. Do you need anything hunni" he asked. "No I'm ok, enjoy your beer" she said putting her arms around him a big hug and giving him a kiss. At that he grabbed the keys to the Jeep and took off up the track. "Right Mont, come on me and you will go and feed the chucks" and off she set with bucket of feed in hand towards the chicken coop. Mary wasn't out long before she started to feel strange "Now is that just me or is he back" she thought while leaning on the fence for support. A few hours went by and the Jeep came back down the track and pulled up outside the house and Frank hopped out to find Monty there wagging his tail to greet him. "Come on mate let's find Mary and they went inside" Hey Mary are you about" he shouted to find there was no answer. He looked around the kitchen and saw the pans on the stove almost simmered dry and he switched them off. "Very odd, I wonder if she's up with the horse, but if she was Monty would be with her," he thought, he stood for a moment thinking "Come on fella let's find Mary" and they went out into the yard. MARY…..MARY" Frank shouted as he walked around outside but had no answer, Frank was getting worried. As he walked around by the barn he spotted her across the yard on the floor by the chicken coop lying very still. He ran over to her to find her unconscious and immediately called 999. It was only a few minutes before the ambulance arrived and the medics took attended to Mary. She was soon stabilised and onto a stretcher being wheeled to the ambulance and made secure in the back with the full attention of a paramedic "We have to take her in straight away to A&E, are you going to follow us down?" "Yes I'll secure the house and I'll be with you" Frank said feeling a sense of panic setting in. The ambulance arrived at the hospital and Mary was admitted to A&E and taken straight into an emergency bay where she was surrounded by staff in minutes. As she was pregnant a call was made to maternity to request a specialist to attend. Sue was on duty when the call came through and she overheard the conversation that the nurse was having over the phone."

Sue is Mr Menon in this afternoon?" the nurse asked "Yes why, what's up?"

"There's a pregnant woman just been brought into A&E unconscious and the doctors are requiring a specialist from your end to help out."

"Ok I'll go and get him, what's the woman's name and I'll get the notes as he'll want them" The nurse spoke to the person on the other end of the phone then replied: "It's a Mrs Mary Scott"

"We're on our way" Sue said "Oh my God what's happened to her" she thought as she ran down the corridor to Victor's office and went in. "Vic they need you in A&E immediately as they have a pregnant woman in unconscious and they need a specialist down there, Vic it's Mary Scott." She said "Oh my God what's happened, go and get the notes Sue and meet me down there straight away." Victor made his way down and found the bay where they had Mary and found that they had managed to get her to regain consciousness although she was still having trouble speaking. The doctors checked her over and found no broken bones or obvious injury and wondered if she had fainted and knocked herself out when she fell. "Mary, can you hear me" the doctor asked "Can you hear me Mary."

"Yes, yes I can, where I am?" she said slowly still coming around. "You're in hospital Mary, You've had an accident, and can you remember what happened?"

"Well I remember I walked up to the chickens and then I just felt funny, now I'm here so other than that I have no idea, no idea at all."

"Well we've checked you over and can see no real harm done but it may be advisable to keep you in overnight, I'll have a word with Mr Menon and we'll decide what to do, the doctor said before turning to Mr Menon. "I'll leave her with you, I'm happy that there's no physical damage done, why she passed out I don't know, may have just fainted and knocked herself out." He said thoughtfully "Ok let me see her and check on the baby then we'll decide whether to keep her in or not" he said before turning to Sue who had now joined him in A&E. "Sue can you get a mobile ultrasound machine please, let's have a look if there's any harm done here" he said while starting to feel her tummy. "Yes ok" and off she went. "Mary we're going to get a scanner and have a look at what's happening with your baby. It is routine as you've had an accident so we want to be sure that all's well" A few minutes later Sue returned with the machine, plugged it in and switched it on. Mr Menon took control and started scanning Mary's tummy, he was slow and methodical. Sue came in close to him and looked at the same screen that Victor was seeing "This can't be right" she thought. Sue didn't like what she was seeing but said nothing. Mr Menon was very quiet for a while and then he eventually spoke. "Well Mary, I think it's advisable that we keep you in overnight for a rest and you can go home in the morning. Do you remember what happened yet? He asked "No, sorry Doctor, my mind's a blank"

"Ok I'll get someone to bring your husband in and get you a cup of tea, we'll be back shortly" and at that he indicated to Sue to follow him out. Mr Menon and Sue made their way to his office and closed the door "What's happening Vic."

"We've lost Sue, lost again, the aliens have beaten us to the foetus, and they've taken it."

"Oh no, how have they done that Vic? Everyone's kept such a close eye on her."

"Abduction and she knows nothing of it, the yanks at RAF Mildenhall are not going to like this one bit." Victor said rubbing his forehead. "More to the point, what do we say to Mary?" Sue added "Creative conversation I suppose, I don't want to say to her that aliens have had your baby, she'll think I'm nuts and have me struck off, I'll have to put the blame back on her, come on let's get to it now" he said opening the door of his office. They made their way back to Mary who was now sitting up and looking comfortable with a cup of tea. "Mary we need talk to you, I'm sorry to ask this but have you had an abortion" he asked "Of course not, why?"

"Your baby has gone Mary, been taken away in a very professional way, what can you tell us of this?" Mary went into hysterics. "What is happening to me, how can this be" she screamed and was crying. "Mary's not had an abortion doctor, she was looking forward to this pregnancy, we both were" Frank said "Well can you shed any light on it Frank, because someone must know something. However if you have had this done it's up to you, but the baby's not there now. I think its best if Mary stays in overnight and we'll keep an eye on her" Mr Menon suggested. Mary turned quite aggressive "I'm not stopping here, I'm going home right now" she said quite harshly. "I don't recommend this Mary, please reconsider" Mr Menon asked. "Come on Frank take me away from here now" she said to him "Take me away from these people." Poor Frank couldn't take in what was going on, nothing was making sense to him and he'd not seen Mary with this aggressive attitude before but he followed Mary's request and helped her out to his Jeep to take her home. They were silent for a few minutes into the drive and then Frank broke the silence "Mary maybe you should follow Mr Menon's advice and stay there tonight," he said. "Don't tell me what to do Frank, I'm going home. I'm fed up of being bossed about"

"What on earth are you talking about, I've not done anything like that with you."

"Yes you have, you thought it was all a joke when I told you of that spaceship and you were sarcastic to the point I stopped telling you about all the other times it came over, you didn't believe me. And think of this, I think its them who have had this baby and if you dare to criticize me so help me I'll punch your fucking head off" she screamed at him. The Jeep pulled up outside the house and Mary got out and leaned on the bonnet getting her breath. Frank didn't know what to do or say "Come in Mary and I'll get you a drink" he said to her trying to be caring. "Oh fuck off Frank" and at that

Mary walked off into the darkness, Frank just watched her in disbelief.

Chapter 18

It was dark and an evening mist was coming down as Mary ran up towards the top field where she hoped that she might see Sol. She was very upset and needed answers. As she arrived she saw Shiloh slowly walking towards her and just for a moment she felt a sense of happiness sweep over her. She loved that horse. "Hello boy, are you ok?" she said giving him a hug. Mary waited, she had a feeling he would be here, and it was a feeling which she could not describe but always came over her when he was in the vicinity. It wasn't long before she was lights appearing through the mist, the dim blue lights which surrounded the rim of the craft. It came in slowly, silently and hovered just feet above the field. It sat there for a short while in total silence, the dim lights flashing on and off. "WHERE ARE YOU" she shouted, there was no response. Mary ran around the craft looking for some sign of life but to no avail. "Where are you, damn you," she said with sadness. Just then a window opened in the side of the craft and a figure stood there, it was him. He looked out at her for a moment before walking away, she waited and then a ramp opened in the side of the craft and Sol walked down towards her. "WHAT HAVE YOU DONE WITH MY BABY" she screamed. "It is not your baby, it never was, it is ours and we are taking it home with us" he said with no compassion.

"It is my baby, we made it while we made love" she said with tears in her eyes.

"What is this love that you speak of?"

"It's when people want each other and need each other and you said you wanted and needed me."

"That is true, when we first came down to this planet I searched for a suitable subject and I found you......Mary cut him off and Interrupted "*SUBJECT*" she shouted "I was just your *SUBJECT* and nothing more?"

"That is correct, I did want you and I did need you but only for our experiments with insemination. When I first saw you and you looked suitable for our experiment we took you on board for examination" he said coldly. "When you took me, I don't remember going with you for examination" she said

"No you wouldn't, you were unconscious at the time and we had you for three of your hours, you wouldn't remember what we did to you then, we wiped your memory and we found you were a suitable carrier for our foetus so we decided to inseminate you. However rather than do that at that time I was interested in how you people inseminate each other in the primitive way so I decided to try it and found it gave me pleasure, most interesting" he said. "You bastard" she said "You've just used me, nothing more than used me, I hate you" she said coldly. "Oh Mary, you really didn't think that there was a future for you and me did you. We may look similar but we are so different. I could not survive on this planet nor could you on ours. We are leaving now and we won't be back, meeting you has been good and fruitful but I will say goodbye now" as he said this he turned and walked up the ramp and it closed behind him. Mary fell to her knees screaming "TAKE ME WITH YOU, TAKE ME WITH

YOU" and crying LET ME LOOK AFTER MY BABY" as the craft slowly lifted away before disappearing in the mist. Mary was crying uncontrollably, sobbing her heart out when she felt hands on her shoulders and a kind voice said "Miss are you ok, are you ok miss, let me help you." Mary looked up but her eyes were filled with tears. She sat up, cleared her eyes and realised………………she was still on the train and the lady from the opposite seat was trying to console her, she had been dreaming all the time, dreaming a very bad dream ! "Well that was some dream you had hunni, you've been asleep for quite some time" the lady said wiping Marys face with a tissue. "I'm sorry, I'm so sorry, I don't know what's come over me and that's never happened to me before" Mary said and she was shaking uncontrollably. A man in a seat across the aisle passed her a bottle of water." There you go love, have a drink" Mary took the bottle with thanks and had a drink. "I don't believe it, I just don't believe it, it was all so real" she thought to herself as she was calming down. "My name's Janet by the way" the lady introduced herself. "I'm Mary and I can't apologise enough for what happened" she said now quite relaxed "Where are you headed?" she added. "Carlisle, I'm having a couple of days with friends, I live in London now but I'm often up here, I love the area, how about you?" she asked "Well my husband and I are from the north but we did live in London for a while too, we've moved back up to Carlisle now though and bought a small farm which keeps us busy" Mary said with enthusiasm. "Sounds good, I'd like to think that I'll move one day, City life gets a bit too much at times I find, one day though you may find me up here for good" she said with a smile "I'll keep an eye out for you then" Mary Joked. Mary and Janet chatted for quite a while and before long the announcer declared that the train was approaching Carlisle so while chatting they used the time to gather their things together in readiness to get off and as the train pulled in they both said their goodbyes and left the train. As Mary made her way to the Jeep she couldn't stop thinking about her dream as to her it was all so real. She spotted the Jeep, walked to it and got in. She felt that she had to sit and think for a while before pulling off "I've never in my life had a dream that was so real,

I can't believe it" she thought while turning the starter and the Jeep burst into life. Frank was working away in the barns when Mary arrived back home, he noticed the noise of the Jeep and made his way to the house. Mary was in the kitchen making coffee as Frank walked in "Hi, how was your trip" he asked. "Well it was ok, but something really strange happened on the train, I had a dream that I spotted a spaceship in the night sky, night after night. Eventually it landed and I met the spaceman and I fell in love. I became pregnant and he stole my baby"

"Really, that's a new one" Frank replied smiling.

"Yes apparently I woke up shouting 'bring my baby back' because in the dream when the spaceman stole it and took it off he took it to his planet." Mary said while taking a drink from her mug. "Interesting, this story would make a good book, you should jot it down" and he winked at her as he walked past "I'm off for a shower, see you in a min" he said as he disappeared. "Good idea" she thought. "Just might do that" A few minutes past and Mary finished her coffee and biscuits and made her way upstairs to get changed so she could pop up and see Shiloh, she entered the bedroom and got undressed to her underwear while looking for her jeans and t shirt and as she did so in walked a naked Frank drying himself off "How fortunate you being here with nothing on, I've missed you" he said smiling " That Frank is VERY evident" she said looking at his groin and smiling. He pushed her playfully back on the bed and fell besides her planting a very passionate kiss on her lips. They made love enthusiastically for a while and Mary felt quite complete and satisfied and afterwards they were just lying on the bed naked and holding each other not speaking but relaxed. "Frank let me go I need to go and get Shiloh his tea and its getting dark" she said pushing Frank away and smiling as he started to get excited again "The Frank in the dream was nothing like this" she thought as she got dressed and made her way out. Mary left the house and went up the track to see Shiloh. As she was walking up she was thinking about the dream and how real it was, how it included people she knew "How can a dream become so real" She thought as she walked up to the gate and lifted the rusty latch. Shiloh was pleased to see her as she was pleased to see him. "Hello boy, come on let's get your tea. We'll go for a good ride tomorrow if you like" she said while rubbing his nose. It didn't take long to sort him out as it was a lovely night and he didn't need his coat on, his hay bag filled and his feed in his bowl she could tell he was happy "See you tomorrow boy" she said before making her way home. The evening went by and Frank and Mary had tea and chatted about what had been happening over a wine or two before turning in. The next day Mary went to town to stock up on groceries and to pay a bill or two. She was walking around looking in the shops when she realised that she recognised the narrow street over the road, it was the street she had seen in her dream on the train. "Well fancy that, there's the street from my dream" Mary had been down there before but found it odd that it should appear in her dreams so she decided to cut down there again and call for coffee around the corner. She crossed the main street and started to walk down the little narrow street ahead. She was walking slowly realising that she had taken no real notice of the shops down here before although one did look a little familiar and as she approached it she saw that it was the bookshop from her dream. "That's odd" she thought as she stepped forward to look in the window. As she looked she could see the proprietor serving a customer and as he did so he looked out towards Mary and waved with a smile "It can't be, It can't be" she said to herself because as she looked she realised it was Mike from her dream "This can't be happening" she thought. Mary stepped to the quaint door and clicked the latch, as she opened the door she heard the "Ting Ting" of the doorbell. "That's the same bell" she thought. Mary went into the shop and pretended to be looking around. The proprietor was writing on a pad but he acknowledged Mary "Morning, if you need any help just call me" he said. "Thanks I will" Mary replied as she kept glancing his way. Just then the phone rang and he picked it up "Hello, Mike speaking, can I help" Mary was astounded "I've got to get out of here, this is weird" she thought and made her way to the door. As she opened it to go out Mike said" Thank you" and waved goodbye to her and as she left she glanced at the shop window and much to her surprise she saw the three books from her dream laid out neatly in a display. "This is really weird" she thought. A week or two went by and one morning Mary said to Frank that she wasn't feeling too good and fancied a lie down. "Off you go then, I'll check on you in a while" Frank said " Ok cheers, see you in a bit" Mary made her way to the bedroom and got into bed still dressed and went off to sleep. A little later Frank went up to her with a cup of tea "How you feeling hun?" he asked. "I can't explain, just a bit funny, If it hasn't cleared in the morning I'll pop in the doctors while I'm in town" she said. The next day they were both awake quite early and Mary said she still felt a bit funny "I'll phone the doctors and get you in" Frank said going to the kitchen and picking up the phone. A few minutes later he came to Mary "They can get you in at two and can you take a water sample with you" he said "Ok" Mary replied. Mary was sitting in the doctors reading a paper having arrived on time "Why do they book you in for a time then keep you waiting 30 mins longer" she thought. The sign in the doctors flashed up Mary Scott room 4, Mary got up and made her way through the corridor to room 4 and knocked "Come in" a voice said. Mary went in and was greeted by Dr Jones, a lovely sensitive lady. "Hi doctor, I've brought a sample as requested" Mary said as she put it on the table "Hi Mary, thanks for that. Would you just wait a moment while I get the nurse to check this" she said as she got up to leave the room. A few moments later she returned and said "Now what can we do for you, your husband seems a bit concerned it appears" She said looking at Mary. "I've just not felt myself lately, just generally off colour, wondered if I need some sort of tonic?" Mary said "let's have a look at you, roll your sleeve up and we'll do your blood pressure" The doctor said pulling out her equipment and putting the cuff on Mary's arm. The blood pressure machine burst into life and the cuff went tight around Mary's arm, while this was happening the doctor took Marys temperature and wrote it down. The cuff went slack just as the nurse came in and handed the doctor a piece of paper which the doctor glanced at and put to one side. "Well Mary your readings are fine and I've no concerns there. You say you've been feeling off" She said picking up the piece of paper from earlier "Well congratulations, you're 6 weeks pregnant" she said with a smile. "What...., I don't believe it" Mary said "I hope this is good news Mary" The doctor replied "Oh yes, definitely, oh yes it's just a shock. Well good luck and I look forward to seeing you a bit more regular now" she said with a smile. Mary got up to leave "Thanks doctor, see you soon" as she opened the door to leave. Mary made her way home feeling rather mixed up and emotional and excited at telling Frank the news. The Jeep pulled into the driveway and Monty came around the house to greet her "Hiya boy, where's Frank" she said, Monty seemed to understand as he ran off towards the barn, Mary followed. "Hiya" she said as she saw Frank moving hay bales. "Hiya, glad you're back you can give me a hand here" he said "How did you get on at the doctors "Well, let's put it this way, there's going to be no lifting from me for a few months" she said smiling and leaving the barn. As she was making her way to the house smiling she heard Frank come running out of the barn "Hey, wait up, are you saying no lifting for a few months, are we expecting more livestock then?" he said excitedly. "Yes darling, we're pregnant" Mary said with tears in her eyes "Wow…. I'm overjoyed" Frank replied putting his arms around her and holding her tight "That's fantastic news Mary, fantastic news, I do love you" he said as he held her in his arms "I'm so pleased Frank, Just what we wanted, a little sooner than we expected but I'm still so pleased. I still can't believe it myself" she said wiping away a tear "Come on I'm stopping work, we're celebrating" he said as he grabbed her hand and took her into the house. "First of all we're having some champagne, then we'll contact Rob and Kath and see if they feel like meeting for a bite so we can break the news" he said as he got the champagne and pulled the cork and poured it into the glasses and handed one to Mary "To us" he said holding up his glass. "To us" Mary said while clinking her glass on his. Mary looked at Frank and was so happy to see him this way, she'd not seen him this happy for a long time and it really pleased her. "Rob, Its Frank, bit short notice but do you fancy an Indian with us this evening……….great, see you at the Taste of spice about 6.30, cheers" he said as he hung up the phone "That's sorted, meet them at 6.30" he said quite excitedly "They will suspect something's wrong as it was you who phoned them and not me" Mary said laughing. "Oh what the hell" Frank said taking hold of Mary again and putting his arm around her and holding her tight "Come on grab the bottle and let's sit outside and think of some names" Mary said as she walked to the veranda. Frank joined her and sat beside her and put his arm around her and there they sat chatting for an hour before getting ready to go out. "Kath we're going out for an Indian with Mary and Frank for tea, meeting them at 6.30" he shouted upstairs "Oh has Mary called then" she asked "No it was Frank actually" he replied "Frank, that's funny, he's never usually the one to make arrangements, we've not forgotten Mary's birthday have we?" she asked while leaning over the upstairs bannister "Don't think so hun" Rob said "I'd better find something to wrap up and put in the car just in case and I'm sure I've got some spare birthday cards somewhere" Kath said in a quiet voice while thinking.

Chapter 19

The door to the restaurant opened and in walked Mary and Frank. "Ah Mr and Mrs Scott how good to see you, please let me have your coats and I will see them safely put away for you" Sanjay said in his usual happy manner. "Frank, Mary over here" It was Rob, he had found them one of their favourite tables. "Hi Rob, Kath, good to see you both" Mary said giving them both a hug. "Hi Frank" they both said as Mary and Frank sat down. "Thanks for the suggestion to come out, I'd just pulled some sausages out of the freezer but this is a much better option," Rob said as Sanjay appeared for a drinks order. "What's brought this sudden decision to pop out for an Indian then, we don't usually get an invite from farmer Giles here" Kath asked "Well Kath' we're having a sort of celebration" but before Mary could finish "See Rob, I told you we'd missed Mary's birthday, I knew it was soon, Oh Mary I'm sorry but I've got you a little something here" She said pulling out a bottle of Bollinger Champagne and a hastily wrapped present, this was typical of Kath. Frank and Mary found this so funny and sat laughing out loud "So what's so funny then, don't you like Bolly?" she said with a look of wonder. Frank turned to Mary "Go on Mary, spill the beans" he said "Kath, Rob, It's so sweet that you're worried about my birthday but it's a month away, the fact is I'm having a baby" and at this she started to cry, happy tears. "Yahoo, fantastic news, absolutely brilliant" Shouted Rob "Oh Mary, Frank, I'm so happy for you both, that's wonderful news, wonderful" Kath said "Sanjay, Champagne glasses please, and let's get this Bolly open right now" Rob shouted over to the counter " Coming right up Mr Rob" Sanjay could never remember Rob's surname. The cork was out of the bottle and Rob poured the bubbly "Here's to Mary, Frank and the little one, God bless you all" and they all clinked their glasses and had a drink. They all had a good evening with good food and Mary was made a fuss of by Sanjay and his staff and presented with another bottle of bubbly as a gift "Right, the meals on me and in return you can follow us to the pub for a swift one" Rob said as they all stood ready to go. "Are you ok about this Mary" Frank asked

"Of course its early days yet Frank, come on lets enjoy this evening" She said in reply and grabbing his arm. The four of them made their way to the Crown which was only a short walk away and as they got there Kath opened the door and they all walked in. There were a number of familiar faces in there tonight, one of which was Alan which pleased Mary and she gave him a big hug. As they approached the bar Rob said "Attention please, celebration in progress at the future arrival of little feet in the Scott household" at that a huge cheer went up in the pub "Oh Rob, did you have to" Mary said punching his arm lightly.

"Of course dear," he said giving her a kiss on the cheek. Alan came over "Mary, Frank what fantastic news, really pleased for you, I've just ordered a bottle of champagne for you" he said "Oh Alan you'll all have me pissed" she replied. "Well soon Mary you'll have to knock it on the head with the booze so just enjoy tonight hun" he said giving her a squeeze. Frank had been ordering a round of drinks for them all and he came to pay. "Those drinks are on me tonight Frank, congratulations" Joe the barman said with a smile. "Crikey Mary we'll have to get pregnant more often if we get drinks like this" he said passing her a wine. Everyone had a great evening, lots of drinks, lots of laughter and it was evident that none of the four could drive so Jody the barmaid offered to run them all home and for ease Rob and Kath stayed at the farm for the night. The next day Frank was up and cooking breakfast for them all, however as they all started to appear it was evident that they all had a hangover and he wondered if they would be able to eat a cooked brekkie. They all sat around the breakfast table recalling the previous evening's event and laughing about what went on, following breakfast Rob and Kath had a lift from Frank back to their car and made their way home. When Frank arrived back Mary was lying in the sun on the lounger on the veranda "I don't feel like it today Frank I'm stopping here" she said settling herself in "No problem, you take it easy hunni" he said as he kissed her and went off to work on the farm. Mary relaxed and felt a little guilty about feeling lazy but in her mind she knew that very little of the farm work was light and she did not want to put this pregnancy at risk in any way. At lunchtime Mary prepared some sandwiches for her and Frank then wandered over to the barn to fetch him in, when she got there he was leaning over the tractor as usual "Frank I've been thinking, we may need to get you some temporary help while I go through this pregnancy, or else how will you manage?" Frank looked up "I know, I've been thinking the same, we'll sort that out a little later, is lunch done?" he asked "Yes, are you coming in" she said as she walked away back to the house. When Frank arrived he found Mary sitting with her head in her hands "What's wrong hun?" he asked "I don't know, I just walked back here and I went all funny, I've never felt that way before, I didn't feel sick, I didn't feel faint it was just a very strange feeling. I had to sit down, but it's gone now, I'll make some coffee" she said as she stood up and made her way to the kettle to make the drinks. Mary and Frank were enjoying the thought of becoming parents. Frank longed for a boy and spoke of teaching his son the art of farming and how to deal with all the animals, and having someone to hand the farm over to when he was an adult with a family of his own. Mary dreams of a daughter, someone to go shopping with and call for coffee to learn about her boyfriends, someone she could help to plan a wedding when she found the right man. "Frank I think the back bedroom with the view over the meadow would make a great nursery, what do you think" she asked. "Whatever you want hunni, if we put a lovely window seat in there you'll have a great spot to sit and tell stories," he replied. "What colour shall we decorate it, a nice shade of pink I think" Mary said smiling "No way, it has to be blue for a boy of course" he said "Ah you wish" she said giving him a hug.

The post arrived and there was a letter from the hospital inviting Mary for an ultrasound the following week. "Frank I've an appointment for an ultrasound next week, fancy coming along? "Yeah sure, how exciting" he said smiling. The week went by and the big day arrived. Frank helped Mary into the Jeep and they set off to the hospital and it didn't seem long before they arrived and parked up. They made their way to reception and checked in "That's ok Mrs Scott, please wait over there on the blue chairs and someone will come to call you shortly" the receptionist said handing her a card to take in. They sat chatting for a while before Mary heard her name called and they got up and walked towards the doorway to the room and went in. "Hello Mrs Scott, my name's Sue and I'm one of the nurses I'll be doing your ultrasound today. What I'd like you to do is pop in the cubical and put this gown on if you would as it makes it easier to scan when there's little clothing to fight with," the nurse said while opening the cubical door. Mary went in and undressed and put the gown on and as she did so she felt as though she'd seen the nurse somewhere before but couldn't place her. When she was in the gown she went out into the scan room and was asked to climb onto the table which she did and made herself comfortable. "Now I'm going to put some gel onto the scanner and then onto your tummy and you may find the gel a little cold I'm afraid," the nurse said as she lifted the gown and placed the scanner on Mary's tummy and began to scan. Frank was watching the screen trying to make sense of what he was looking at. The scan seemed to go on for a while before the nurse spoke to them" Lovely, everything is just as it should be, all the vital signs are fine. You have a very strong baby on the way, are you wanting to know the sex" she asked "Well I hadn't really thought of that but if it's ok with you Frank I think I'd rather wait for the surprise, what do you think" she asked Frank " No let's wait, I'd like the surprise too" he said kissing her forehead "Very well, If you hold on one moment I'll print a photo off for you" the nurse said as she pulled the print from the printer. As they left and were walking back to the Jeep Mary was feeling on air, she was so happy "When we get back to the village let's have a pub lunch "she said while putting her arm in Frank's. "Good idea, let's do it" and they Jumped into the Jeep and made their way back. During the ride back Mary was thinking of the day and the trip to have her scan when suddenly it dawned on her. "Frank I know where I've seen that nurse before, It was in my dream on the train, It was her I'm so sure of it, so sure it was her, but how could that be?" she said "Oh, come on Mary, how could it be, Just someone who looked like her, you're imagining things" he said.

"No Frank its really funny, since that dream happened I'm sure I've seen a couple of the people who were in it, it's like I'm living in a mystery movie."

"Ok, start to jot things down when they happen, maybe someone is trying to tell you something" he said

"Could do, it's just seems strange," she said quietly. They arrived home and Mary was thinking of things she had to do and decided that Shylo was first on her list so off she went with Monty by her side as escort. Mary pushed past Shiloh and made her way to the hay store and started filling his feed bowl and hay bag when she started feeling strange, a feeling that she had experienced once before, but one she couldn't describe, but she knew she didn't feel right. She stopped for a moment and thought about it and then slowly started to put Shiloh's food out. She walked back to the gate and looked back at him enjoying what she had put out then she lifted the latch walked through the gate and locked it behind her. Mary stood for a moment leaning on the gate, still wondering about the strange feeling inside her and then it happened. Mary looked up and in the sky and saw the very light that she had seen in her dream and it was heading her way, as it got nearer it seemed to stop for a while and she just stood and looked at it and then it just vanished, like someone had switched a light off "That's just like the light in my dream, but surely it can't be, no it was probably a police helicopter" she thought. She slowly walked back to the house and walked into the kitchen where Frank was having a drink while reading the paper. "Frank, remember me telling you of that dream I had about the spaceman coming and taking my baby?" she asked. "I remember you mentioning it yes" he replied "Well I've just seen a light in the sky, just like the one in my dream" she said. "It was probably the police helicopter, it's been about quite a lot lately at night, don't know why though" he said looking up from his paper, come on sit down and I'll make you a brew. The next few weeks were quite busy as usual, john the tanker driver had been a couple of times, Frank had been working hard and had been to a couple of auctions and generally everything was running well. Mary felt quite content and happy, she felt she was living the dream. "Mary would you like a pub lunch, I know I've a lot on but I want to do some paperwork this afternoon so we could have a break" he asked "Yes ok, come on go and get changed"

"Ok, won't be long" Frank drove them to the Crown where they settled down enjoyed a nice lunch while chatting about the future for the farm and the forthcoming baby. There were not many people in and they quite liked it like that today, they were happy to have their own company for lunch. Later in the day Frank was busy sorting through the paperwork. He knew it was a job Mary was capable of doing but he was trying to take tasks off her as he wanted her to relax and enjoy her pregnancy. The early evening was approaching and Mary was aware that Shiloh would want his feed. "I won't be long Frank, I'm off to feed Shiloh"

"Ok, take it easy and be careful"

"Come on Monty you can keep me company" Mary and Monty set off for a leisurely walk up the track to the top field. Mary walked quite slowly and enjoyed the evening air, there was a slight mist coming in which made the countryside look beautiful, he fingers ran through the tall grass as she walked. Monty spotted a rabbit and set off after it. She knew he wouldn't catch it or if he did he wouldn't harm it, he was a very friendly dog. She arrived at the top field and Shiloh was standing looking over the gate, as though he was expecting Mary to come. "Hello matey, come on let's get you fed" as she opened the gate and pushed past him and made her way to the feed store where she filled Shiloh's hay bag and his feed tray. Shiloh was rubbing his nose on her as though he was thanking her for this, Mary liked the affection. Monty came up and he and Shiloh looked at each other and Shiloh bent his neck down and licked him. Mary thought it lovely how these two were friends. When Mary had finished she walked over and sat on her little bench as she often did to take in the lovely evening. For a while she was lost in her thought when she realised that she was beginning to feel a bit strange but she couldn't put her finger on what it was. She felt in her pocket and realised she had her phone with her and could call Frank if case this feeling got worse. Mary sat hoping the feeling would go but as she did so she noticed in the sky the light, the strange light from some weeks earlier and the same light from her dream on the train. As she watched it she noticed that it was slowly coming over the hills and would pass over the farm. Mary watched it and could see no detail, it was Just an orange ball of light. It slowly passed over and disappeared from view over the hills on the opposite side of the valley "Wow…..It's here again, how strange is that, I wonder what it is?" She thought, then realised that the strange feeling she had experienced had gone completely never thinking that the two were connected. Mary made her way back down to the house and walked in the kitchen just as Frank had made a pot of tea "Hiya, Just in time, sit you down and I'll get you a cup" he said "Thanks, how about some cheese and crackers too"

"No probs, you just relax and I'll get some for you"

"Frank I've just seen that unusual light again, it came right over the farm, quite high though I must say."

"Well if you think about it the RAF have been flying around quite a lot lately, I bet its some training going on" he said as he put a mug of tea down. "Yes I suppose so, it's a lovely evening, come up with me one night and we'll sit in the dark together and watch the night sky"

"Ok will do, we'll take some champagne

"Sounds great" Mary said as she cut the cheese and made crackers. The days were going by and Frank and Mary were enjoying seeing her tummy grow and getting ready for the day when the baby arrived. The decoration in the nursery was coming along well and the usual teddy bears and woolly toys were beginning to build up. The décor was neutral because they do not want to know the sex of the baby. One morning Mary had a call from Kath about meeting for lunch and they arranged to meet in the Crown for a change and have a pub lunch. Mary got ready and made her way to the pub In the Jeep where she found Kath already there looking at the menu with a bottle of wine in the cooler on the table "Hi Kath, sorry if you've been waiting. I just don't seem to be able to get ready as quick these days" she said as she sat down. "It's ok, I've only Just arrived, here let me pour you a drink"

"Thanks, I need one, now let's have a look at the menu." Mary and Kath chatted while they perused the menu and chose their meals. Jody the barmaid came over and went through the specials with them. The girls placed their orders and chatted away until the meals arrived. The food in the Crown was always consistent and they both enjoyed their meals as usual. "Kath I had a very strange dream on the train coming home and I don't think I've told you about it"

"Oh right, what about"

"Well it was about me starting to see a light in the night sky which turned out to be a UFO, then I met some people in the dream and the spaceman from the UFO, became pregnant and he flew off with my baby into space."

"Had you had a drink or two before you got on the train?"

"No Kath I hadn't, but the funny thing is this. I've seen that very light in the sky recently a couple of times, it's the same light, I'm sure of it."

"There's a lot of military activity at the moment for some reason, could it be them flying around." "No I don't think so, and also what's very strange is that I've recently met two people who were in the dream too, I know they were, there's a bookshop around the corner not far from here and in my dream I slept with the owner. Now I've been to the shop and it's him, he was in my dream. I feel that something out of this world is going on, I feel as though I've entered the twilight zone like the TV show"

"Are you sure about this Mary, really sure?" asked Kath "Yes I am, it's all too much of a coincidence Kath, something funny is going on I think".

Chapter 20

Mary and Frank were up early and it was a lovely morning, the sun was shining and the birds were singing. Mary stood outside on the veranda with her coffee and thought how lucky they were to be living in such an idyllic spot, Mary loved it here, Frank was sitting drinking his coffee in the sun before starting work. Mary passed him some toast. "Right Monty, first things first, let's have a walk up to Shiloh and take him for a walk, see you in a bit Frank, when I get back I'll cook us a proper breakfast" and off they went at a steady pace. Mary enjoyed the walk and the solitude up to the field and it pleased her when she saw Shiloh waiting for her by the gate. "Hello boy, fancy a walk around the farm, we can go to the meadow" she said as she pushed passed him to get through the gate. Mary made her way over to the store and prepared Shiloh's food for when they got back then they all set off around the track, Mary let Shiloh walk on his own as she knew he was totally safe around here. As Mary was walking around enjoying the scenery and watching Monty chasing the odd rabbit she noticed how busy the traffic seemed on the lane up in the hills behind the farm, some of which were parked in the lay-by which was up there. Looking a bit closer she also noticed a black van which was also there with the cars "What a coincidence, Stop it Mary you're beginning to become paranoid" she thought as she carried on walking. Eventually Mary appeared at the meadow and made her way in. Mary though the grass looked beautiful and settled herself down in a nice spot and sat watching Monty rolling around on his back and Shiloh eating the grass. Eventually she lay back and closed her eyes for a few moments, opened her blouse to catch the sun and relaxed with her thoughts "I'll just have five" she thought. Mary felt the wet tongue of Monty on her face "Oh for goodness Monty, can't a girl have five minutes, Oh come on lets carry on" and she got up, brushed herself off and called Shiloh "Ok guys come on lets go" and at that Mary made her way around and down to the farm, she decided to take Shiloh down with her so he could have a change of scenery. When she arrived she was surprised to see Frank looking a little agitated "Where have you been hunni, I was getting a bit concerned" he said to her

"I've only been up to get Shiloh and we had a little walk and five minute in the meadow before we came down here, its nice to be missed though" She said smiling and giving him a kiss.

"Mary you've been gone for three hours"

"Impossible, you're having me on"

"Mary you left here at about eight, now look at your watch"

Mary did and was shocked, it read 11.15.

"What the hell's happened, I must have fallen asleep, but I can't have done, I only closed my eyes for a moment and then Monty licked me"

"Well I'm glad to see you safe, by the way I've had my breakfast" he said as he walked off. Mary walked inside and clicked the kettle on and sat by the breakfast table while she thought about what happened, then she glanced up at the mirror and looked. "Mary made her way outside to Frank "Frank, look at me, look at me closely" she asked "What do you see?"

"A gorgeous wife" he replied "No Frank, look at me. You say I've lay in the Sun for three hours but I'm not even red, the Sun's not caught me at all."

"Mary, you may have lay in the shade"

"No I didn't, I was in the open all the time." Mary walked back to the house and finished making her drink before flopping down into the sofa. "Hold on a minute, in my dream I disappeared for a few hours and it ended up that I was abducted……no that's nonsense, it was only a dream, but then there are the coincidences earlier with the people who I've seen. Now I am getting paranoid" she thought. Mary decided that she had better put her feet up for a while before walking Shiloh back up to the field so she grabbed her book, her drink and settled on the sofa to read a few chapters. The time passed by and Mary was engrossed in her book. She loved reading when the time allowed and was really enjoying the book she had and didn't want it to end. After a while Mary started to feel funny, she had experienced this feeling before but couldn't put her finger on what was wrong, it was a very strange feeling and she felt that if she was to move off the sofa she would fall over so she stayed where she was and waited. Eventually the feeling passed and she felt reinvigorated and full of energy again "How strange is that" she thought anyway enough reading, come on Mont let's get Shiloh back to his field" and at that she got up and made her way out of the door with Monty running ahead. "Frank I'm going to take Shiloh back up to his field, if I'm longer than half hour will you come to me please" she asked "Yes ok hunni, are you alright"

"Yes I'm fine, I must just be over tired, see you in a bit" then she kissed him and took hold of Shiloh and started to make her way up to the field. Shiloh seemed to be pleased that they were back as he walked briskly towards his gate. Mary lifted the latch and pushed it open and in he went, he knew his feed had been prepared earlier and he made his way to it. She closed the gate and leaned on it for a while just watching Shiloh enjoy his hay and Monty standing watching him. Suddenly Mary felt that feeling sweep over her again and she clung onto the gate "What's wrong, what's causing this" she thought and then she heard the sound of the quad bike coming towards her and as suddenly as it came the feeling went, it was Frank of course. "I've not been missing again have I" she asked "No, I watched you walk off and I've been a bit worried about you so I thought I'd give you enough time to get here then come and give you a lift back, hop on" Mary did so thankful of the lift, Monty ran after them with a big stick in his mouth happy with his find. Mary and Frank spent the rest of the evening relaxing and chatting with a few glasses of wine. "Mary I'm getting a bit worried about you, I can't make out whether you're losing the plot or something?" Mary laughed "I'm ok Frank, I think this pregnancy is playing tricks on me and I am tired more often now, in fact I'm off to bed" she said as she closed her book. "Ok, I would like you to take it a bit easier though"

"I will Frank I promise" she said as she made her way upstairs. Mary stood in the dark by the window looking out into the night sky at the stars "What a wonderful night" she thought and as she was looking at the stars she noticed one which stood out brighter than the others and watched it for a minute or two before opening the window to get a better look. "I don't believe it, it can't be surely, it's that light again" just then it vanished "How odd" she thought. She got undressed and climbed into bed. Mary lay there realising that Frank would not be up for a while and was enjoying the space in the bed to herself before nodding off. Next morning Frank was already up and out when Mary woke. She made her way down stairs and decided to cook him a full breakfast "Shiloh can wait a bit this morning" she thought "I'll give Frank a treat". Mary made them both a hearty breakfast which they both enjoyed and then after she had cleaned up the dishes she went off to get changed. A little later Mary was in the kitchen putting on her boots and she started to feel funny again. This time the feeling didn't seem to last long and suddenly vanished and then Mary walked out to Frank "I'm going to book an appointment with the doctor, Frank, these feelings I get are beginning to bother me."

"Good Idea, soon as possible hunni" Frank replied.

"They're not there today so I'll call in the morning. Have you got something light for me to do for you as I want to help you a bit today" she asked "Are you sure, I mean Pete will be here later to give me a hand as you know."

"Yes hunni, I'm fine and if I get tired I'll tell you"

"Well ok, there's a bucket of nutrient feed pellets there, they need to go to the field where the sheep are and scattering in the feed troughs, are you ok with that"

"Yes I think I can manage that hunni, I'm not dying you know" she said smiling at him as she grabbed the bucket and walked off. The field was up the track in between the farm and Shiloh's field only a short walk but even so Mary took her time. She opened the gate and let herself in and scattered the pellets into the feed troughs. "I may as well see to Shiloh while I'm here" she though. On seeing something going on the sheep started to come over to investigate. Mary made her exit and closed the gate and started to walk to Shiloh but as she did so it happened again, the feeling, it was back only this time it was so strong Mary leaned on the fence so as not to fall over and as she did so she saw in the sky the orange light and she watched it as it seemed to get closer to her, she realised that it was heading her way. As she watched it slowly started to change from an orange light into three orange lights and a triangular shape and it was landing. All of a sudden it made sense to Mary what was happening, the dream wasn't a dream, it was a premonition, all the coincidences now made sense. Mary screamed and started to run, she could see the triangular shape very clearly now "Oh my God, Oh my God it can't be…….Please God no, don't let it be, Please don't let it be, the feeling of dread went through her like a knife………………

It's happening, It's really happening……………….She Knew why it was here, it was here for her baby…………Mary ran like she had never ran before, she ran really hard down the track towards the farm screaming "FRANK…FRANK" she shouted sobbing. Wondering what was happening Frank ran to her "FRANK, FRANK" she screamed "They're here, they're here, they've come for my baby" she sobbed "Don't let them take me Frank, Please don't let them take me!" Mary said with floods of tears coming down her face "My dream Frank, it was a premonition, they want my baby" Frank took her in his arms and looked up in the direction from where Mary had come and a cold shiver went through him as what he saw scared him, the unbelievable sight of a spaceship. A cold shiver went through him as what he saw scared him beyond belief, he held Mary very tight and close to him as he stared at the unbelievable sight of the large triangular spaceship hovering just above the fields "Run Mary run, as fast as you can" They started running towards the Jeep, when they got to it Mary jumped in followed by Monty and locked the door and Frank paused and looked up. The ship was just sitting there about 10 feet above the ground "Oh my God" he said under his breath before he jumped in the jeep and started to drive away at great speed. Both Mary and Frank knew that the chase was on and he was determined that the Nordics would not get hold of Mary no matter how long or how far they had to run. "We have to get away from here right now; Pete can look after the place. "I love you so Much and I'm not going to let them get you, I promise, but we have to get away and hide" he said "I love you too but hurry get us out of here now "she screamed, tears running down her face. The jeep sped off up the track and out onto the main road and disappeared from sight. They are frightened but they knew the chase was on and they were now on the run until the baby was born.

Chapter 21

The radio in the black van burst into life "They're on the move" a husky voice said slowly into the mike. "Ok, follow them" came the reply from the radio in the darkness of the van. The engine started and they made off down the road at speed so not to lose sight of the landrover. "Frank what *we are* going to do" Mary said in a shaky voice.

"I don't know yet, let me think while I try to get us to the motorway" Monty stuck his head between the two of them seeming excited that they were going on a ride. They made their way through the lanes heading for town, from there they could pick up the signs for the motorway. Franks mind was awash with all sorts of thoughts, what was happening to them, who could help them, what could he do to protect them, where would they go? All the time scanning the sky to see if they were being followed by the craft. Eventually the road took them through to Carlisle where they picked up the motorway and headed South not sure of where they were going. "I'm scared Frank"

"Me too hunni, but I'm sure we'll come out of this ok" They drove for a while in silence, both lost in their thoughts then "Mary do you have your phone with you?

"Yes why"

"Phone Kath or Mike, ask them if they still have that flat they let out in Kendal, we could make for there. That will let us get our thoughts together" Mary pulled out her phone and charger from her bag. She pushed the charger into the socket in the car and plugged her phone in. Noticing she had a decent signal she called Kath.

"Hi Kath"

"Oh hi Mary, we were just talking about you, what's up?

"Kath we're in deep shit, we're on the motorway heading north, do you still have the flat you let out in Kendal, if so is it free?

"We do and it is, is that where you're heading. What's wrong, what's happened?

"I can't explain now" Mary said trying to hold back the tears "Can we use the flat please, it's urgent?

"It's all yours as it's empty at the moment. I'll text you the address and postcode, when you get there go up the stairs to the front door, you will see a little cupboard by the side of the door. Open it and you will find the key safe. The code is 1955, let yourselves in and make yourselves at home, I'm sure you'll work the heating out and there's a bit of bedding in the airing cupboard. Call me when you're settled"

"Oh thank you so much, speak later" A few minutes later Marys phone pinged and it was the text from Kath with the address and postcode. Mary put this into google maps and off they went. It wasn't a long drive but far enough away for now and it was late when they arrived. They made their way to the flat and let themselves in. Frank threw his keys down and flopped onto the sofa. "I'll have to pop to find a shop Frank, we need some shopping as we've got to eat"

"Yes ok, I'm too tired to think at the moment. Just see if there's a takeaway to save us cooking"

"Ok back in a min" Mary stepped out into the busy street "We should be ok here for a while, no one could find us in this town surely" She thought. As she walked to the shopping area she was unaware of the black van which had pulled up in the street a little way up from the flat. Mary returned with a takeaway and shopping to last a couple of days while they thought what to do. They had a meal and a bottle of wine, and just tried to relax after the stress of the day. Monty fell asleep in front of the gas fire. The next morning they chatted as they were cooking breakfast. "What are we going to do Frank, who can we talk to? She asked "I don't know. What good is going to the Police, what could they do, would they believe us, is anyone going to believe this?

"What about the military?

"Yes but which part, where would we start. Mary, I still find it hard to believe this is actually happening. Please let me wake up in a minute from another bad dream"

"Frank, remember when those jets were flying around and Dave spoke to the drivers of those black vans?

"Yes, some sort of exercise going on I think he said"

"Suppose it wasn't, suppose the military already know about the ships visit to us. Why was the exercise in the vicinity of our farm, why were the black vans positioned so they could see our farm and our movements? Frank the military are on to this, they know, why they have not contacted us, what are the vans doing, what do they know, Frank I'm really scared now"

"We had better give Kath a call, she'll be wondering what's going on" Mary called Kath and unloaded all what was happening, they were talking for quite some time. Kath said she couldn't believe what was happening but offered any help they could give. "Kath, would you pop to the next farm to George and Ethel. No need to give them details but would you ask them to feed Shiloh till we get back. Make up some story of us having to deal with a family emergency or something"

"Yes of course, If I knew about horses I'd do it myself for you"

"Yes I know you would, also you don't know where we are if anyone asks, ok?

"No probs, call me if you need anything, what about the rest"

"Thanks Kath, chat later" Mary put the phone down, thought for a while then started crying. Frank moved over and put his arm around her "Try not to worry, hun, there must be a way out of this "

"Yes but how, what's going to happen. We have him after us, we think the military are up to something, who do we talk too Frank?

"I don't know, at the moment I just don't know. I'll give Pete a call, he'll have to look after the rest of the duties at the farm himself for a while" Frank picked up Mary's phone and dialled. "Hi Pete, It's Frank. Pete we're in a spot of bother, we've had to head off urgently for a family crisis mate, can you look after things for a short time while we're gone please. If you need to get any extra help I'll pay you whatever it costs. George and Ethel are going to look after Shiloh so you no need bother with him mate"

"No problem Frank, leave it with me and you relax and concentrate on your family, I'll be fine. Call me in a few days if you like"

"Cheers Pete, bye" Frank was trying to sound as normal as possible as not to attract any undue attention or make Pete worry about them unduly. "Ok, everything at home is taken care of, now we just have to worry about ourselves" The rest of the day was spent indoors with Frank and Mary keep going over the same conversations about their dilemma, but still not coming up with any answers and it was beginning to show as they were getting a little irritated and snappy with each other at times with frustration. However, the evening came in and Frank lit the fire and put some logs on and Monty settled on the mat to enjoy the heat. They then snuggled on the sofa in silence each with their own thoughts. Meanwhile, outside the sound of tourists and locals enjoying the nightlife of the town was evident. There was a lot of traffic going up and down the road, all passing a black van parked nearby. The radio in the van burst into life "Any movement" came a voice with authority "Other than her getting some shopping no Sir, nothing at all" was the reply "Ok, keep your eye's peeled and wait for instructions but report in if things change" The radio went dead before they could reply. The van was in darkness other than the glow from someone's cigarette. The next morning Frank had just got up to make a drink when the phone rang, It was Rob "Hi mate, what's up" Frank said while wiping the sleep from his eyes. "I've thinking about you two all night and I'm concerned about you. I think I've an Idea you'll like"

"Go on Rob, what's that?

"I checked my emails and a Tenant of ours has given us notice on a cottage we have. He's moved out now but has paid us for the rest of the month, it's free now. The nice thing is it's in a very secluded spot, you would be able to chill a bit perhaps, bit of a drive but I think it would be better than that little flat"

"Sounds good, Where is it ?

"It's in a village called Hawes on the A684, I'll text you the directions and leave it with you, like the flat there's a key safe and I'll let you have that number as well. When you go down the lane to the cottage from the village you will be really private. It's there for you just go if you like"

"Bless you Mike, I'll keep you informed, chat later" the phone went dead. "Mike's just offered us a place in the country, isolated, feels we may be happier there for the time being, what do you think?

"I think we have two very loyal friends there Frank, I'll leave it with you"

The day started with bright sunshine and Mary took her cup of tea and looked out of the window and wished she was looking out over her farm. She leaned on the wide window ledge watching the passers-by going to and fro while enjoying her brew. Then.......something caught her eye.

"Frank.....Frank, come look at this"

"What's up" he said as came up behind her. "That van parked there in that row of parked cars, I'm sure it's the same as the ones we've seen before"

"Are you sure?

"I think so, or am I getting paranoid?

"Let's not take any chances, we should use the cottage we've been offered, trouble is if it is them they'll just follow us. Let's see if we get an opportunity" Rob said while looking through the curtain thoughtfully. "Ok let's keep our eyes on it this morning, want some breakfast" Mary asked as she opened the bacon and turned the gas cooker on. Frank looked at her and felt concerned at how calm she seemed. "Yes ok, that'll be good, I'll make a fresh brew" he said as he filled the kettle. The day was really no different than yesterday, same worries, same conversations still no solutions to satisfy their thoughts. They kept an eye on the van which didn't show any sign of movement at all. Then things changed, the sound of an almighty bank made them both jump and shoot to the window. They looked out on a road accident which blocked the road causing traffic to back up blocking in the van. Without saying a word to each other they grabbed their things and ran down to the side door of the flat where the Jeep was parked and got in and started it quickly, into gear and sped up the ally onto the next road away from the jam. They knew the van couldn't possibly follow them, they had got the opportunity they wanted. About an hour or so they arrived at the village and followed Robs directions to the cottage and pulled up outside. Mary looked at it and was lost at how lovely it was, all private and secluded at the front and open fields to the back. "Look Monty we'll go for a walk shall we" Mary said rubbing his head. They made their way inside and made themselves as much at home as they could considering they were travelling so very light with little belongings. "Just how many properties do they own Frank? Mary asked "I've no idea, never thought to ask them, but I could live here, it's gorgeous, wonder what he charges for this per month?

"Look here, the tenants left in a hurry, there's still stuff in the fridge and cupboards, fancy a cuppa she said as she kissed his cheek and grabbed the kettle. She looked out of the window at Monty sniffing around the garden. "Oh God is this ever going to end so we can be normal again, I'll never take anything for granted again" she though, just then she was brought back to reality by the kettle clicking off. A few days had gone by and this was spent in endless conversation of what to do mixed with a little laughter but plenty of tears. The phone had been very busy with calls to Pete to find out about the farm, if he needed anything, if there were any problems. Pete was very good, never asked them a question of what was going on. Mary and Kath had talked a lot. Kath was trying to be as supportive to Mary as she could be in this situation but Mary realised the between Pete, Kath and Rob all of them quietly must wonder what the hell's happening. "One day I may be able to tell them, I hope" she thought. The day went by and evening came in, it was going dusk with a lovely red sky. Frank had chopped some wood for the fire and was busy lighting it and Mary was just finishing off preparing some tea. Both of them were stopped in their tracks by a knock on the door. They looked at one another as obviously they were not expecting anyone. Whoever it was knocked again, they both froze. They had to answer as it was obvious the cottage was occupied at this time as the lights were on and the dog was barking "Who's this" Mary said "Well , only one way to find out" Frank said as he slowly made his way to the door and hesitated before opening it. He pulled the old fashioned bolt and clicked the latch and slowly opened the door. Frank was surprised to see a tall elderly gent, very smart, long coat and a trilby with the look of an Insurance salesman standing there. "Can I help you" enquired frank

In an educated voice the man replied "You must be Frank Scott, mind if I come in" and without waiting for a reply he pushed past Frank and walked into the Kitchen where Mary stood looking worried "Ah you must be Mary, put the kettle on would you" he asked as he took off his long coat and folded it before putting it aside "Who are you, what do you want" asked Mary. "Well Mary I'm Commander George Gregory, Mr Gregory to you, of the Ministry of Defence and I've travelled a long way to see you two" he said while making himself comfortable. "What can we do for you? Frank innocently "Come now Frank, we all know why I'm here" he replied

"How did you find us" Asked Mary

"Well Mary you did manage to give us the slip but we have our ways of finding people and you were not a problem on that score. Now shall we have a cup of tea as we have things to talk about and before you thing about nipping off again through the back door I will tell you that this area is surrounded and we will not let you go, so try to relax as we're on your side now" Mary and Frank were quiet while Mary followed his wishes and made them all tea and coffee before sitting down at the table with Commander Gregory. "You've got yourself in a bit of a pickle Mary and the question is what we do about it" he said casually while taking a sip of his tea. "What do you mean we, this is our problem, for us to sort out" Frank said trying to be defiant. "Oh Frank, We know why you've been running but let me put your mind at rest, they are no longer are after you, they've gone, you Mary are no longer of any use to them. They have gone in search of another host, like many of their kind searching the world over for young women that have had no children that they can impregnate and then when the time is just right steal the foetus to be transferred into one of their own females to be raised as a hybrid on their own world" he said while getting comfortable "You mean I know longer have to worry about them coming back at all. Why am I of no use to them then, I'm still carrying a healthy baby inside me? She said rubbing her tummy. "Good, I'm pleased you're ok Mary with all the stress you've had. They had to monitor you carefully and come back for you at just the right time, timing for them is crucial, when they came for you they didn't expect you to run like you did. This took your baby over their critical timing and it became no good for them. It's a little like boiling and egg and wanting it runny, a few seconds late and it goes hard, not what you want" Commander Gregory was beginning to relax now and the feeling was spreading to Frank and Mary, they were feeling a little better in his company "What do the aliens do with these hybrids, what's the purpose, why do this? Asked Frank with interest in his voice. "Simple my boy, when they are grown to an educated adult they send them back here to earth. They will look just like you and I, perfect human forms. Then they get into high power positions where they can learn about us or manipulate mankind either into better peace or war. If you've been to the bigger cities you probably have passed one in the town but you wouldn't know. They are here and have been for a long time. What's happened to you now happened a lot in ancient times and from the mid 40's through to the 70's. We can't stop it, but we can try our best to control this. We don't want to completely stop this because humanity has advanced so quickly with what we have learned from alien technology from crashed or captured spacecraft, you've only got to look at the modern things you use, mobile phones, computers etc" The commander relaxed and took another drink from his mug "I can tell you briefly about this as you now have come a part of us, the system"

"What do you mean" Frank asked

"Well they have gone and we now need to take you under our wing. Mary is carrying an aliens baby Frank, you are not the biological father, get used to it. When it is born and growing it will be completely normal to you, you will learn to love him/her, you will have fun educating him/her and getting to know their friends. Your lives will be completely normal and hopefully very happy. But your child will have exceptional talents, what these will be we can't say at this time but we will have to monitor their upbringing"

"I'm not happy about this at all, we didn't want those aliens in our lives and now we have you saying you'll be involved in the upbringing of our child, I just don't know what to say, this doesn't seem right at all, I feel so confused" Mary said with tears in her eyes. The Commander took on an authoritive voice and sat up in his chair "Let me be very blunt and to the point Mary. To stop the aliens taking the child we were going to step in and take it ourselves and use a military female as host. That is the importance of this situation, but we realised that time had run out for them and decided that the baby could now stay with its rightful Mother, which is obviously much better but has to be monitored by us"

"For how long will this go on" Mary asked Commander Gregory thought for a minute before answering and began in a relaxed manner "For all their life. Your child will be directed to have the best education, all paid for by us. When they enter the commercial world and set out on a career we will have already sown the seed of which way they will go. They will find that attractive Job offers come their way which in turn will mean they will be unknowingly directed to work for us. From this time on we will be able to monitor their growth, lifestyle, interests etc., and also learn from the intense knowledge which we feel they may have to take humanity further forward. You as parents will want for nothing, you will be well looked after"

"What shall we do now, I think we're both very confused by this" Frank asked calmly "Go home" The commander said "Go home and get on with your lives and look forward to the birth of your beautiful baby, everything else will just fall into place. Now it's nice to meet you both but it's unlikely that we will meet again. I must leave now but I wish you all a very happy life from now on, "Goodbye" he said as he grabbed his hat and coat and made for the door. The door opened and Mary and Frank realised that there was a large black car sitting quietly with the door already open. Commander Gregory got, waved and closed the door, all the windows were tinted so no one could see the occupants. The car very gently pulled away and made its way up the lane and disappeared into the darkness. The next day Mary and Frank packed up what things they had and made their way home to the farm. As they pulled up Pete walked up to meet them. Mary opened the Jeep door and Monty jumped out scampered off as if pleased to be back. "Hi folks" said Pete wiping his hands on his dirty rag. "Is everything ok? "He asked in a concerned manner. "Yes Pete, everything's Ok, thanks for looking after the place. We'll fill you in on the recent happenings another day but at the moment we just want to settle back in" Mary said to him. Mary and frank were tired. The last few days had really taken it out of them and they just now wanted to relax for a while. Mary made her way out onto the veranda and settled into one of the easy chairs, Frank appeared a few minutes later with a glass of wine for them both and sat in the chair next to her. Without saying anything they just relaxed and sat watching the setting sun both lost in their thoughts of what was to come………………

The end……………………for now ?

Printed in Great Britain
by Amazon

need is desperate," Dr Church wrote from one mission centre. "Some missionaries say they have no real fellowship with the Africans nor, sad to say, fellowship with neighbouring missions. We pressed them to remember that we have not come to preach Revival, but just to go more deeply into what real walking with Jesus means and to be more Christlike and more broken, that's all."

At a place near Blantyre, "Apparently the Africans present were staggered by William Nagenda, as an African, giving his testimony about his home and money. Then in the evening they all went down to a meeting in Blantyre (four miles from here). There was a wonderfully free time. There were Europeans from the government, business and banks - not many, but just those whom God seemed to send. Afterwards, being driven home, a man leaned over to William in the car and said, 'William, God told me to repent at the Prayer Meeting, but I refused. He showed me my white man's pride in refusing to carry your bag at the Airport. I'm sorry, and He has cleansed it.' A little thing, you may say! Yes, but it's those little things that hinder the Holy Spirit's blessing."

"It's been a strange time for me," reported Dr Joe Church later, "I'm still in bed with a severe ulcerated mouth, the worst I've ever had. But I am having a good time, reading, praying and writing. Perhaps I talk too much and God is showing me the place of intercession. At our prayer time around my bed, Dora and William both claimed complete victory over the subtle sin of - what do we call it? - the 'Are-we-doing-what-Joe-wants' sin! That is rather a long title for it, but it came as a real revelation from God and once repented of and cleansed, we were free and rejoicing again. Oh the joyous liberty of the children of God, when we are as simple as little children with Him over sin. That sin could have cramped this tour. It is easy in teams to be held up by each other.

"William has reported to me a conversation he has had

Letter for this tour, Dr Church wrote:

Thursday, 8th September at Guebwiller.

We began the Convention with a team of six ... There were several things that had to be put in the Light before God and talked over ... William and I began the first meeting with testimony based on the story of Philip and the Ethiopian ... The hall was packed and there was great hunger. ... Dr Pache gave the Bible Reading on 'revivals in the Old Testament'. William followed him, stressing the need of resting and letting God do His work of Revival in us - at once, with no waiting. In the evening I drew the 'Not 'I' but Christ' picture on the blackboard and spoke on 'the stiff neck'. William followed. Today we have been on 'The Cross'. Once again hearts are melting before the love of Calvary. There have been many tears and wonderful scenes of rejoicing."

Saturday, 10th September at Guebwiller, France.

"A still more wonderful day! Dr Pache took the Revival in the Book of Acts as his Bible reading. After a break we gave time for testimonies ... William closed the meeting with his testimony of how he had tried to fight 'the old man' in his own strength and what a failure it had been until Nsibambi had told him to rest - to rest in the finished work of Christ. I have never seen such a joyful conference as this outside Africa."

Friday 16th September at Basle, Switzerland.

"Praise God, after much prayer and heart-searchings in the team, God has broken through. We went back again to the Cross, stressing the question of relationships. All Revival is held up by sins of lack of love to one's neighbour. These sins must be put right; then there is no need to go on praying. Revival begins."

The team spent some time in Germany before returning to France and then to England.

In November 1951, Dr Joe Church, William Nagenda and Dora Skipper visited Nyasaland (now Malawi). "The

congregations in theirs ... That is South Africa!" Quest 212

The team for the first tour of Switzerland in January 1947 was again all-white: Dr Joe Church, Rev. Lawrence Barham, Rev. Bill Butler and an ex-missionary of the Ruanda Mission, Mlle Berthe Ryf.

Dr Church wrote: "About forty pastors, evangelical leaders and their wives who had been touched and drawn by Berthe's testimony, were gathered with great expectancy to meet us at a mountain pension above Vevey called Chalet Beaumont on the first evening. The Spirit of God came down on our three-day gathering ... There were reconciliations, embraces and abandoned entering into new life." Quest 223

"We found pastors and evangelists from far off, Roumania, Hungary, Czechoslovakia, Italy, also France and Belgium" recorded Dr Church. This prompted the Rev. Bill Butler to conclude one of his addresses: "God loved the little country of Palestine with its hills and valleys and chose it wherein His own Son should die for the world, and the Gospel should go forth. God has chosen another little country, Ruanda, set in the middle of Africa, from which to send out the Water of Life. May it be that small but still free Switzerland with all its heritage will be chosen of God to carry the Water of Life to needy Europe?" Quest 225

During 1947 and 1948 the team of Dr Joe Church, William Nagenda, Canon Lawrence Barham and the Rev. Yosiya Kinuka, joined with missionaries of the Ruanda Mission on leave and leaders from this country, notably Roy Hession, to visit Keswick and other conventions and speak at many meetings in the British Isles. A notable result of the ministry of these years was to establish a team which proclaimed, and testified to, the truths which had become so powerful in the revival in Africa.

The team for the second French and Swiss Tour in September 1949 included William Nagenda. In his Diary-

Chapter 8

Witness worldwide

As news of revival in Rwanda and Uganda reached other parts of Africa and beyond, there were calls from churches and missions in these places for the leaders of revival to visit them with the news of what was happening. Reports of these visits were recorded in special tour reports and also in *Front Line News*, a periodical circulated by the Ruanda Mission. From these reports it is possible to gain insights into what God was doing in Rwanda and Uganda from the way events were described to others.

One of the earliest calls from areas beyond East Africa came from South Africa in 1944. A serious problem arose, however. "The convenor of the Cape Town Keswick Convention, Dr Moore-Anderson, had written to me on May 8th 1944, inviting three of us to come. ... Someone put the need of evangelical Cape Town succinctly: after visits by a number of well-known preachers what was needed now was a team in action ... especially a team of black and white working in absolute oneness. But after waiting till the last minute for the permits we were met with nothing but blank refusals for William and Yosiya to go." Quest 209

Dr Joe Church commented on the tour: "There was warmth, personal talks, decisions, but we felt a deep under-current of resistance against the insuperable barriers of colour-bar and sectarian exclusiveness. We went out to meet the 'coloureds' in their church, and African

foundation for a life that is wholly revived. "When the Blood cleanses, the Holy Spirit fills", became a glorious, daily truth, whatever may be the psychological or physical state which accompanies it.

The fact of experience is, however, that that level of spiritual life is difficult for a Christian to maintain on his or her own. This failure is not due to any lack of provision on God's part, but due to the weakness of human nature. The answer to this weakness is *fellowship*.

The privilege of fellowship is the joy of oneness in Christ that was won on Calvary. The responsibility of fellowship is, in the phrase loved by Dr Joe Church, "keeping each other to the Highest!" His autobiography reflected his "Quest for the Highest". This 'highest' is more than that which is morally right and true. It is the attitude and behaviour of the person who is 'conformed to the image of Christ', claims no rights, rejects no-one, is servant of all, and seeks the highest good of all others.

It is part of the heritage of the Mission that missionaries who served in it learned the joy of a deep oneness with their fellow missionaries and with African Christians. They also learned the cost of keeping each other to the 'Highest'.

'Continuous revival' may not be a true description of the Christian individual and fellowship when 'revival' is defined in terms of dramatic, extraordinary manifestations, but it expresses the profound experience of every fellowship where 'the Blood of Christ cleanses and the Holy Spirit fills' each individual and each seeks to 'keep each other to the 'Highest'.'

7 Relationships in fellowship

It is all too easy, particularly in the powerful movements of the Holy Spirit in revival, to believe that if other Christians do not see things as you do, they must be fighting not only against you but against God. It is the witness of many of the missionaries who lived through revival, that the preciousness of the fellowship which they enjoyed, with it's joyous experience of sins forgiven and the indwelling presence of the Holy Spirit together with a deep oneness with both fellow-missionaries and Africans, was an outstanding memory of those times. It appears equally true that other missionaries, equally devoted in their service for God, who, for whatever reasons, did not share that same sense of fellowship, often felt that they were excluded by the 'inner circle' and even the most important biblical terms were sometimes assumed to have different shades of meaning.

Part of the *heritage* which the Mission values so greatly is the experience of it's missionaries having worked as a team, even when the depth of individual experiences has been expressed in different ways. The precious truth lies in two forms of intolerance! Firstly, an intolerance of anything which is sin, which deceives or is done 'in the dark'; anything which is not an expression of love, genuinely seeking the best for others. Secondly, an intolerance of anything which creates false barriers between those who are in Christ, at whatever stage of their spiritual development they may be, expressed in an attitude of humility and 'brokenness' which embraces people with Christ's embrace.

It is the experience of God's unifying power in fellowship which proved such a strong basis for the conviction that, in this revival, God had revealed His purpose for all Christians, that is, *continuous revival.*

When a Christian learns what it means to repent of *all* sin, to trust in Christ for forgiveness and cleansing, and to welcome the Holy Spirit into every part of life, there is the

ness is obstinacy, or rather, to be 'stiff-necked' or unyielding."

'Brokenness' is saying to God, "Yes! You are right and I am wrong" and then taking the lowly path of confession, restitution of wrong, and apology to anyone harmed. It is the reaction of Christians when people take advantage of them, showing little or no respect for them or their possessions. It is the response of the one who forgives another but is not forgiven in return.

In August 1948, Miss Barrie wrote: "Last week we got back from the Gahini Convention; the days there were amazing and for me a time of learning many things. We were once again pointed back to the Cross and the Way of being broken and humble as THE way, the only Highway. How easy to write this but how Satan hates it to be real; but unless it is real and vital in our living and working together, with the precious Blood cleansing moment by moment, what is the use of meetings and more meetings, institutions and organisations, here and at home?"

It was in the 'striving together for the Gospel' and facing the strong convictions of those for whom their 'grey' areas had become gloriously 'black and white' - for the 'blacker' that sin is seen to be, so much the more joyously 'white' is forgiveness and reconciliation with God, that were learned the lessons which form part of the Mission's heritage

Two wedges that Satan used powerfully to split the fellowship were illustrated by the experience of Festo Kivengere in Tanzania. "When Festo said he knew Christ personally, and that Christ had saved him from sins," wrote his biographer, "the church leaders believed he was saying that he was holier than everyone else in the church, that he was a special kind of Christian." [Coomes.143]

The second dividing wedge was identified by Festo Kivengere himself. In the Christian faith, "It isn't a case of whoever is not for you is against you, but of whoever isn't against you is with you." [Coomes.148]

concern is to be continually in fellowship with Him. Sixth, Therefore I abandon controversy or argument. It is no solution to our problems to join the Abaka. This obscures the real essential of being more deeply united to Christ and would only perpetuate divisions.

"Seventh, people do need correction, but I want to learn how to move them by prayer, not by authority or argument, so that their convictions are based on what Christ has shown them, not on what I have ordered or argued. Eighth. Towards all, love. So I long for the "rivers of living waters" to be flowing and this doesn't mean an effortless attempt to be 'hearty', but spontaneous effortless living under the control of the Lord Jesus Christ, and in the continuous consciousness of His presence."

Many missionaries have expressed how great was their appreciation of the fellowship which God gave them when working together in revival. Such an effective witness to the grace of God could not go unchallenged by the Enemy. The clear stand for saving truth and openness in relationships, which was the great strength of those whom God used so powerfully in revival, was fought by Satanic power working through human weakness. It is significant that the term Abaka was later dropped and the most common term for a 'saved' or 'born again' man or woman was 'mulokole' - a Ugandan word meaning 'a saved one'.

The strong, sometimes almost harsh, unwillingness to accept anything less than the 'highest' in all relationships appears to contrast with a willingness to 'bend the neck' and accept in all humility that one is wrong. This characteristic of God working in revival is called being 'broken' - before God and before one's colleagues and friends.

A distinction made by Peter Guillebaud, quoted elsewhere, is worth repeating. "Humility and brokenness are not the same thing at all, though they may overlap. The opposite of humility is pride, but the opposite of broken-

African *Abaka* accepted those missionaries they felt were also *Abaka* but were very critical of those who they felt were not truly repenting of their sin, 'walking in the light' with their colleagues - missionary and African - and sharing their zeal to reach the lost who were heading for hell if they were not reconciled to God. The acceptance or otherwise by the *Abaka* became a divisive issue, even among those missionaries who were determined not to allow anything to spoil their oneness in Christ and in the proclamation of the Gospel.

One of those for whom this issue was very distressing was Dr Algie Stanley Smith. He saw that unity was essential for a clear witness to Jesus Christ and His saving Gospel. Because of this he refused to be associated with the *Abaka*, despite the great sympathy he had with their stand for truth and openness and their evangelistic zeal.

He wrote in his diary for 30 December 1938: "Looking back on the events of the past few weeks, the Lord seems to have given me new light and a new hope which is already being realised. The points briefly are these. First, I am convinced that among the leaders of the *Abaka* movement, there is no fear of doctrinal differences. Second, that we ought to be profoundly thankful to God for the *Abaka* movement and for these leaders. It has been through them and not through the more prosaic people that God has brought about the spiritual awakening in Kenya and Uganda. This doesn't mean as some unwisely say, 'They are always right'. Third, these differences between us will never be cured by argument, accusations or memoranda. Fourth, it is only Christ who can do it. I think it is to drive this home that He has allowed all previous efforts of both sides to fail. We must really believe that He can do it. Fifth. The only way for us is to get to a new place of surrender or self-abandonment before Him, pleading to know our worthlessness and getting a new conception of the meaning of faith. Our only

is a pure one. Have you ever known a newly converted boy at home who has not made mistakes! They have made mistakes but God has spared us all these years from any real error, I am thankful to say. As Samuel Chadwick says, 'Fire cannot compromise' ... Some of our missionaries have 'sat on the fence' or openly criticized from the beginning. Little may be detected in the chatty superficial letters of Ruanda Notes but out here where the light of the Holy Spirit is blazing brightly, nothing can hide and hidden motives are laid bare mercilessly."

The *Abaka* did not see themselves as an exclusive clique, but simply the fellowship of those who were willing to face the light of God's truth in their lives, individually and with each other. Any barrier or distinction between them and those who did not join them, was not a human one in which they decided who should or should not belong. It was a God-made distinction between those who let God work in them in revival light and power, and those who did not. Their desire was that that barrier should be broken down and that all should be one in Jesus, in a unity which they had found so real.

Dr Godfrey Hindley explained the *Abaka* by the fact that "those who were influenced by revival had such a deep desire to see all their friends live a holy life that they themselves wanted. If they saw something that was not right in another missionary, they would tell them and that was resented by some people. I think that many who were affected by revival were hard on occasions in the way they dealt with each other. However, I have seen missionaries, who, although converted, received this challenge and were completely changed. Sometimes the challenge was hard but if the Spirit of God was in it, it brought them new life or they became very angry."

The fellowship between missionaries was not the only one - that between missionary and African was also at issue, and this was not so simply resolved. Some of the

who had burning hearts to pass on the Good News to the 'unsaved'. To those 'on the outside', it was a closed clique of those who believed that they alone were right and that they had to put everyone else straight.

In July 1938, Dr Algie Stanley Smith wrote from Kigeme, "This evening I met with many of the bakuru (leaders), men and women. I was looking forward to it, and was asked to start by giving a story of the Kisenyi Conference, which I did. Then in a very humble, but direct way, one after another they told me what they thought of me and my work. My weakness and softness towards all and sundry had made them associate me with those against revival. It had given many people a handle to say that they preferred my religion to that of the Abaka. It proved that I was a hypocrite and a coward. I didn't give the Cross the place it should in my teaching, and generally gave soft soap to people instead of reproving them of sin and warning them to flee from the wrath to come. I have been increasingly conscious that these things are true, and it certainly brings to an end all pride in anything I have done. We have just come away and it is 12.45 midnight. Tomorrow I must give a clear testimony. But I can't manufacture a sense of reality in my faith in the lost state of those out of Christ, nor can I make the Cross as essential a thing as it ought to be."

"There is a large and growing number of Christians on every station," wrote Dr Joe Church, in November 1938, "called sometimes the 'abaka'. These men and women have had a definite experience and often go off at once to witness to their friends. Two hundred went off from Gahini last August and it was three of this great band that got as far as Buhiga and was the cause of the trouble there, or rather the devil was!

"No one denies that there have been errors of judgement, and mistakes on the part of these young and enthusiastic *Abaka*, but also remember that their motive

do those who, in the fellowship, are 'walking in the light' with God and with their colleagues react to those they perceive to be 'in darkness'?

Three years after the outbreak of revival at Gahini, The Rev. Geoffrey Holmes wrote of a worrying development: "Gahini is our oldest station in Belgian territory, having been started in 1925. From this part have gone forth hundreds of keen Christians to other areas in Ruanda and Urundi to spread the knowledge of God's love for us. We should be grateful for this and I am sure we are. Gahini Christians really have given of their best for the extension of God's Kingdom in other areas. But today at Gahini we are faced with problems for which we crave not only your prayers, but the prayers of Christians in other parts of Ruanda and Urundi which I feel Gahini has done so much to help.

"At Gahini a new thing has happened - not suddenly but gradually, over a period of several years. The result is that today here there are two 'camps' - those who are in with the 'abaka' (a word meaning in this dialect, 'those who glow') and those who are not in with them. Actually here at Gahini most of the native Christians are in with this new group. There is no real fellowship between those who are in this group and those who are not. "Some of the Christians are so taken up with their own spiritual struggles that they have very little time for the heathen round about and no real message for them. In consequence the congregations are falling off both here at Gahini and in the out districts."

The African word for 'those who are on fire' is *Abaka*. It was that name which was used widely in Rwanda and Burundi, particularly in the early stages of revival, to refer to those whom God had clearly and evidently revived. It very quickly acquired two very distinct meanings: to those 'on the inside', it was the fellowship of those who were 'saved', who were 'walking in the light' with each other and

gether."

The depths to which barriers had been broken down were illustrated in a letter from Dr Kenneth Buxton, dated 17 April 1950, on his and Agnes' return from leave in the UK. "When I think of our return to Buye at the end of last year I wonder whether it was a foretaste of what it will be like when the Friends of Ruanda meet in Heaven those in Ruanda for whom they have prayed and worked but whom they have not yet seen. It was like a family reunion; after nearly two years separation we found that we were still one in Jesus. Though all of us had passed through testings we were made near to Him and so near to one another with no barriers of fear and jealousy which separate black from white and man from man, yes, and Christian from Christian too, for in the Light 'the Blood of Jesus Christ cleanses' these away and we find, in actual practice, fellowship with one another in Him. So now on earth, but one day you at home and we out here will join around the Throne of 'Him Who has loved us and washed us from our sins in His own Blood."

Colour prejudice is not at times easy to distinguish from other forms of intolerance and deeply ingrained attitudes require a great work of grace to eradicate. Nevertheless, in revival God showed His power to perform that miracle when there was a recognition that such attitudes were sin and repentance and forgiveness sought.

The liberating experience and powerful witness of fellowship between 'saved' men and women of different cultures - in this case, black and white, European and African - who are prepared to 'walk in the light as God is in the Light', is an important part of the heritage of the Ruanda Mission.

This fellowship between missionaries, between Africans and between missionaries and Africans also contained the seeds of conflict. True fellowship is impossible without 'light' and light cannot exist where there is darkness. How

cultural differences, in spiritual matters and in the church we are equal. 'I have called you friends.' The African can have a deep, even mystical, yet practical experience of Christ, and understanding of the Faith and the Scriptures which equals and even may surpass ours. Therefore the attitude of colour superiority in the church of Christ is out of place, and so, except in schools, is the parental or authoritarian attitude. This does not mean that we encourage the Africans to despise the Europeans; and they won't, as a rule, if they know that we don't despise them. We also come to them, knowing that we cannot work without them, and we have definitely to accept the idea of Aggrey's device; the black and white keys of the piano. In every possible way we work to forward African leadership and responsibility."

A remarkable convention of missionaries and Africans from different missionary societies which were by then working in Rwanda and Burundi took place at Mutaho, in Burundi. Referring to the other societies - Danish Baptists, American Free Methodists and Evangelical Friends - Dr Kenneth Buxton commented: "It was the first time that we really got together and they learned from all of us something about revival and the way of fellowship, and they were very ready to receive it. I remember at that convention, one of their senior missionaries, coming round with Joe and laying hands on all of us. They were ready to receive it but I think that one of the great things, as the other Missions learned from all of us, was fellowship with Africans. Until we met together they kept their Africans very much at arms' length. Some of them would have a barrier across the drive and no African could come beyond that and they would not have them up on to the verandahs either. They had to be two steps below, far less have meals together. At Mutaho, with Yosiya Kinuka and others, they learned what they were missing by the lack of fellowship with Africans. So it was mutual learning to-

The strength of opposition may be gauged by the fact that this criticism of 'fellowship' at Kigeme went beyond the Home Council to the General Secretary of the CMS. Happily he accepted the explanation given by Joy and Doris. "Max Warren asked me about it," said Joy, "he really wanted to know and I explained." Then she went on: "If someone was very opposed we were sure that they were going to be the next ones touched by the Lord. It was those who were opposed who reported these things home.

It was natural that the oneness which God gave to missionaries and Africans over spiritual matters should extend to other areas. A group of leaders - missionary and African - would meet to share the responsibilities of decision making for the hospital, school or church. Often this group would include leading Africans whom God had 'touched with revival'. It would also inevitably exclude some leading Africans and even missionaries whom it was felt were not really 'in fellowship'. "All the important decisions at Gahini," one missionary complained, "were decided by Joe Church and Yosiya Kinuka as they sat on Joe's verandah each morning."

This reaction from missionary and African was repeated elsewhere. It could not be denied, however, that God singularly blessed the close working together of missionaries and Africans as they together studied God's Word, 'bared their souls' to each other, prayed fervently together 'in the Spirit', and sought God's leading together in every aspect of their lives and work.

At times spiritual coldness would set in, the fellowship would be weakened and its testimony less powerful. Nevertheless, the joy of close fellowship with God and with each other and the impact of its powerful witness were undoubted.

To quote Dr Joe Church when writing of 'An understanding relationship with the African'. "While we have various technical points of superiority to the African, and

Nsibambi helped him to see that that was not true teamwork."

The following year, Dora Skipper wrote from Gahini: "Our hearts are full of thanksgiving to God for His mercy and forgiveness. Holy Week was one of absolute victory in practically every heart. I should think you could almost count on your fingers those untouched by the messages. ... The greatest thing is, I think, that He has made us all one. White and black."

A month later, Dr Decie Church commented: "Since Easter Sunday, God has been dealing with us Europeans as much as with the Africans and in exactly the same way. We all now, black and white, feel the same sort of guidance about the small things of life, things in the olden days we would have said were just childish and could not affect our communion with Christ. We often laugh at the way our organisation has gone to the winds."

The powerful witness of a true oneness between missionary and African was not to go unopposed. Some missionaries felt that to take this too far would be to compromise home life and open the way to abuse. So strongly was this felt by some that some strange stories reached the UK about the nature of some of the missionary-African gatherings.

"When we were at Kigeme," said Joy Gerson, "Doris (Lanham) and I were the only two at that time who were one with the Africans. We were most provocative probably. We were trying to follow Jesus." She describes how a group of people were brought to Kigeme by one missionary couple and a fellowship meeting lasted all night. They had not expected the meeting to continue like that and so they had followed their usual evening custom. "We used to change and put on our housecoats which went right down to the ground," she explained, but it got to England that we were having orgies with the Africans in our nightclothes!"

ethnic differences bridged by the reconciling work of the Cross.

But what of fellowship between missionaries and Africans? It was not so much a question of whether 'revival' *could* bridge the different cultures of European missionaries and African nationals, but *should* it? It was natural for missionaries to feel that their homes were their 'castles'. The requirements of health and hygiene made it necessary for their standards of living to be above those of most of the Africans, but not so high that they could be considered as unnecessary luxury. This was not, however, the reason why many missionaries would not allow Africans into their homes; their missionary commission did not require it, so it was reasoned. The verandah was as far as they felt it necessary for their African colleagues to 'invade' the privacy of their homes.

Then came revival and God did a powerful new thing. He brought the deep fellowship enjoyed between missionary and missionary, African and African, to missionary and African. As with the other 'new things' that God was doing, it brought great joy and ... *conflict.*

In June 1936, following an invitation to Dr Joe Church to form a team to lead a mission at the Mukono Theological College, a group gathered to pray and plan. Dr Church wrote: "We were twelve Africans and four Europeans who met at the Bishop's house at Namirembe for a quiet weekend, Friday 19th to Monday 22nd to pray and plan for the convention at Mukono. Simeoni Nsibambi and Yosiya Kinuka were the African leaders. It was a new thing in those days for Africans and Europeans to be accommodated together in the same house. We went on until midnight, on the lawn, in the moonlight, putting things right which were between us and praising for burdens rolled away. There were very personal things that we had to share. For example, an older Canon of the church felt that it was his task to start and end every session!

Chapter 7

Relationships in fellowship

Everyone is, to a greater or less extent, a product of his or her culture. The missionaries of the Ruanda Mission were almost all English, having received an English education with all that that implies. They were from a conservative evangelical background with a strong sense of call from God to "Go into all the world and preach the Gospel, making disciples ..." On the field, the relationship between the missionaries and Africans was that of evangelists and teachers of the Gospel to receivers of the message. When Africans were converted, they were encouraged to join the ranks of the evangelists and teachers and express their evangelistic zeal to their own people.

God used the message proclaimed and taught by the foreign missionaries to 'save' many Africans from the 'kingdom of Satan' and to give them 'new birth into the kingdom of God'. That was, after all, the purpose of their going there. When God began to work in reviving power two things followed dramatically. The first, God fulfilled His promise, "I will put my Spirit in you" giving vibrant spiritual life to individuals. Secondly, God began to weld people together in quite unexpected ways. Fellowship between missionaries deepened, despite - even perhaps, because of, conflicts. Africans found their inter-tribal or

To quote Dr Harold Adeney again, "To me, the great spiritual heritage of revival so far as church structures are concerned, is the way that God raised up men in all three countries like Bishop Festo Kivengere, Archbishop Erica Sabiti (Uganda), Rev. Yona Kanamuzeyi (Rwanda) and Rev. Paulo Rutwe (Burundi), and put them in positions of church leadership and through them shone brilliant light through the whole fabric of the Anglican ecclesiastical organisms. Sadly, some men of high spiritual calibre and effectiveness were spoilt and became cold when entrusted with the responsibilities of ecclesiastical office."

God works out His purposes in the faithfulness of people to the light He gives them. The experience of the Ruanda Mission is that God gives leadership qualities to many otherwise timid and fearful characters. He then uses them to great effect when, with a daily testimony to His saving grace in their lives, they fulfil roles in the recognised structures of the local church. The spiritual effectiveness of the leadership, as of all other members of the church and fellowship, depends on the extent to which those who form it are prepared to *take the sinner's place* and allow God to work in them as He will.

Others saw their fellow-workers who claimed to be 'in revival' as to be so dazzled by what they experienced as to be incapable of seeing their own faults and rejecting the excesses. How could God build a church on such unbalanced foundations?

The answer came in the increasing understanding of the *grace* of God as He worked in different personalities. At first, it was that grace in the individual which was such a revelation, but increasingly that same grace was recognised in God's dealings with others and accepted as such.

The reality of that personal encounter with the living Jesus Christ and of the cleansing power of the Blood of Christ was the testimony of many missionaries. Dr Ken Buxton said, "Through experience and through learning their real meaning, words which had only been words before became real - terms such as brokenness, and repentance and the Blood of Christ. Not particularly suddenly, but slowly, they took on a new meaning.

"There were crises. Particularly one day, I remember, when an African dresser came and wanted a talk with me and he said very graciously, 'I have something to tell you doctor. When we Africans come to your door you are always like a signpost.' I said, 'What do you mean?' 'You are like a signpost and you are always pointing to the way out.' That hit me very hard. I had come a long way, so I thought, to be a missionary in Africa and I was being a signpost pointing them away. But it was a work of the Holy Spirit gradually teaching me the way of true repentance and I saw that a lot of it was pride in my own heart, and pride in the developing medical work and the reputation the hospital was getting and so on. All that I had to be broken down on and repented of and the joy of meeting together with other Africans when I myself took the sinner's place with them at the Cross, made all the difference, to me, and then to the fellowship in the hospital, and we began to work together really as a team."

'dead'?

Dr Joe Church, a strong contender for the 'layman' side, commented: "By this time the new stations were being opened up and the newly converted Gahini evangelists were the volunteers who went to open up the work - they were the backbone of the whole Ruanda advance. ... The Ruanda missionaries were all the time (until now) held back from full support by this lack of oneness on the 'mission', there was wonderful revival blessing, such as we had never even heard of before then, at many stations, such as Wesley describes happened at some places in early days. - but the 'fearful', 'not expedient' section came in force and sent out a Keswick speaker to visit us. He failed to appreciate what God was doing ... His message home was one of praise for revival blessing but he pleaded 'We must have more parsons!' He missed a wonderful opportunity of fanning further the flame of revival - all he did was to dampen it down, make the battle harder."

Dr Godfrey Hindley remembered what often happened in the early days on a Sunday: "It was quite common for people to go through the Church of England service on a Sunday morning and then a crowd of revived Africans would get together outside and start singing and testifying. They stuck to the service but their real joy and worship was outside and so, after a time we said, this is ridiculous. Let's have the thing inside; remain in the service but have the type of service which benefits them. One day the Bishop of Uganda came along to Shyira and he said, "Should I have known that your station was a station of the Church of England, because I saw no evidence of it?"

At root, the challenge was to the basis of true fellowship in the Spirit. It was very difficult for some missionaries to accept that God could work through those who, in their perception, were 'fighting revival'. If revival was of God, then to fight revival was to fight against God, so it seemed.

practice."

The issue gave rise to a crisis in 1935 just as God was beginning to bless His work with revival. It was generally accepted that there was a need for strong leadership in the newly emerging church and someone to fill this gap was found in the Rev. Arthur Pitt-Pitts. He had been with Dr Len Sharp and Dr Algie Stanley Smith as students at a UK Keswick Convention in 1910 which God had singularly blessed to them all. Happily the nature of the controversy did not centre on the person - Arthur Pitt-Pitts was much respected and loved by the founders of the Mission and others who knew him when he was working first in Uganda then in Kenya. The issue lay elsewhere.

Two questions had to be resolved. The first: if leadership in the newly emerging church was needed, why was it necessary to go outside the Mission for a 'parson'. Why not appoint a competent, spiritually qualified layman to the task. Secondly: if a 'parson' had to be appointed to be archdeacon, why did he also have to be the head of the Ruanda Mission in Africa.

According to CMS rules, following the practice of the Church of England, an ordained person always held the highest position of authority in any Mission situation however senior and experienced the other laymen there might be.

This particular situation was resolved when Arthur Pitt-Pitts was made Archdeacon of Ruanda-Urundi and Dr Algie Stanley Smith was appointed Field Secretary of the Ruanda Mission.

As God worked in reviving power throughout south-west Uganda, Rwanda and Burundi, the problem did not disappear, in fact it became greater and led to deeper conflict. God was indeed, raising up a Spirit-filled leadership there. Was the new emerging church to be built on that leadership or was it to follow rigidly the structure of a church in England, which was believed to be largely

power of God to forgive and cleanse from the defilement of sin, intentional or unconscious, and to restore fellowship with Him.

This taking the sinner's place was a humbling experience which brought into relief an unsuspected aspect of missionary activity - that of leadership in every form of ordered life, from the hospital to the church council.

The founders of the Ruanda Mission were doctors. In the eyes of the Church of England they were 'laymen'. This preponderance of the 'lay' element in the Mission over the 'clerical' continued and, in fact, increased. There was never any doubt in the minds of the early missionaries that the goal of their medical and educational work was the establishment of an indigenous church. The problem faced from the beginning was to discern what was to be the form of that church and how it was to be led. Was the leadership to be drawn from the church structures as they developed - clergy, archdeacons, bishops - or was the 'fellowship of the revived' to be the source of spiritual leaders? It was in seeking to resolve this problem that the issue arose which was then commonly referred to as the 'parson/layman' controversy.

The setting for this has to be traced back to the character of the Church of England at the time that the Ruanda Mission was formed and developed. In England, the Rector or Vicar ran his parish. His role in the church structure gave him great authority in the affairs of the parish. "This clerical domination and Anglican emphasis," explained Bishop Dick Lyth, "seems incredible in these days but was very true then. However, I think you should be fair to those early clergy and mention briefly that: a. England was still in the twenties, in the grip of clericalism, and it was a CMS regulation that the parson, however junior, had to be head of station; b. that the Mission's supporters were Anglican, and missionaries were therefore compelled to introduce an Anglican form of worship and

stration for work of the Spirit. 2. Undue emphasis and endless repetition of past sins, particularly of a sexual nature, in mixed audiences. We feel it to be an unhealthy focusing of attention on unwholesome things, rather than glorifying the Saviour and a positive testimony of victory. 3. Judging of other groups because of their non-participation of these excesses."

It was very evident that, in revival, when God convicted of sin and forgave the repentant sinner, there was a driving force in many to make a public declaration of what was happening. Often that open confession led to a powerful presentation of the truths being proclaimed: that God cannot tolerate sin in His relationship with people and that in the 'blood of Christ' He grants total forgiveness to the repentant sinner.

"It is clear now that the peculiar element in what happened was not so much that people *truly repented of their sin*, important as that was, but in addition to that they *confessed openly before others that they had truly repented of their sin, put right wrongs committed, and been forgiven.*" The importance of the testimony lay in the fact that the one making the confession had *taken the sinner's place*. A truly humbling experience but one which gave all the glory to God and to Him alone. It is particularly humbling for anyone in a leadership position. However, God not only honours such a testimony but it brings the liberty of not having to 'act' something which one is not.

It is easy to believe that to show oneself to be a Christian who needs to go to God time after time to seek His forgiveness, is to be a poor witness. Surely a missionary, particularly a senior missionary, who admits to failure in his or her life is a poor testimony to the power of God! Not so! Revival revealed in very clear terms that the person whose testimony God uses powerfully is one who is prepared to 'take the sinner's place', to acknowledge truthfully his or her utter dependence on the grace and

Peter Guillebaud said: "I remember, in 1948-49, in the middle of a terana (fellowship meeting) a girl got up, trembling, in tears, and poured out a story of immorality, immoral behaviour. Nobody batted an eyelid, nobody shut her up, the power of God was present. She was under conviction, it had to be exposed and dealt with. But, at the same time, people who were doing this in a trivial, light-handed way, were opposed. You can't talk about things like that in this way. Some things you cannot repress, others you must speak out about. You can talk about things in such a way as to provoke the very things you are talking about."

Reactions among the missionaries varied from those who felt that they ought to trust God to lead the Africans to the right balance of what should or should not be confessed in public, to those who appeared to be against any public confession except in general terms and that only of the assurance received that sins were forgiven.

Evidence of the wisdom of the former emerged as African leaders came to exercise a strong authority in fellowship meetings but it was not always so and many missionaries were very perturbed. The matter was referred to the Home Council.

Dr Kenneth Allen reported that the 'Revival Controversy' had been discussed in September 1947 at a committee meeting of the Alliance of Protestant Missions of Ruanda-Urundi. A Minute read: "The Alliance is united in thanking God for all the evidence of His working in all our Missions in deep heart-searching revival power. We are determined to throw ourselves heart and soul into this movement. We will cooperate with our African leaders in all that is good; and discourage all that tends to evil. But as an Alliance we wish to express our united disapproval of the following excesses of the Revival Movement:- 1. Dancing and swaying of the body while singing. We feel it to be a dangerous tendency to substitute physical demon-

open confession of sin constituted the repentance, it became very clear that God's forgiveness did not depend on the public admission of having sinned, but it was a powerful witness to those who heard it. The exception occurred when the sin being confessed had harmed someone, that confession to that person, where possible, constituted part of the repentance.

The second question produced a stronger reaction. "The blood of Jesus cleanses from *all* sin" which had been confessed to God and about which there was a genuine repentance. But was it right to confess openly *all* sin to the extent of relating all sins in detail in a public meeting? This question presented a dilemma for the missionaries. God was so clearly working in great power among those who were making some of the most detailed confessions and yet this did not appear to be justified biblically because of its effects on some, particularly sensitive, characters.

In 1938, Dr Algie Stanley Smith talked over this matter with William Nagenda and Yosiya Kinuka. He wrote in his diary: "I seem to be resisting William and Yosiya inwardly, though in many things I agreed with them. I suppose my underlying fear rests partly in the fact they are not prepared to state that 'sexual' confessions in detail should not be given to mixed audiences. They say, in effect that they won't dictate as to what the Holy Spirit may or may not tell a person to say, and we must be willing to say anything the Holy Spirit tells us to say. Yet the main thing is that we must get together, and trust the Holy Spirit, and in Him trust one another."

Commenting on the practice of exposing the nature of the sins openly before others, one missionary wrote: "The public confession of evil thoughts, evil desires and even deeds, described in minute detail cause one's cheeks to burn with shame."

Referring to an incident which occurred ten years later,

blood of Jesus purifies from *all* sin' became a glorious reality.

In Africans, the same Holy Spirit not only revealed to them the same truth that had become precious to missionaries, that *all sin* separates the unrepentant sinner from God and that *all sin* is 'cleansed by the blood of Jesus', but He also appeared to drive them to confess those sins not only in the privacy of their hearts to God, but also openly, in public.

Without any instruction being given from either missionary or African leaders men and women would stand up and say, "I want to repent ..." and would follow that by describing, sometimes in great detail, the sin of lying, theft, deceit, hatred, slander, or whatever, which they had committed and of which the awfulness before God was overwhelming. God used such public declarations to bring about a deep conviction of sin in the hearers.

The meaning of the Greek word used in the Bible for 'confession' means "to declare openly by way of speaking out freely, such confession being the effect of deep conviction of facts". Vine 244 To confess sins of which one had repented, openly and in public was, therefore, undoubtedly biblical. Two questions arose which became the subject of questioning, if not conflict.

The first questioned how far forgiveness by God was *dependent* on the open confession of sin. Many Africans gave a clear impression that they believed that they had to 'repent in public' before they could be forgiven. Because the Africans frequently preceded their confession in public with the words *Ndashaka kwihana* ... "I want to repent ...", the 'act of repentance' of sin became confused with the 'open confession' of that sin. Was it that, in fact, the African, moved by the Holy Spirit was really meaning by that phrase: "I want to confess *before you,* all the sins of which I have repented *to God* ?"

As there are no biblical grounds for claiming that the

Chapter 6

Taking the sinner's place

The effects of revival in the individual were simple compared with those in the life of the Christian community. Reconciliation with God was the glorious experience of many, reconciliation with each other, equally glorious, required effort and discipline and followed a more tortuous path.

One of the first effects of revival in the individual was the inward compulsion to confess in public what had been confessed to God and for which forgiveness had been received. "If we *confess* our sins ..." So begins the verse in 1 John 1 which has acquired such a deep and personal meaning in revival. That "God is faithful and just and will forgive us our sins and purify us from all unrighteousness" has been the joyful experience of thousands of Africans as well as missionaries.

Prior to revival, *confession of sin* was considered by most missionaries to be a very private matter between the sinner and God. It was 'to say the same thing' as God does about those thoughts and actions which He calls 'sin'. That is the root meaning of the Greek word *homologe*. Faced with the penetrating light of the Holy Spirit, dark corners of the mind and heart were lit up and thoughts and actions were revealed to be sin which had, previously, been considered as of little significance or irrelevant. 'The

to do so harshly or publicly before there has been a personal, private approach produces very counter-productive reactions.

The heritage which we have received from the revival experience points to the need for everyone to *see Jesus* at a deep level, and for that to be reflected in concern for the spiritual welfare of others in the fellowship. And that includes the assurance that it is right and, in fact, necessary to express that spiritual concern for others by challenging them about something they have said or done, provided such action stems from a genuine love for the person, concern for his or her spiritual welfare, is done humbly, in private and after much prayer.

'Seeing Jesus' begins in the individual, but the effects of that reviving vision overflows to a deep concern to 'see Jesus' together with other Christians.

Africans. It seems clear, however, that some judgements were made and expressed by some missionaries, for whatever motives - a loving concern for the spiritual state of a colleague or a more critical challenge to their spiritual profession - which created enough mental and spiritual turmoil to warrant appeal to both the Bishop of Uganda and the Home Council.

Whether because some missionaries felt that some of them were not 'born again' or because they could not come to terms with all that revival required of them, a strong feeling surfaced that those who did not agree with what was happening in revival should 'go home'. In 1944 Dr Algie Stanley Smith wrote: "When we turn to the idea of anyone going home, I look upon it as unthinkable. I love and have a deep appreciation for everyone in the Mission, my appreciation differing according to their gifts. I can see how much we need each other just as we are, and as God will make us, and how our different gifts fit in. For *anyone* to be sent home would be a tragedy and a defeat, especially in view of the repercussions on the African church, it would be disastrous. As I have prayed over these things I have truly felt like praying, as Moses did, 'if not, blot me I pray Thee out of Thy book'. As for any party being sent home 'that I may make of thee a great nation', don't we all say, as Moses did, 'Never; for won't the heathen say 'the Lord was not able'''.

Looking back on those days, a number of missionaries later confessed to an 'unChristlike' harshness in expressing their judgements however much they may have felt motivated at the time by strong desires for purity and holiness in the fellowship. We can, however, only judge others by what we see and hear, and that provides an imperfect basis for judging their spiritual state. Does that preclude, therefore, any challenge of others as to whether they are 'saved' or not, whether they have been 'born again' or not, or whether they have 'seen Jesus'? Clearly

and women like sheep without a shepherd - so many still out of Christ, millions on their way to hell. I do not say, they are not born again, but they are blind to see the need all around. The daily routine is done with all perfection, but what about the perishing souls? How many cry about things today? I do not know; but I know that many are very happy because the devil has blinded them to the terrible needs of our fellow-countrymen. May God open our eyes. The Word of God in these days needs men and women who are conscious of the great debt they owe to the Lord Jesus. This will open our eyes as born-again ones, to the baptism of the Holy Spirit and fire, also it will open our eyes to see the need all around us. How can one help weeping and crying when we see such a great number on their way to hell! God is very good to me in these days, because He has shown me just in a small way of the need of the world today. I feel very very sorry for Jesus, having died for the salvation of His people, to see so many going to hell. He is crying!"

This seemed a hard challenge from an African, one of many for whom men and women had given up their all at home in the UK, in order to come to a distant, foreign land in order that they, those Africans, may be saved from the very destiny they were now accused of not really appreciating.

There was, however, a further side to this challenging which created a great deal of heart-searching. Whether stated explicitly or inferred from remarks made without that meaning intended, some missionaries understood themselves to be judged by their fellow-missionaries as being 'unsaved' or not 'born again' and therefore unfit to continue on the mission field. It was claimed that such accusations were made not only in the confidentiality of private conversations but also in meetings in the presence of other missionaries and Africans. Some allegations were traced to misquotations made by some trouble-making

problems arose when one 'revived' person genuinely attempted to discern whether another person was really 'saved' or 'born again'. If the indications seemed contrary to such an assumption they often felt constrained to make every effort to challenge them to full repentance and faith in Christ.

This kind of challenge from Africans was strongly resented, at first at least, by some missionaries. Yet, seen from the African point of view, there was a justification for that kind of action, as Dr Joe Church realised: "When one of these really born again Africans sees a missionary cold and opposing, after a time his patience is exhausted and there comes a day, perhaps when he is taking a ticking off, when he quietly says, 'Excuse me, Sir, are you really born again, or not?' What he means by that is, 'Your life looks so much like that of other nominal Christians that I really wonder if you have ever had the experience I have had.'"

There were deeper issues too. One of the striking characteristics of many Africans newly 'saved' was that the Holy Spirit in them gave them a driving concern to show others what they had seen so clearly - that they were lost 'in sin', perishing in darkness and on their way to hell - eternal separation from God, until He, in His grace and mercy showed them the 'blood of Christ' shed for them on the Cross so that they could be 'saved' from that destiny. "Could anyone," they appeared to ask, "who did not share that desperate concern claim to be 'born again' of the Spirit of God?"

William Nagenda expressed this concern in a letter written in May 1938: "God has been showing me in these days, that many workers in Ruanda, and elsewhere are lacking a very important thing in their lives, that is, to see the perishing of people. Many clergymen and doctors in Ruanda are quite content with what they see now, they never seem to see fields whitening unto harvest, or men

others, often for racial or social reasons.

In the light of God's searching holiness, anything, however apparently small or trivial, which came between a person and God could not be tolerated. There was only one 'way out' and that was by deep repentance for all that was seen to be sin, confession to God, restoration to anyone wronged, and forgiveness received through the 'blood of Christ'.

So profound was this new conviction of the radical nature of conversion to Christ as being 'born again', 'saved', 'a new creation', that a revised Doctrinal Basis was drafted for the benefit of candidates offering for service with the Mission. The candidate should have, it was proposed: "An earnest desire for 'revival'. By this, one means that the worst enemy of Christ is a lukewarm and powerless Christianity, irrelevant to life; that Christianity is not a philosophy - but Life received through heart repentance for sin, and faith in Christ crucified and risen; that the Cross of Christ and the shed blood of Christ are the only grounds for our acceptance before God, our pardon, and our continuous blessing. Revival involves a life of transparent sincerity, of immediate acts of repentance to those we have wronged and it stakes all on the conviction that the victorious, Christ-like life is possible here and now, not by struggling but by yielding and 'dying' to sin and living unto God."

That draft change was not incorporated into the Doctrinal Basis in that form because it was recognised that that level of spiritual insight could not be expected of all those offering for service. Some of those who drafted the revision had, when they had joined the Mission, been blind to the full truths that they were now proposing as necessary for others!

Seeing Jesus for oneself proved to be a great revelation to missionary and African alike, but with it came a driving desire to see others enjoy that same experience. The

not bluffing, but up he would jump and would point out where it is.

"That is what happens when we have seen and understand the meaning of the 'Blood of Christ'. That is, we *know*, as the Greek word expresses it. We 'know by experience'."

The testimony to new birth in Christ of some of the Africans came as a shock to some missionaries. "It has been a deeply humbling experience," wrote Dr. Algie Stanley Smith, "for one has been shown something of the poorness of one's previous experience. These men and women, who have been literally 'born again' are, some of them those whom we looked upon as our brightest trophies, yes and we wrote of them in Ruanda Notes; and yet on their own confession they were stealing, drinking or committing all manner of sins unknown to us."

Dr Stanley Smith, albeit a founder and senior missionary, highly respected by both missionaries and Africans, wrote in his diary on 24 July 1938: "I preached in Church to a big crowd and really felt I must tell of my deep regret at having given people an 'urwitwazi' (stumbling block) to refuse a religion of uncompromising hostility to sin."

One after another," said Joy Gerson, "we were really convicted of thoughts and imaginations that we all had to get right about."

The 'leaves of the tree of sin', to quote the illustration of the African quoted above, were the open, visible sins of lying, thieving, adultery, hatred. When these were stripped by confession, repentance and faith in Christ, there were revealed many 'branches of sin' which had hitherto been regarded as of no great significance - 'white lies'; deceiving exaggerations; unkind words; sharp, barbed comments; 'petty thefts' of employer's time or goods; jealousy of other's positions and abilities; destructive criticism, which is, in truth, 'slander'; unwholesome frivolity; pride; lust for wrong sexual experiences and material goods; rejection of

better than his cow and today he has gone over with his wife to her home, to make a full confession to the in-laws and to say that he forgives them freely and they can keep the cow. It is hard to imagine a harder thing for an African to do, especially as they are heathen and will consider him quite mad, but God is doing this sort of thing these days. I wonder how many of our English brethren feel that they have no peace with God as long as they have a debt, by thought, word or deed, against their fellow men?"

At Gahini, a further development was to be repeated many times in Uganda, Rwanda and Burundi. Joy Gerson (later Mrs Berdoe) recounts how, in the girls' school some of the newly converted or 'revived' girls insisted on burning blankets, returning stolen goods and destroying objects associated with sinful behaviour. "The Lord has shown us that we have got to bring out everything that we have been given to do with sin".

Dora Skipper recounted the action of one of the teachers of that school: "Abisagi could not get free from bad thoughts which kept coming back to her. On Wednesday night God made it quite clear to her that she was to burn all the things that were in any way connected with the past sins. We all met in school and after Abisagi had explained why each thing had to go, we went outside and she burnt them all. Through that act of real separation God spoke to a great many people. The clear proof that all this is real, is that peace comes as soon as the things have been destroyed."

"We often told the Africans about the game the children play in our country called 'Hunt the thimble'," explained Dr Joe Church, "When each child had seen the hidden thimble, he could sit down and rest. Sometimes a younger child would be slow and frustrated and an older one would come and help. Then suddenly, with a shout of joy, the perplexed one would say, 'I've seen it!' There might be tears of joy. The child can be challenged to see if he was

Referring to the events of 1936, Dr Joe Church wrote: "About this time, many of us Europeans had gone through new humbling experiences of the deeper blessing and meaning of the Blood of Jesus in giving full salvation and one or two even went so far as to say they had never been born again before."

Reflecting on the momentous events which occurred in the girls' school at Gahini in 1936, Miss Dora Skipper wrote in April of the following year, "God is still doing wonderful things for us all. As an African said to me the other day; 'Those sins which used to seem so big, like stealing, adultery and drunkenness, I see are only like the tiniest twig on the top of the tree, perhaps the leaves. When they have been plucked off, God is able to show us the deeper things that are destroying our lives.' This man's particular trouble was 'cows'. To the African, cows represent his saving Bank; he sells the calf to pay his poll tax. As soon as he has saved up about 70 or 100 francs, instead of putting the money in a Bank, he will buy a cow; so a cow is probably the thing nearest to his heart."

She went on to relate the story of one African church teacher in whom God was working with convicting power but who could not find the peace of reconciliation with Him. When he had married he had paid the dowry for his wife with a cow that did not belong to him. His wife's family discovered this and a row ensued. As a result he harboured a hatred against that family, even while he was leading a small congregation as a church teacher! "This week God got down to a much deeper work in his heart. He came to my room a couple of nights ago and beads of perspiration stood out on his face as he explained that God had done a new thing. He had touched the thing that was nearest to the root of his heart, and now he knew that he had to give that cow willingly, though he still felt that they should have been satisfied with the one he had given them from another relation, he saw that he must love God

that is when you learn that all you need is Jesus!"

"The work of Revival spread all over Rwanda, Burundi and Uganda because the people of God didn't leave the work of God to the Pastors or Europeans," said the Rev. Yohana Bunyenyezi, remembering the days before he was ordained. "No! we all realised that it was our job to spread the Gospel; women with babies on their backs - I remember some who went from Shyira to Buye on foot! Girls used to go. Men used to go, without cars, just on foot, on bicycles, on lorries. It made the Rwanda authorities like us and give us sites, because God's people went to them and repented of not paying taxes or disobeying laws and they made restitution."

Whereas, in the earlier days of revival, there were great manifestations of God's power at conventions and large gatherings of people, as the years went by, so the same power was at work in many small fellowships, in homes between husbands and wives and their children, in hospitals and in schools. The Gospel preached was a very simple one but its effects in people's lives were dynamic indeed.

love and of various forms of pride which had been blinding them to the truth. The chief opponent of the other big matter, a very senior man indeed, suddenly saw his attitude as family pride and fear of giving offence in breaking an age-old heathen tradition in a marriage question; the cloud lifted from his face as he cast it all down before the Lord, Delegates were shaking hands all over the room as barriers fell flat, and songs of praise rang out. It was a considerable time before we returned to 'business', but this was business for eternity, and in the strength and spirit of that victory the other business was despatched at record speed."

In 1961, Dr Ken Moynagh reported: "Our school children began to be blessed and some were saved. Little groups of them would meet, in the open air or in their homes, to read the Bible and pray together. The Head of our school told us that he found such a group meeting under some coffee trees - girls of between eleven and thirteen squatting on the ground with their Bibles open and some of them weeping under conviction of sin. He spoke to a junior teacher with them and she explained that she had discovered the girls were meeting on their own and she felt that the Lord was calling her to join them. Many were helped at this time, both in the central school and in the surrounding out-schools."

In 1959 and in the early 1960s Rwanda was shattered by a revolution which resulted in thousands of men and women being killed. In later years further political strife led to even greater numbers being massacred in Uganda and Burundi, and more recently, again in Rwanda. In these violent upheavals, many Africans who had come to a living faith in Jesus Christ have lost their lives or have been driven from their homes to be refugees elsewhere. The testimony of one refugee witnesses to the reality of the God who worked in reviving power in these countries: "When you have lost everything and all you have is Jesus,

another long journey, 300 miles to the south, to Burundi for the Matana Convention. These are land-marks in the history of the Church out here and it would take a book to tell you of all the testimonies and praise that went up to God at these gatherings."

It was not only in services or fellowship meetings that God gave such strong evidence of his reconciling power. In July 1950, Miss Lindsay Guillebaud reported a remarkable church council meeting: "Last week our local Church Council held its half-yearly session. On Tuesday, the meeting was troubled. Two very important matters had just been settled but there was a sense of defeat. Unanimity cannot, of course, always be attained, but the 'people of God', the inner circle of spiritual leaders, do count on being of one mind. And now they were not. The great majority had been perfectly clear about the right course of action, but a very few, in each case those personally concerned, had been resolute in opposition. They seemed blind to the fact that they were adopting an unspiritual attitude, and the Council was distressed; harmony had gone.

"But then came a sudden change. What happened? I believe it was only made possible because of a few simple words of apology. First a missionary expressed regret and accepted responsibility for an ambiguously-worded minute (it was not his own wording), which had led to misunderstanding and so to wounded pride; then the whole Council, previously on the defensive about it, accepted the responsibility corporately and apologised to the person concerned. Not only did his attitude immediately change, so that he repented of his fighting spirit and asked the Council's forgiveness, but the Spirit of God came upon the whole gathering and turned it into a Fellowship Meeting. Difficult points were at once solved in the new outpouring of love: 'No house? Oh, you can have mine till your new one is built' - and one after another repented of lack of

Revival worked miracles in families. Especially was this evident in African society where, as elsewhere, the man is normally very dominant.

Sometimes in startling ways in big convention meetings, often in small groups of people in some hillside gathering, God gave encouraging indications that He was still at work putting His Spirit into the least likely people. In March 1947, Dr and Mrs Kenneth Buxton wrote from Buye, "Last Sunday ... we were walking away from a service, held under the trees, as we still have no roof on the Church. In front of us were two ordinary Barundi women, talking away together. As we drew near, we heard a conversation very much like this:- 'We were in darkness and in death, but God has saved us.' 'Yes,' said the other, 'we were in a terrible way because of our sin, but Jesus has brought us out of darkness into Light. Praise God ... His Blood has saved us and given us victory over sin and the fear of death. Praise God!'

"So they talked on as they went home, bubbling over with the joy of salvation, two of many who are His witnesses in the heathen villages."

Returned from one of his tours in 1948, Dr Joe Church, reported continued progress at Gahini: "The banner of 'The Highest' still flies at Gahini and news of people being saved and satisfied comes in daily. Revival is only living victoriously day by day, in other words, 'Walking with Jesus.' This has been the subject of our last two big Conventions. ...

"There have been four Conventions since I got back to Gahini. At all of them we met the Lord afresh face to face and were revived. The first was the Alliance Convention on lake Kivu at Kumbya, in January; then, in July, the big African Convention at Gahini like the one that was held at Kabale in 1945 (described in the book 'Jesus Satisfies') Then I took Yosiya Kinuka to Kampala for the Uganda Convention in September... We have just returned from

Although they had heard the Gospel many times many of them were complete heathens in their hearts and lives. But during the latter part of last year God did wonders for some of them; they brought their heathen charms and burnt them among much rejoicing; sins were confessed and restitution made of things stolen."

Ten years after the momentous convention at Kabale in 1935, a second was held there in 1945. A crowd of some 15,000 gathered from Uganda, Rwanda and Burundi. With the theme *Jesus satisfies*, speakers referred to the 'cup which overflows', an illustration taken from Psalm 23.

"I saw many weeping," wrote Dr Joe Church, "There is no thrill in the world greater than seeing hearts melting before the love of Calvary. Faces relax, peace pervades, abandon comes in and men yield to the pleadings of their Saviour. Many times we have seen this as the Spirit of God descends upon a gathering ... People who have really seen it cannot speak lightly of the movings of the Holy Spirit and Revival. It is too sacred."

In the early days of revival, the leading African speaker was William Nagenda. In the latter period, that mantle fell on Festo Kivengere. He was to bring to his ministry, which eventually spanned the continents, a breadth of insights gained from experience of the past and the matured thinking of his colleagues.

An important part of 'our heritage' lies not only in the fellowship of the many African men whom God used but also in a less publicised aspect of their ministries. It is the names of the *men* that are best known. For many of the missionaries, however, it was not simply the fellowship and testimony of William Nagenda, Yosiya Kinuka, Festo Kivengere, Yona Kanamuzeyi and others which was valued, rather it was the testimonies of William *and* Sara, Yosiya *and* Dorokasi, Festo *and* Mera, Yona *and* Mary Kanyamuzeyi ... through to Yusitasi *and* Marion Kajuga.

him whether he should ask the missionary to accompany him to confess to the garage owner. Yohana said, "No if you do that the garage owner (a European) will think that it is the missionary who has prompted you. Go with Jesus only, that's real victory."

So Toma found his boss.

"Sir, I've come to repent," he confessed

"Repent of what?" his boss asked.

"I'm a thief. I've stolen many, many tools over many years."

The European boss looked at him and said,

"Are you an animal?"

"Yes, sir, I am," Toma replied,

Shaken at this reply, the Boss forgave Toma and made him the manager of the garage!

Toma joined Yohana and Aida and the team at Bujumbura grew as men and women were won for Christ by their testimony to the reality of the Gospel they preached in that most unlikely of places.

It was also in 1944 that Dora Skipper recounted continuing expressions of revival among the girls who came to the school at Gahini from Rwanda and Burundi. "A fresh blessing of the Holy Spirit is being outpoured upon the hill this week; and many girls have been helped, but the Barundi need much prayer, that they may learn really to love Jesus. They are so down-trodden and so fond of money and position that they find it hard to want to follow Him; for it means breaking with much that they hold dear."

At Buhiga, Drs Harold and Isobel Adeney were in temporary charge of the station. "It has been great to see God working. There has been a new hunger for the Gospel in many parts of the district. A particular encouragement has been the way in which the Spirit of God has been working in the kraals quite close to the mission and amongst many of the labourers who work here day by day.

'Camp Meeting'.

Also, at Shyira, "People from all our stations and from the Belgian Missions met and knew themselves as one Church ... At this Convention there were many reconciliations and a new certainty that we are all in one team at this great time of Revival ... One son of the county Chief came to the Convention to see what it was like, and while there was convicted. He repented of, and produced for burning, the tip of a horn he had bought for 400 francs with which to bewitch and kill his cousin who he thought might be attending the same Convention. Only the power of the living Saviour can deal with the feuds there are in Ruanda. There were many other spiritual victories among us all."

At that convention, Peter Guillebaud spoke on 'famine in the world' from the prophecy of Isaiah applying it particularly to Bujumbura, the capital of Burundi and the need for a witness in that city. Yohana Bunyenyezi heard that address. Through it he heard God say to him: "It's you I am calling. It's you I am calling." He asked Aida his wife, "What do you think about it?" She replied: "If I were a man I'd be off!" So they set off to begin a remarkable work in a very difficult place. They lived in a tiny hut and were led of God to do some extraordinary things, such as standing together at a cross-roads at 5 pm when people were going to their homes from work. They replied to questions about what they were doing and told everyone who would listen, the Good News of Jesus Christ.

Soon encouragement came when a man called Toma visited them at night: "I feel many sins in my heart," he said. "I am a thief. In the garage where I work I've been stealing spare parts for years, lying about it and then selling them."

"Pray and listen to what God says to you, and what He convicts you of, repent," Yohana said to him,

A missionary called to see Yohana. Toma discussed with

these students were, burning the blankets which they had stolen, and destroying bad letters from girls and much else." Something remarkable was happening. These young men were overcome with the awfulness of their sin, they were repenting of it to God and confessed it to each other. There was testimony to forgiveness and a new reality of the presence of Christ.

And there was singing! The story of Pilgrim in John Bunyan's 'Pilgrim's Progress' in its Kinyarwanda version, *Mugenzi,* had been an inspiration to many Africans. Now it came to life in a new way. "God gave us a new hymn that day", said one of the students, "about the way in which 'Christian' came to the Cross and his burden of sin rolled away for ever, and of the certificate he received at the Cross, which was worth so much more than any certificate you could get from the Church or school." Verse after verse was added to the hymn in the picture language of 'Pilgrim's Progress' but drawn from the students immediate experience of God working in them. And after each verse the chorus:

Bless'd Cross, bless'd Sepulchre, bless'd rather be
The Man who there was put to death for me.

All the students experienced the reviving power of God in their lives. Some of them were saved then and immediately entered into the reality of a living experience of Christ. "Out of this time of blessing," remembered one of the students, "there sprang a new bond of oneness and light between us who were saved, African and European, and a new cooperation in and out of school, worked out through the Blood of Christ."

Two conventions in 1944 were remarkable for the wide range of nationalities which gathered together and for the depth of spiritual challenge. In July, at Mutaho, in Burundi, Danes, Swedes, Americans, Canadians and British and various denominations - Baptists, Methodists, Friends and C of E - joined together in a memorable

bringing divisions among us. It seemed as though with one sweep of the Pierced Hand of His Love and Power, Christ has blotted this out by bringing home to us the terrible reality and danger of spiritual pride. At the Annual Meeting at Buye, 'great stones were rolled away,' and we are waiting to see in what way God is going to come among us again in Resurrection Power.

"The old message of broken-hearted repentance for sin, of simple self-despising clinging by faith to Jesus Crucified, the call to a bold, deathless, uncompromising, uncomplaining, embracing of the Cross in a life utterly poured out for Christ and for men in the power of the fullness of the Holy Spirit, this is what we have been recommissioned to proclaim and to minister and to live before men. What a Gospel!"

The newest mission station, Buye, in Burundi was developed rapidly. On the medical side, Dr Kenneth and Agnes Buxton supervised the building of the hospital. Rev. Lawrence and Julia Barham trained church teachers and ordinands in the developing Bible School. It was a spacious site and buildings, albeit simple in character, were easy to construct. It was here that was organised the first course for the training of school teachers drawn from Rwanda and Burundi. Run by Peter and Elisabeth Guillebaud, it was to be the scene of a remarkable outburst of revival.

On a Friday evening in April 1944, God began to work among the students. An overwhelming sense of the presence of God came upon them in their dormitory. All through the night they were deeply convicted of sin, confessed their sins and put things right with one another. In the morning it was raining and so they could not go into the school garden to hoe as was usual on a Saturday. Peter knew nothing of this as he was working on his car. Then, at midday, Peter went out to meet them. "I did not know what had hit me," Peter recalled. "There

lives of these people."

The first meeting of the Inter-Missionary Advisory Church Council on which the majority were Africans, was held on the 2nd February 1940. "It was wonderful to see the emancipating power of spiritual oneness in Christ." commented Dr Hindley. "Our people found it difficult to conceive of a Church which had no Bishop, used no Prayer Book or, like the Friends, practised no external Sacraments. But the manifest signs of the Spirit's working made such differences appear trivial and our oneness in Christ the supreme fact. The meetings were remarkable for frank speaking and love for each other and much misunderstanding was removed."

In 1941, a number of students from the Theological College at Mukono in Uganda, made a witness tour of Rwanda and Burundi. They included William Nagenda, John Musoke, Nasanayire Mukasa, Yona Mondo, Yakobo Badokwaya and Yohana Bunyenyezi. "We went from Mukono to Gahini on our bicycles," remembered Yohana Bunyenyezi. "We spent three days at Gahini and then went on through Kibungo towards the river. There were no more roads and often we carried our cycles and cases. Near the river I fell in the swamp and was almost lost, but Yakobo Badokwaya held on to the case on my head and gradually I climbed out by holding on to the papyrus. ... We went on to Buhiga ... Butare ... Kigeme ... Nyanza ... Shyira and from there to Kabale. On that journey God taught us many things. He taught us the love of the brethren and we experienced a great awakening in our hearts because of the amazing work of God we saw wherever we went."

"1943 has opened with a great and growing hope of Victory." wrote Dr Algie Stanley Smith, "For we too have been given much encouragement. Into the message and method of 'Revival' there had crept a hardness and exclusiveness which were closing doors once open and

on his plot of land when he heard a voice calling, "Dawidi! Dawidi!" He looked round but there was nobody there. He returned to his hoeing.

"Dawidi! Dawidi!" again the voice called. He looked round and again there was no-one there. He panicked, dropped his hoe and dashed off to find Hans Emming, the missionary in charge of the station.

"I'm hearing voices." he explained. "Somebody is calling me and there is no one there!" Hans looked at him and said, "Have you talked to anyone else today?"

"No!" he replied.

"You haven't talked to Benjamini?"

"No!"

"You are the third person," Hans went on, "who has been hearing those voices calling you by name."

Those three men were all saved, all became pastors and leaders in the Baptist church in Burundi.

In 1939 Dr Joe Church wrote: "I realise that I have not told you anything about the wonderful time we had at the Burundi Convention at Musema. The Cross of Christ and the Power of His Blood shed for us was the central message. Over one hundred went back to their stations having openly testified to a new vision of Jesus as their Saviour."

In November 1939, Dr Godfrey Hindley wrote: "It has been said that we often write of our own experiences and not of our work. Well, we have learned in these days that it is our own relationship to Jesus that really matters and then God can work, so that is the reason why some of our letters have been more personal. But we nevertheless rejoice in what God has been doing through this land. Everywhere you go there are real live bands of Christians who have a sure foundation, a certain knowledge of their own salvation and a desire to make it known to the heathen. This has been born, not of exceptional work by the Europeans, but by a real vision of the Cross in the

selves to much prayer. While we were at Gisenyi, when no European was on the station, revival came. As soon as I returned I sensed the new atmosphere by the look of joy on people's faces, and the enthusiastic hymn-singing which went on in various places throughout the day. The senior Christians soon arrived to tell me of many remarkable happenings and finished by saying that it was their sins which had held up revival at Buhiga."

"A wonderful thing happened while Dr Joe was at Kigeme on Friday night," Miss Dora Skipper wrote home in June 1938. "A man on the hill had made up his mind to stab another because they had had a quarrel. The man whom he was plotting to stab woke in the night and felt an urge to pray, so he and his wife spent most of the night praying for the salvation of the man. The other man began to dream and great fear came upon him and he woke up and threw his dagger away and came to confess to the leaders of the church."

Three weeks later she wrote from Gahini, "Nothing special has happened here. At least it would seem special to you in England as souls are being born again every day and the whole hill is ablaze with the joy and power of the Lord. We are getting almost used to conversions now they are happening daily."

Peter Guillebaud reported how, throughout 1938 and 1939, teams went out from Gahini, in Rwanda, crossed the river Akanyaru and walked into neighbouring Burundi "witnessing to ordinary people, leaving the missionaries out of it, and gossiping the Gospel. The teams were mostly made up of women whom some would consider to be 'nobodies'! When the Holy Spirit began to work all sorts of things began to happen. Dreams and visions and all that kind of thing."

One of these teams turned up at Musema, a station of the Danish Baptist Missionary society. Soon afterwards, one of the Africans there, Dawidi Nkurikiye, was working

ago the trained midwife and another senior boy were marvellously convicted and converted. How, why, when or where, I cannot tell you, but both are now bursting with joy."

From Matana Dr Len Sharp wrote: "At the usual Sunday morning service on the 13th. June, many came under deep conviction of sin and about sixty stayed on to an after-meeting. One by one confessed aloud to God and sought His mercy. We had the great joy of explaining the way of salvation, and hearing one after another accept Christ and praise Him for forgiveness and salvation."

A year later, remarkable incidents were still being reported as men and women were faced with the demands of a holy God and shown the way of reconciliation through the Blood of Jesus. At the same time, the sense of fellowship between the 'revived' was deepening.

In June 1938, Rev. 'Pip' Tribe wrote to Dr Algie Stanley Smith telling of great blessing at Kigeme where they were having "great fellowship and Butare is deeply moved. Such an answer to prayer."

Also from Kigeme came an interesting story of the man who had stolen Dr Stanley Smith's clothes when he had first gone to Kigeme to inspect the site. "He has been a reader for some time, but a week or two ago he began to be deeply convicted. ... Muhaya (the local church teacher) tells me he is trying to get the money to pay back for my clothes! He is said to be a new man quite transformed."

In July 1938, an important Mission Conference was held at Gisenyi. After that had taken place, Dr Bill Church wrote from Buhiga, "The Revival, which has swept over other stations in varying degrees left Buhiga superficially touched only until July. Before we left for the Conference at Gisenyi all our Christians were cold and depressed, almost to the degree of being morbid. There was, however, one hopeful sign, they were deeply concerned and convicted about the state of the station and gave them-

Ezekieri Kayonde, (later Rev. Canon). "When God saved me in 1937" he recounted many years later, "there were many sins I had committed and I had debts I had not repaid. I first heard the Gospel in 1925 when I began to attend school, but I despised it. It went against my character as there were things in it I did not like. Then, in 1937, I saw that the Son of God had given Himself on the Cross for me, I saw that I was a sinner who should be destroyed. I was shown Jesus crucified on the Cross for me. He wore the crown of thorns for me. It was my judgement He suffered. I repented and asked Him to forgive me. From that moment I knew that I had to die with Christ, that I had to speak for Him. And God enabled me to confess to the Chief that I had stolen cows, money, cloth. 'Now judge me,' I said to him, 'I am in your hands.' The chief looked at me and said, 'You have done rightly to come to me. You have stolen these things from me. Now, as God has forgiven you so I forgive you. Now you pray for me that God will forgive the sins I have committed.' We praised God as we sang 'Yes' ashimwe' (Jesus be praised). We were able to tell of the grace of God which has very great power. God enabled me to end that debt, but my real debt was to Jesus Christ who had paid all my debt on the Cross."

There were many other testimonies of the powerful conviction of sin which overwhelmed men and women in the schools and hospital at Gahini and of the joy of sins forgiven and indwelling of the Holy Spirit. Largely unorganised, the witness to the Gospel which radiated from Gahini was truly a missionary outreach of Africans to their fellow Africans.

Miss Doris Lanham reported a 'wave of blessing' that had reached Kigeme. "Only one of our hospital boys cared at all, and he was on fire. But, in January, God began His work and two of the junior boys were saved and others became restless and miserable. Then about two weeks

cannot fully understand, coming from a Christian land."

The consolidation went on. Rev. Cecil Verity wrote from Gahini, in June 1937: "Last year many got their first awakening to what a life in Christ Jesus was meant to be, but although many then got in at the Wicket Gate, like Christian in *Pilgrim's Progress*, few got to that place where they saw the Cross and their burden was rolled away. Then, also, as many have admitted, confessions of sins were made, especially sins which were known to others, but there were left in the life other things known only to God and the individual himself or herself, which were unrepented of and the consequence was that many did not get into a place of peace or power and so went back into sin.

"And now at last God is bringing home to us all, we white people as well as our native Christians, what the real meaning of repentance from dead works and faith in Christ really involves. God has been searching us out and there is hardly one of us who has not been found wanting. When God starts to show a man what he is really like, the process is often acutely humiliating and we begin to see ourselves as we really are, miserable sinners. All the props seem to fall and respectability, that so often masquerades as Christianity, is shown to be hollow until the soul in desperation cries to God for deliverance and forgiveness.

"During Holy Week a Mission was held while all our evangelists were in and the schools also present, resulting in deep conviction of sin and public confession ... During that time from a hundred to a hundred and fifty came confessing their sins as of old before John the Baptist at Jordan."

The Evangelists' Training School at Gahini, was the centre of teaching for many who took the vibrant message of salvation to the districts around. Some of the evangelists trained there were posted as church teachers to other, more distant parts of the country. One of these was

ten or more at once, were praying (not shouting but agony from deeply convicted hearts): 'Lord save me from (mentioning his or her particular sin) for Christ's sake, Amen.' And there was absolute liberty. No one thought or cared for anyone else, no one noticed if any one else was praying - the church was three parts full - each saw his sin and saw the Saviour; it was too wonderful to describe, but it seemed something like the collapse of Jericho.

"On Friday, Saturday and Sunday, time was given for confessions and witness. At last it became so impossible we took the girls to school and they went on from 6 to 10 pm and, after a few hours sleep, they rose at 2 am until 6 am. No excitement now in Church. William and Yosiya were almost brutal in refusing to allow anyone to confess, except he kept to the point and yet, though some were made to sit down, there was a constant stream for hours and the same in the girls' school. No excitement, the girls and women standing quietly waiting their turn to confess the sins that had made them slip back since June, or which had kept them from repenting at all and all felt the same. 'Christ is a wonderful Saviour', 'I see now He has saved me'. There must have been hundreds confessing. We wrote down the names of about 50 in the girls' school we felt were genuine, and William jotted down those he felt were genuine in church and he knew their names and heaps he did not know, and he had a 100 names on his list afterwards. ...

"I have wondered whether there must be two times of definite blessing; because in June, what we saw was the fight to get the devil out, a mixture of power, but what we saw and felt last week was a new experience of real victory over sin in the heart through the Blood of Christ. I think the revival is like our experience of the entry of the Holy Spirit only, perhaps there must be more distinction here because of the absolute bondage of Satan these people dwell in until they turn to Christ. It is something we

him letters telling what they were doing and also that God would perhaps, call them to go to Matana. They were just to be led, in which case they might be delayed a week."

God's timing is perfect, however, and the visits of that team were to produce lasting effects in the places visited. At Kigeme, Mrs Tezira Rwabuhungu, wife of the Rev. Erisa Rwabuhungu, described the remarkable events which took place then. "We experienced revival," she said, "we saw awesome things, we trembled, we wept and when we saw the cross and were filled with joy we sang and sang."

At Gahini, Easter 1937 proved to be a time of particular rejoicing. "Our hearts are full of thanksgiving to God for His mercy and forgiveness," wrote Dora Skipper, "Holy Week was one of absolute victory in practically every heart. I should think you could almost count on your fingers those untouched by the message ... The power of God was different this time from that in June. In June we all felt that there was a great fight in the hearts between the devil and God on the hill. A great deal of confession was brought about by exciting hymns and shouting prayers late at night. There was an electricity and fear and excitement everywhere which was frightening. But this time, from the start on Wednesday, there was a terrific power of God, calm, full of power, quiet and strengthening. No shouting, no hysteria. Nagenda gave a very powerful address on Wednesday morning; with a black-board illustration on 'sin'. The names of various sins being just the branches; the illustrations looked as if they had been done for him by Joe. Yosiya followed him with his quiet but very searching manner, Eriya and Blasio too were amazingly strong, they never wasted a word and one felt that God was just hammering home His message.

"On Thursday morning, Cecil Verity spoke, put things right, and that seemed to break through the last fortification; a time of prayer followed and all over the church,

Chapter 4

Revival in Rwanda and Burundi

In early 1937, a team of Africans, including Yosiya Kinuka and William Nagenda, set off from Gahini to visit Shyira for a few days with the intention of returning in time to resume normal working in the hospital and schools on the following Monday. It proved to be the start of a much longer tour. "They (the team) found at Shyira that they were all praying for and waiting for a blessing," wrote Dora Skipper, "they did not know from where it would come. They only held meetings, I think, on Wednesday and Thursday, but people went down like nine pins ... On Friday they felt they must go to Kigeme as they had not told us of the date of their return. We did not really expect them until Monday.

"At Kigeme they found people praying for a blessing. William and Yosiya went into a house at night where they heard them praying and found that they were just beseeching God for blessing (though they did not know the team had arrived). Everywhere they went without our sending any notice - they meant to stay just for the week end and get home on Monday, but on arrival they were greeted with the news that all the teachers were coming in on Monday and Tuesday and coupled with that, on their arrival they found a Gahini runner at Kigeme who had taken letters ahead there of Joy's and were able to give

handling was hers or belonged to the school.

At the nearby Bible School, a Mission was held. Joan went along to listen. "The men were saying how God had convicted them of misappropriation of money, borrowing money from one account and then not paying it back. I knew that I was doing the same thing and could not excuse myself at all. So I asked God to forgive me."

She then attended another meeting at the Bible School while the other missionaries went to the monthly English speaking service. "After the speaking there was a time of testimony and I felt God telling me to tell the folk there that I had been forgiven for muddling up the accounts and for using school money for my own things. But how could I stand up and say that? Hadn't God forgiven me? No, I could not do that. I would lose my reputation. But at that point Jesus reminded me of Himself on the Cross, and I saw that even though He was the Son of God, He made Himself of no reputation so that I might be free, and I saw that His Blood was shed for that very purpose of taking away my sin and iniquity. ... James Katalikawe translated for me as I was too overwhelmed to speak in Lukiga. I was soon to be overwhelmed, not with my guilt and fear, but with the most amazing joy and peace - so much so that on several occasion I had to ask Jesus to reduce it or I would burst - it was more than a human frame could hold. I had heard people say that 'the blood of Jesus does not cleanse in the dark' and I certainly did not know that deep release until I told others what Jesus had done for me. But that was just a beginning, it was as if the Holy Spirit went for a walk through my life and showed me one thing after another that stopped Jesus from filling me."

For missionary and African alike, revival meant a new way of living. And it was all concerned with relationships with God and with others. Revival also brought a driving concern to witness to and share that reality throughout Kigezi and beyond.

Bufumbira, 50 miles to the west of Kabale, there was a sudden moving of the Holy Spirit in the boys' and girls' schools. The blessing began when a saved master apologised to a boy during a singing class for getting angry with him. Thereupon the boy stood up and confessed that he had hated him for it, and both of them accepted the Lord's forgiveness and were reconciled together. A wave of conviction then spread through the school. A day or two later, another master who had backslidden for several years was taking religious instruction in the girls' school when he suddenly said, 'I am going to give you my testimony', and then and there he came back to the Lord. There were some thirty children in those two schools who were blessed at that time ... from the start they became the enemy's special target."

Joan Hall began work as a teacher at Kabale in 1953. "I remember when I first arrived how struck I was by the peace on the face of one particular person who worked at the Kabale Preparatory School. I remember asking myself what I could give to such people. ... Sala lived down the hill from me in a little shack, her husband was an alcoholic and was not always kind to her. She had had a large family of 17 children, every one of whom had died before reaching two years of age. Yet she could come up to the Tuesday or Thursday fellowship meeting and with a beaming face tell of all that Jesus was doing for her. And not only that, she would say, almost with tears in her eyes, 'we sometimes feel sorry for you Europeans. You seem to know it all in your heads, but I know Him in my heart'."

As headmistress of a school at Kabale, she had to face a personal crisis and share it with the school. With many things happening in the life of a busy school, she had not always kept strict account of monies received and spent, and while not knowingly misappropriating any, there were times when she did not know whether the money she was

Margaret Clayton arrived in Burundi at the end of 1938 and worked there until moving to Kigezi in 1941. At a convention at Kabale, she wrote, "I heard Simeoni Nsibambi speaking. He emphasised that 'sin is sin' and this brought me to a new place of repentance of sin and fullness of the Holy Spirit and I discovered the joy of deep fellowship with fellow-workers. I am very grateful for the insights I gained then: that sin must be faced, recognised for what it is and ruthlessly dealt with in oneself; we are continually in need of God's mercy and forgiveness and this forgiveness is available, it does not depend on our effort but on the mercy of God. Where the Blood of Christ cleanses, the Holy Spirit fills. I have also found the 'bent neck' and the 'V' for Victory 'Yes, Lord' of Dr Joe Church's illustrations a great help to me."

Through the 1940s and 1950s, the districts of Kigezi and beyond, into Toro and Ankole, experienced waves of God's saving power. The extraordinary events decreased in frequency, but they still occurred at times of gatherings of Christians and in response to a proclamation of God's saving Gospel and testimony to its outworking in ordinary lives.

Over these years, many missionaries experienced the loving concern of Africans as they worked together in leadership positions, in schools, in hospitals and in outreach evangelism. "It was with Ugandans who had been influenced by revival that we missionaries had such great fellowship in the gospel," wrote Miss Lilian Clarke. "Through them many of us were 'touched by revival' after we had been some years in Africa. Their faithful witness and their loving concern for our spiritual well-being testified to the strength of their Christian character. As a consequence of their love for us the Mission itself was blessed as we testified to the way the Lord had blessed us through them."

In 1955, a missionary reported: "At our chief centre in

the women to do everything in connection with milk and milk pots. So I took the milk pot and then I did something else that I had never done before - I knelt before her and very tremblingly I asked her to forgive me for the way I had mistreated her.

"Poor Erina! She knew what was going on at the church and thought that everyone was going out of their minds. She had never gone to church; she did not want to go to church; she wanted to have nothing to do with it. But here, she thought was real madness. How could her husband give her anything? She asked him to get up, go away and take the milk pot with him, alarmed that madness had actually entered her home.

"For a while Erina kept to her old ways refusing to meet with people from the church, but Yeremiya prayed for her ceaselessly. One day he was working in his garden when, to his great astonishment, he heard some loud singing coming from inside the home. Erina had always refused to sing with these 'mad' people. But as she was preparing the milk pots, God had spoken to her, and as she asked Him to take her life and cleanse her and fill her with Himself, to quote her own words, 'it seemed as if all I could do was to shout and sing ... a great light shone around me and I knew that there was a living God after all.'

"But what was Yeremiya to do about the fact that he had two wives? He and the other Christians that he talked to thought they would not go to the missionaries - they were known sometimes to have their own rules - but after thought and prayer, he knew that he should look after both his wives and their children, but he should be married to only one of them. As Erina had become a Christian he married her."

Sometimes it took several years, even for missionaries, before the truths which so clearly animated many revived Christians became real in their own experience. Miss

and I was determined not to do that. I sat on the floor at the back of the church (there were no benches or chairs then).

"You can imagine my surprise when the very first speaker began to speak about cows. As a cattle-owner my attention was captured and I found I had to listen; I could not escape. The preacher was speaking from Isaiah 1: 'The ox knows his master, the donkey his owner's manger, but Israel does not know, my people do not understand.' As the talk went on I realised that that was true of me. I could go out into the field and call the cow I wanted and it would come to me because it knew me. And the preacher was saying that God is there; He understands and actually calls me. This was something new. For us God was remote. We had to try to find Him and do things in order to make Him happy. This was new that God wanted to come near to me and make me happy.

"Many thoughts went through my perplexed mind. I stayed in church all night and so did many other people. Some were crying out and screaming, and I think I cried out too. In the early hours of the next morning I went home, and I said, 'God, if you are God, and if you are calling me like I call my cows, then please help me to come to you, and please show Jesus to me.' Then I began to see and understand His call and respond to it.

"There were many things that were wrong in my life that I truly thought they could never all be put right, but one of the first things that Jesus showed me was that I had not been loving to my wife, Erina. I had treated her more like a slave than a wife and had actually beaten her and I knew that I must go and say sorry to her. I felt that I should give her a token of my sorrow and so I got a milk pot and filled it with fresh milk and took it to her. This was strange to her. You see, I had never ever given her anything; I had always expected her to give to me. Not only that, but in our tradition it was always the work of

3 Revival in Kigezi

Yeremiya Rwakatogoro told his story to Joan Hall: "I never dreamed that I could ever be travelling along these roads in a car to preach the Gospel. The first time I came across here was to go from North Kigezi to Rwanda. I had heard that the cows from there were better and more beautiful than our own. So down there I went to see if I could find one that I liked. I spotted one and waited until nightfall to go in and take it and then walked with it the hundred or so miles to my home. At home there was great rejoicing at the gift I had received. They really believed it was a gift. After I became a Christian I came back along this road several times, the first was to take back the cow I had stolen together with the calves it had had!

"But the hardest thing was not taking back the cow; it was something different. In our area we heard what was called a new religion from Rwanda and we knew that our leaders disliked it very much. People we knew well, some were relatives, suddenly started to go to church. More than that they started to say that God was saving them from things I did not want to be delivered from. Some came to my home and actually apologised for some of the things we had been doing together and they said that they would no longer be doing them. That shook me and frightened me. In addition I found that these people seemed to be happier and freer. I felt that part of me did not want to be free from the things I was doing; after all, I was enjoying them. I felt that my case was hopeless and that nothing could ever get me out of the habits I had formed.

"As Festo Kivengere said, 'You hate those people and you love them at the same time.' That is how I found it. Many were, after all, my relations. Eventually I decided to go to our nearest church where there was a Mission going on, although we did not use the word Mission in those days. I knew that people were falling down, and then saying all sorts of shameful things that they had done,

must own up to the Government too and he must do what he wants. I knew that I had been given eternal life though I am still on this earth because I have agreed that Jesus should save me. The policeman and those present wept, as did my wife whom I had recently married."

After further questioning the policeman said, "Let us pray. Please God make me like this man. Please save me." He repeated this prayer two or three times. Eventually Daudi Ikuratiire was excused punishment because there was no evidence against him except his own testimony. That testimony was to have a profound effect on many in that district.

Prior to his conversion, Daudi had heard Dr Joe Church preaching about the power of the blood of Jesus to destroy sin. "I asked myself," Daudi said, "how long will I hold out like this? So I asked Dr Church: 'Is there any sin that is too hard for the blood of Jesus?'" He learned that "the blood of Jesus cleanses from *all* sin."

When he had repented of his sin and confessed it in public as he had confessed it to God, he knew with absolute assurance that God had forgiven Him. "All that I feared," he testified, "the people, the ridicule and so on seemed somehow to be below me and I was right up above them and I stood on my two feet and confessed all those things as they were. Sin was dethroned in my life because the blood of Christ washed all the sin away."

Not only was Daudi Ikuratiire's testimony greatly used at that time but continued to be so for 33 years as he cared for his second ailing wife. "There is not another woman in the village who has been loved like me. For 33 years God has used him to keep me alive." She confessed shortly before her death.

The testimony of another man who was converted in the 1940s gives a remarkable insight into the way God worked in the lives of Africans with the background of their own cultural attitudes and customs.

stunned silence. He had killed his wife because "I knew that she had found out about my misconduct with another woman and I didn't want her to let the church people know as I would lose my job. The child awoke in the middle of this and I knew that the child would say what had happened to my wife so I killed her too."

The whole team was deeply moved as they all realised the seriousness of what Daudi had done; they knew that murder was punishable by capital punishment. Daudi knew that he had to confess his crime to the Government and so wrote to the Authorities in Kabale with a copy to the police.

On the following Sunday, at Kinyasano, Daudi Ikuratiire related how God had met him and confessed before them all that he had done. The speaker who had preceded him at that service, Mr Yeremiya Rwakatogoro, remembered: "As Daudi stood up and told what God had done for him we were quite overcome with grief, because we knew that he was saying goodbye to us. As he spoke it was as if there a great pit opened up before us, as if there were spears everywhere. There was an almost physical movement around us that is hard to put into words. God's presence was almost tangible." Both the Saza and the Gomborora Chiefs who were in the congregation left in the middle of the service.

Relating his experience years later to Miss Joan Hall he said, "You see, it was overwhelming when I realised that it was the power of God, not my power. I had completely made up my mind never to reveal to anyone those things in my life. No-one knew what I had done and I was determined that no-one would ever know. I knew what the results would be."

"Why did you own up to killing your wife and your child knowing that for this you be killed yourself?" asked a policeman later when he was being questioned. He replied, "When God had forgiven me for that sin He told me that I

Church. The leader, Mr Betsimbire replied that that they stayed outside. They did not enter the church. The DC then asked the priest, the Rev. Father Peresiiti to give his version of the incident. He told how the visitors had arrived singing and this had stopped his people from singing and dancing. 'When I came to see what was happening they turned to me,' he said, 'and preached to me, and even dared to say that I had sin. Truly, do you think I have sin?'

"'You have no case,' the DC concluded, 'From what you say they found the children playing and they played, they found them singing and they sang and as for saying that you are a sinner, truly you are. And I am, and your children are too." The prisoners, now freed, left for Kinyasano overjoyed.

God's reviving work received a great impetus from the remarkable conversion of Mr Daudi Ikuratiire. He was for several years a church teacher in charge of the churches in Rujumbura. As the church leader in the area he joined a team that started a series of visits beginning at Kyaruryenje then went on to Katwekamwe and Murama before returning to Kinyasano. The team arrived at Katwekamwe as evening came on and almost immediately the Holy Spirit worked in great power. People cried out as they confessed their sins. Others brought out and burnt fetishes and various articles that had been used in divination to ward off evil spirits. These included cow horns and snakes' heads. They were all brought out and burned publicly.

That night, having seen and felt all that was going on, Daudi could not sleep. About 2 am he was overcome with a sense of guilt at the depths of his sin. Later that morning, as the leaders were talking and praying about who should be the speakers for the meetings that day, he confessed to them what he had done: he had murdered his wife and his child. The rest of the team listened in

3 Revival in Kigezi

On Tuesday morning, 15 men and women presented themselves to the Saza Chief and they were imprisoned in two rooms, one for the men and the other for the women. "Each morning they were taken to different parts of the river to wash and then to clear the compound of the Saza Chief where his house had recently been completed. Any Christians who came to them were beaten but non-Christians were allowed to stay."

One of the visitors was Mr Stefano Kanyumba. On arrival he greeted the prisoners with "Tukutendereza", (Praise the Lord). The Saza Chief heard this and asked him, "What sort of a fool are you?". He replied, "I've been fooled by sin". The Chief then ordered a guard to beat him. This he did with such force that he fell to the ground with blood flowing from nose and mouth. He appeared dead. When the Christians saw what had happened they wept and said to the chief, "Kill us too if you like". The prisoners were forbidden food until the evening when the women were given something to eat. They sang as they ate and this amazed the guards.

"That evening, at about 10 pm, the chief guard, Mr Geoffrey Kahiriita came out of his house crying and calling out. He came into the prison and knelt weeping in front of the Christians. He asked Jesus to forgive him and he was born again, and there was much praise."

"On Friday night there was a strong earth tremor and the prison began to shake. All the prisoners except the Christians began to shout. Each of the Christians felt that the Lord was telling them that they were going to be freed the following day.

"On Saturday, the District Commissioner of Kigezi with police escort came to Rujumbura particularly to hear the case against these Christians and to learn how they had been rude to the Priest at the Roman Catholic Church.

"When the prisoners had assembled before him he asked them if they had forcibly entered the Roman Catholic

ledge of each other and each other's problems and difficulties and praying over them together."

At Easter 1941, a series of meetings began and ended at Kinyasano with the intention of strengthening the Christians and of sharing the Good News with those who did not know Christ. They first met together on the Tuesday before Easter at Kinyasano for prayer together and a sharing of testimonies. Then on the following days many of them went to the churches nearby of Rukondo, Nyaruiizi, Kyatoko and, on Good Friday, Katwekamwe. "The team was large and the joy was great as they went along singing new hymns which they composed as they went round."

On Easter Sunday there was a great service at Kinyasano at which God's presence was felt very powerfully. When the service was over they felt that God was telling them to go to preach at Nyakibare, not far away. When they arrived there they saw people coming out of a Roman Catholic church singing and dancing traditional dances. The people from Kinyasano went on singing the songs they had been composing and the local people looked at them "wide-eyed and agog to know what was going on". This gave the visitors an opportunity to preach the Gospel to them. The Roman Catholic priest came out to see what was happening. The visitors continued to preach and even addressed him. He was furious with them because they said that he was a sinner. Very angrily, he mounted his motor-cycle and roared off to report them to the Saza Chief. Eventually the team from Kinyasano returned home.

The Saza Chief then sent a soldier to Kinyasano to arrest those who had 'invaded' the church area at Nyakibare and had been abusive to the priest-in-charge. The soldier was persuaded to return to the Saza Chief with the promise that those concerned would report at the Saza headquarters the next day.

the reality of its power in the lives of many relatives and friends, in 1941, Festo Kivengere finally bowed in repentance and faith before the Jesus Christ he had tried to ignore. "I got off my knees, still crying, but now with joy. No more guilt, no more shame. God was no longer a threat. Christ was no longer an embarrassment. He loved me! I started singing and shouting. I sang all the little songs I'd thought I'd forgotten like 'Jesus loves me this I know'. They had now, for me, a new meaning! I just wanted to praise and praise." Coomes.101

The reality of Festo Kivengere's testimony combined with his command of the English language and leadership qualities brought him to the fore. He was invited to join the team of leaders, first as translator then as speaker. In this way he shared in the deep fellowship enjoyed by William Nagenda, Simeoni Nsibambi, Rev. Yosiya Kinuka, Rev. Ezekieri Balaba, Dr Joe Church and others.

In the years that followed in Kigezi, teams would be formed to go out to spread the good news of the Gospel to everyone in the district and far beyond. As numbers grew so the teams divided to form others to visit new places. "It was at this time that the pattern of meeting regularly twice a week, excluding Sundays, began. At Kinyasano, the Christians met on Wednesdays and Fridays.

"Every Wednesday, the brethren would come from all over the area to Kinyasano especially to be fed with the Word of God, to pray and to share God's dealings with them personally. Each Friday the Christians met in their own churches. So people jokingly said that each Wednesday was time to smash and to repent of any sin that the person had been troubled by on Monday and Tuesday, and each Friday was to expose what the enemy had been doing on Thursday! So each week there were three meetings: Sunday, Wednesday and Friday. This greatly deepened the fellowship and oneness among God's people, and it strengthened the preaching because of a greater know-

churches where they were situated. ... The breakthrough came with the conversion of Festo Rwamunahe, headmaster of the school (Makobore, near Kinyasano) and almost immediately by that of his second master and friend, Festo Kivengere (later Bishop). During the years that followed, nearly half of all the schoolmasters were saved. ... One evidence of what the Lord was doing was that books, pens and other things stolen from the schools were being returned. In the accounts of the schools I frequently had to start a column headed 'conscience money' for refunds by teachers and pupils, sometimes after a long period. For repentance always involved putting things and relationships right."

It was in 1940 that this move of God among school staff began at Kinyasano where the two main schools of the Rujumbura district were located. In that year new staff, fresh from training college, were located there. The Christians among them joined the existing Christian staff to "become a strong team together and did a lot of preaching in both schools ... Both those in the school and those in the church had strong bonds of fellowship and oneness. They often ate together and they regularly shared together not only in food, but also in fellowship, reading the Bible, praying, helping each other with personal and general problems, confessing their faults and praising together. They continually sought to be open and honest with each other, to read the Scripture and give a testimony of what Jesus was doing 'for me'.

"During the school year 1940-41 some of the school children were touched by all that they saw in the teachers. They saw their peace, their joy, and the great oneness they had and this brought some of the students to faith in Christ. They repented of the sins they had committed and confessed them openly. Some went to apologise to their teachers. Those were great days."

After reacting against the gospel for some years, despite

At Kinyasano, Dr Church preached using the pictures of pin-men which he drew himself. In this way he explained the power of the blood of Jesus Christ to wash away everyone's sins, if they repented of them, and so give joy and peace instead of sadness, weeping and sorrow. There followed a great release of joy and people began to sing, "What can wash away my sin, nothing but the blood of Jesus." Eventually people left to go home rejoicing.

The districts of Kigezi and Ankole are next to each other. "Because of the great work of preaching and because of the large numbers of people coming to the Lord from different parts of both Kigezi and Ankole, a great bond grew up between the Christians of these districts." A few Christians from Kigezi decided that they would visit the Christians in Ankole. These included the Rev. Erica Sabiti who later became the first African Archbishop of Uganda.

The team arrived at Kinoni, in Ankole, in September 1939 and found a crowd awaiting them from different parts of Ankole and even beyond. A remarkable feature of this 'mission' was the absence of any great physical manifestations of revival, such as falling down, weeping and crying out, but a great sense of a deep understanding of what God was doing. "We all seemed like educated people," said one who was there, "We cannot explain in words what salvation meant for us or what our understanding was at Kinoni. The only thing we can say is that it was very powerful as God revealed to us the depths of sin that had never been repented of." The oneness, love and understanding between the 'brethren' of Kigezi and Ankole was wonderfully cemented.

Writing of the situation in Kigezi, the Rev. 'Greg' Gregory Smith commented: "In the very early years of the Revival in Kigezi (i.e. from 1936), many of the school teachers were untouched and very few new teachers returning from their training in other parts of Uganda were saved. The result was that the schools were drifting away from the prayer and testimony.

On the Sunday of that weekend at Kinyasano, the team was by then so large that they divided into smaller teams and went out to nearby groups of people, preaching the same Gospel and seeing the same results - many, many being drawn into the Kingdom of God through repentance and faith in Jesus Christ. Some stayed on in the churches because they felt that their sins were so great and so many that God could not forgive them. It took time for them to realise and accept the limitless grace of God to forgive the repentant sinner, however great and however many may be the sins.

When the news of what had been happening in the Kinyasano area reached Dr Joe Church he wanted to go there and see for himself. At the request of the Rev. Ezekieri Balaba, a meeting was arranged by Mr Daudi Ikuratiire, the Pastor in charge of the churches in Rujumbura, at Kyamakanda in July 1939

A huge crowd had gathered under the trees when the team, which included the Rev. Ezekieri Balaba and Dr Joe Church, arrived. They began by singing some hymns. Almost immediately many people fell to the ground. "Mr. P Kitabire started to speak, seeking to explain what people should do, but they seemed as if they had been frightened and were in a state of shock. People were falling down, weeping and crying out. Dr Joe Church saw that the people were unable to listen and understand so he spoke a few words of comfort in Kinyarwanda and this was translated by Yeremiya Betsimbire. He looked on the people with much grace and compassion."

Among the trees under which the congregation was sitting was a particularly big one. "At that time a strong gust of wind blew. To the astonishment and fear of the people, the tree began to fall and some thought that it would fall on them. Dr Church asked everyone to wipe away their tears and to go to Kinyasano."

walked away for about a quarter of a mile in order to get some of the crowd to move, and then finally we returned to the church.

"On our return we found about 50 people in church. I started by asking one woman whom I knew had been crying when we first arrived, why she had cried, and I got back a very clear answer, because of the 'condemnation'. I asked her why she was condemned. She replied, 'Because of my sin before God'. She then added that she had found Jesus at the service we had just held. We saw that to deal with all the crowd before us was hopelessly impossible in the time that we had, so I left the church and went back to Kabale to ask someone else to take the chair for me and I returned to the gathering to find both Dr Symonds and William Nagenda hard at it. Many seemed to lack assurance of salvation and we gave several words on this point."

In 1938, the Rev. Lawrence Barham, who had been a leader of the work at Kabale, was located to Buye, in Burundi, to begin the pastoral training of clergy there the following year. The church leadership at Kabale was then in the hands of the Rev. Ezekieri Balaba. A team led by him visited Kinyasano in April 1939.

"They started preaching on Friday and the Holy Spirit fell on all who were in the church. Many fell down, others shrieked or called out, and sometimes they had froth in their mouths. This was all brought about by the deep conviction people felt as they saw their deep sinfulness."

On the following day many were saved, among them were some who later became church leaders and their wives. Immediately these newly converted Christians were drawn to join the team and share in the preaching and giving their testimonies. Those just saved found they were wholly accepted by the older members of the team. A great sense of fellowship in Christ grew among them and in the years that followed many meetings sprang up for fellowship,

before, there is a very high standard, and the sense of sin is immense. It is impossible to go into details in a letter, but all I can say is that I am humbled as I see the growth and zeal in these people whom I came to help. In many cases it is they who are leading and we who are following. I can only give one or two examples of recent happenings. A fortnight ago at morning prayers for the patients, three women with chronic ulcers gave their testimonies. They spoke with such conviction and joy that we were deeply moved. It is just wonderful when one realises that they probably came from heathen homes."

At about the same time, Archdeacon Pitt-Pitts wrote describing the events of 13 April 1939: "Muyebe is about 8 miles from Kabale station and we arrived there a little before 2 pm and found about 700 people outside the church. We counted the crowd ourselves and made it this number in round figures. But I soon saw that the important matter was not this crowd but the people who were inside the building. About a dozen people, some men, some women, were there with their faces to the ground, crying and crying. I went with William Nagenda and spoke to them trying to comfort and help them one by one. This seemed to have very little effect, so we went outside and started the service. We sang the hymn twice, "Come every soul by sin oppressed", and one by one the weeping people joined the crowd. We each gave a message. William spoke first on Repentance, I followed with a message on 'Jesus of Nazareth passes by', and Jack Symonds spoke on 'the Cross'.

"The meeting then closed and I said I wanted to see the people who had been weeping in church when we arrived, also anyone else who wanted to know how to be born again, but I did not wish anyone else to come into the church except those two sets. I did not wish people to come with just their testimony to give as our time was limited and I wanted to help those who needed help. We

but they were given renewed liberty and boldness in preaching, and so the Gospel penetrated even more deeply in parts of Ndorwa, Rukiga and Bufumbira.

At about the same time, several Christians felt that they should go and pray at the home of the Saza Chief, Mr Karegyesa, because his daughter, Ruusi, and his wife, Agnes, had been saved. When he saw them the Chief was furious and had them beaten and put in jail. This kind of opposition did not stop the witness of the praising Christians. A number of prison soldiers were converted through such testimony.

The concern of the Rev. Ezekieri Balaba, the Principal of Kabale Normal School, for the church centre at Kinkiizi resulted in a team, led by him and the Rev. Lawrence Barham, going there in December 1938. Many people gathered there from all over that district. As the Gospel was preached, the Holy Spirit came in great power and many men and women were saved.

A remarkable feature of this visit was that, among the manifestations of God's reviving power, there was a striking healing of skin diseases. In the ordinary way, women suffering from that kind of disease would use a local oil. Now something extraordinary was happening. "On Saturday they met again and many came to Christ. The Holy Spirit fell upon everyone - the fit and the sick, men and women, young and old, those from near and far, and those suffering from skin diseases were healed. People were in awe of this. And so the light shone at Nyakatare and the Gospel penetrated Kinkiizi. Many folk were enlightened by the light of the Gospel and threw away their charms and fetishes. Churches and schools were built and God was praised."

Dr Jack Symonds recorded that, in April 1939: "When we arrived back at Kabale we found that a new wave of revival had started, which has been going on ever since. The work this time, seems to be much deeper than ever

that they became very angry, beat him three times, tied him with ropes and carried him to Rukungiri where he was put into a government jail. Later he was released and pronounced not guilty of any punishable crime.

In September 1938, the church teacher, Mr Rwakyanga, took a number of his supporters to Nyabiteete to meet with members of the churches at Kitoojo, Nyakabungo and Kasheshe. He asked the saved people to stand. "We hear," he said to them, "that you are upsetting the whole district; you cry out at night and prevent others from sleeping and you say that you have been healed of your sins. Whoever told you that sin could be healed? Don't you know that sin cannot be healed? It is part of the blood of a person just as milk is when it is mixed with water. You have not been healed of your sins you have become insane!"

"We *have* been healed of our sin," they replied. "If we are insane, we don't really mind. We are in our homes living normally and we are dealing with our affairs in an orderly way. We say with absolute confidence that Jesus Christ is our Saviour!" Although forbidden to preach in church, they could not be silenced. In fact one local teacher, Mr Kibandama, a 'born again Christian' allowed them to continue.

That same year, a number of chiefs and subchiefs complained to the District Commissioner about "the people who had been saved and were mad. They explained that these people preach against others, exposing sin, and that makes those who go their way, weep, shout and call out in church. They also talk about unseemly things that should not be mentioned."

As a result, some of the leaders of the Kabale team, including Charles Kakira, and many others were put in the Saza prison at Ndorwa. They remained there a week while other Christians did not cease to pray for them. When they were released, not only was their joy very great

through long years of tradition and superstition." It was astonishing to see the power given to people to break with these and other customs related to their animistic superstitions once they had come to Christ.

One local man, Mr Rwakatogoro, joined the team but it was obvious that things were not right within him. Well after midnight he fell under deep conviction of sin and was laid prostrate "until he agreed with the Spirit's words and he repented of, and confessed his sins. Some people from his home came in the morning to see what was happening. They heard how he had been saved. He told them how sin had been a barrier between him and them and he wept as he told of all that happened. Some listeners were saved then and there.

As the time for the new term at the Kabale Normal School approached, the members of the team from Kabale urged those who had come to faith to carry on the work of the Gospel before returning to their training school. Those who came to faith as a result of this series of visits showed great vision for sharing their faith and a great spirit of self-sacrifice and urgency in their witness.

It was not all joy and singing, however. There was a strong opposition to such preaching which God confirmed with evident signs.

The church teacher of Kyamakanda, Mr E Garyaharibusha, started a group of people in opposition to anything to do with revival and especially opposed the preaching of Mr Y Betsimbire, his assistant church teacher. He taught that the revival ideas of salvation were useless because baptism gives a person all that is needed. Mr Betsimbire could not be silenced, however, so powerfully did God work through him.

Mr Garyaharibusha then took Mr Betsimbire to the senior teacher of the area, Mr Kosia Rwakyanga, accusing him of being disobedient and insane. Mr Betsimbire continued to preach in such a powerful way to his superiors

On the 21st September they left Mahwa and walked to Rumbugu where they found the church teacher and his congregation waiting for them. They sang some of the hymns that had recently been composed by the saved ones among them and "through the hymn singing, the Holy Spirit convicted many people and again some fell down in conviction of sin."

The next day the team went on to Rwenyangi. They arrived in the evening and, finding many people waiting for them, they began to preach and give their testimonies. "As soon as the team opened their mouths the Holy Spirit worked. People fell down, some weeping and some shouting. Some left the church in fear. " The local sub-chief was converted. He later gave up his government post and became a church teacher and remained a faithful Christian until he died.

From Rwenyangi, the team went on to Nyakarira to arrive as it was getting dark. They found a crowd of some considerable size waiting for them and as soon as they began to speak, the Holy Spirit came down in great convicting power. Many were so amazed, even frightened by the manifestations of God's power they witnessed, that they stayed in the church building all night. Some joined the visiting team.

The next morning the team went on to Nyabiteete. Almost immediately the church teacher came under deep conviction, fell to the ground and was saved. "Many husbands and wives fell to the ground, sometimes crying, sometimes calling out, but all of them were calling to Jesus to save them. Mr Mugyeru, Mr Bwagwaya and their wives and Mr Kyebiteete ran from the church when they heard people crying and screaming. They were also frightened when they saw the women tearing off and throwing away bangles from their legs and no longer covering their faces with their cloths. These things were amazing and frightening because they were breaking

Chapter 3

Revival in Kigezi

Throughout 1937 and 1938, there were signs of God working in the Kigezi area, usually in unspectacular ways as the Gospel was preached and witness given to His saving power. However, from time to time, extraordinary events would accompany this preaching of the Gospel and testimony to a personal experience of God's working.

In the school holidays of September 1938, a few people from the area of Buyanja and Kebisoni became convinced that they should themselves do something to reach those around them with the Gospel. They invited a team from the Kabale Normal School to visit them. Led by Yeremia Betsimbire, a Mission began at Kyamakanda on the 16th September. "That very day many responded to the Gospel. The most amazing thing was that the head church teacher of that area, who had been opposing and arguing against the team and their message of salvation was saved on that first day of the Mission. He then joined the team!"

After the Mission, the team went on to Karuhembe then, over the border to Mahwa, in Ankole, where a large number of people had gathered. "In the evening they began to preach and the Holy spirit worked in great power. Many men and women fell down and many started to confess their sins. The people at that church have never forgotten that visit."

giving this man agonies of shame and distress of mind. This is not emotionalism; it is stern conviction of sin by the Holy Spirit, and it fills us with awe."

From the Convention at Kabale in September 1935, to the end of 1936, there were dramatic manifestations of revival centred on Kabale in Uganda and Gahini in Rwanda. In every case, the cause of the extraordinary happenings was seen to be a deep conviction of sin - specific sins - and these were seen to be a frightening barrier between the sinner and God. And this was accompanied by a great sense of danger that if there was no repentance and reconciliation with God only a dreadful Hell remained. Then, when there was confession and repentance, there was a deep joy of sins forgiven and the assurance of the life of God within. This powerful convicting work was far greater than any human being could have brought about. God was at work, there was no doubt about that.

In Uganda, the leaders, the Rev. Lawrence Barham and the Rev. Ezekieri Balaba formed teams from the students of the Kabale Evangelists' Training School. In Rwanda, similar teams from the Gahini Evangelists' Training School were led by Dr Joe Church, Yosiya Kinuka and William Nagenda. In both these centres the numbers of team members grew as witness to revival truth was taken into the districts.

A remarkable and humbling feature of what was happening, as seen from the missionaries' point of view, was that much of the zeal for witnessing to immediate neighbours and to those further afield, came from the Africans, and not only the leaders but many of the ordinary, often newly converted, Christians. The call to "Come to Jesus for forgiveness and peace" seemed, to be followed, almost immediately by "Go! Tell what God has done."

The extent of the activities was so great that separate chapters are required for the events in Kigezi, Uganda and beyond and those in Rwanda and Burundi.

Monday 27th July we spent with the teachers and evangelists going through Bible teaching, with Archdeacon Pitt-Pitts to advise, encourage and help."

In view of what was happening in the district around, Cecil Verity called in the church evangelists to encourage them and, at the same time, to warn them of the wrong kinds of excesses. "He had a difficult time," Dr Joe Church wrote, "while he was talking to them and giving them advice and I rather think warning them against emotionalism, several reprimanded him and then began to pray; and many were so broken down and weeping that he had to go out of the school room and leave them and continue his meeting outside under the trees.

"The teachers told us that these outward signs were happening all over the district and that the Roman Catholics were saying that we were encouraging 'devil worship'. But the pagans were saying that the Bazungu (white people) had bewitched them."

"It was in 1936 that I was saved," stated Sira Kabirigi, later to become a school teacher, "but I did not then see the power of the Blood. I was defeated by my sins. 'Sin is defeated by the Blood,' I was told. I said to myself, 'How can the Blood do that? Then, in 1937, I understood. Pshaa! I saw that the Blood put an end to sin. I could not myself change into something else."

That only God could make that sort of change in a person was brought home to the Rev. Lawrence Barham the day before he set off from Kabale for a safari visiting the churches in the Kigezi district in November 1936. A gardener came to him, he wrote, "and with great beads of perspiration standing out on his forehead told me of a few small things he had stolen from me. I should have been inclined to think them of no importance, but he told me of how he had lost all peace, and had had to face up to going to prison for theft if he confessed. I realised afresh that even what we should call petty pilfering is sin, and was

but I fell into sins of various kinds and slipped back spiritually. In 1936 things changed completely. There was great blessing. The teachers Ezekeri Nyakarashi and Esai Nyamuhigo loved to call the young men together to hear the Word of God. Often they would wake me up to go and pray. There was much blessing in those times of prayer - we got up at 4 am or even 3 am to go to the church to pray, there was such seeking for God. So, in April 1936, I really understood what salvation was. I realised that there was perdition and that there was new life for those who trusted Christ. I was completely changed. I saw my sins as sins indeed, and prayed that the Lord would help me to repent, and those I'd sinned with. One day, in our chapel, God helped me to get up and confess and ask forgiveness of God and of others. I don't know how, but God took over. There was such love spread around and we had wonderful times. I was invited to Dr Church's house where newly saved ones used to come to pray, to be brought into the family and know one another. I felt my life completely changed. There was great power then."

The Sunday services at Gahini were often times when there was a great sense of God's presence. Archdeacon Arthur Pitt-Pitts visited Gahini a month after the startling events in the girls' school. Dr Joe Church wrote of Sunday, 26 July: "Pitt-Pitts spoke in the morning, the church was packed out, about a 1000 at least. I carried on at midday and spoke on the Holy Spirit. When I had finished several began weeping and crying out all over the church - one lying flat on the ground for about ten minutes. I made people sit and then got Pitt-Pitts and Miss Skipper and others to help the people out quietly. I closed the service at 2.30 pm and told those under conviction to stay behind. About 200 stayed and clearly that was one of the most wonderful days at Gahini. They were praying quietly and weeping till dark at 6.30 pm. I did not stay all the time. 15 to 20 were saved. All that day and

thick darkness and the hopelessness of their sins.

"Margaret Cyambari has come right through; she held out though she trembled for two days and could eat nothing and only yesterday she let Jesus have His own way in her heart and today she is radiant. She says she really believed that I was so fond of her I'd persuade God to let her into Heaven when I got there! Some of the things they revealed were amazing. Quite a lot have not come through yet but the awful tense feeling is over and now there is peace."

"Blessing fell on the school while I was still there," said Marianne Kajuga, one of the girls in the school. "The place was shaken as by an earthquake. People started weeping. I saw them weeping, falling on the ground, they frothed at the mouth, people lifted them up. In fact Dora (Skipper) came and tried to stop it to no avail! She called others but they couldn't do anything either. I especially remember one day, I think it was Saturday. The girls went out to cut the millet, but as they cut the millet they sang and sang the hymn 'Dukanguke! dukanguke! (Let us awake! Let us awake!) all day until they had finished.

"When evening came some began to weep, others stood around to watch them, some began to repent of their sins. I looked on. The Holy Spirit swept through the school and I think that everyone was touched, they repented of sins without fear. God began to help me too. I felt I loved Jesus, that He was my Saviour and that He died to save me. I realised that apart from God we would perish. I knew that He was knocking and wanting me to open the door. So Jesus saved me while I was still small and I went on bit by bit. I understood more and more of the Gospel and that I could walk with Jesus."

Yusitasi Kajuga (later Canon) who became the husband of Marianne, was in the Evangelists' Training School in 1936. Because of his evident abilities he had been given a leadership role. "I suppose they thought I was a good man

the night for sleep and that if they wanted to work for Him they must be rested and ready."

Dora Skipper gave her own description of those events: "This has been an amazing week. I have never seen anything like it. I have heard of it and always thought it a form of hysteria but it is uncanny. A person is suddenly taken with shivering. He thinks that he has fever. Then suddenly an awful sense of fear and then his sinfulness comes before him. The teachers came in and told me about it and I thought that they just got terribly excited and went off the deep end and upset each other.

"Sunday night was absolute pandemonium but all agreed afterwards that it was the devil, not Christ. I heard a noise starting on Monday at 3.30 am, so went down to quell it before it became uncontrollable but found Geraldine in charge and they were all sitting round and two girls crying and shaking. I removed Nyiramukobya and took her into the school to talk to her and she shook and shook and cried out uncontrollably, "I am so frightened. I'm so frightened". I got her to bed and told her to trust Jesus. He would drive out the devil. Then I went back to stay in the room and they were perfectly orderly. Geraldine impressed on them that God was only heard with a still small voice. Then they prayed and as they went on praying quietly, suddenly the girl who did the cooking started to shake violently and began to cry uncontrollably, so I removed her while they went on praying and put her to bed. All the day there was a fearful tense feeling and excitement everywhere and both Joy and I felt shaky for no reason. We came to the conclusion that it was a real fight going on between Christ and the devil.

"Tuesday evening all who were all right went to bed but others were left on the grass or in the class rooms. One here and another there, just writhing like the maniac when Christ came down from the Mount of Transfiguration, but all say that afterwards they were conscious of the girls. They seemed much calmer then and they prayed and prayed. They each seemed to have a revelation of sin and it was shattering. All Monday Miss Skipper was seeing the girls separately. At first a lot of them were rather hard, but by the end of the day, public opinion seemed to be that it could not have been of God that they should break the windows and desks in God's school, and so waste God's money. That must be wrong."

"After supper on Monday it started again, there were little groups all over the place with girls foaming at the mouth and seeming quite desperate. They were taken to bed but again on Tuesday morning Miss Skipper was with them in the school very early as they had all gathered to pray.

"All Monday and Tuesday, the girls were harvesting the amasaka (millet) which was much better for them than sitting doing lessons at this time. It all seemed to be so perfectly planned and timed. Tuesday night again a few of them were out shaking and one or two were foaming again, but it was much quieter. And whatever happened, once they were through it, they seemed to be different people.

"Wednesday seemed to be the climax. They spent the morning cutting millet, then they had all the afternoon to settle themselves up, to pay debts, to make things right with other people and to pray alone or with others in the daylight. At about 7 pm, Miss Skipper went down to the school. I went down too, and have never been in such a meeting. We sat all round the room and we had as many lamps as we could muster. God was there and He spoke.

"One or two girls began to shake but they were taken out and helped and everyone was quiet. There was no emotion then and no demonstration but there was great power. Many of them prayed, but quite quietly. Then they all went to bed and there was quietness. Both Miss Skipper and Geraldine had been stressing that God gave

were all throwing themselves about, they were absolutely uncontrolled, some were laughing, some weeping, most were shaking very much and they seemed to have supernatural strength. The powers of darkness seemed to be right on us. It felt like being in hell as though Satan had loosed his armies. As soon as she could drag them out, Miss Skipper got hold of the girls and spoke to them. Some were genuinely frightened, others were angry that they should be stopped in the middle of their experience of, as they believed, God. They were really and truly seeking Him, and it was just there that Satan got in and nearly turned all their seeking to evil. Gradually they were taken to their beds, some of them still very hysterical, others quiet but hurt in their hearts that they had been stopped.

"Mr Verity came in at last, having tried to break up a similar gathering down the hill, but Miss Skipper was the only one who could do anything to calm them. She learned from some teachers next day that this is really a heathen custom connected with marriage. On the night of the wedding, girls go with the bride and get into the same state until, at last, the bride gets worked up in the same way and then she goes to her husband - it had all got hopelessly tangled in their desperate longing to find God and be free from their sins. It was very late when eventually they were more or less settled down, but all the night there seemed to be singing and shouting from several places.

"Apparently it began in the school by four girls being dead earnest about getting right with God then and there, but others, mostly those who were quite heathen, came in and those who were really praying said that the Spirit went then.

"Very, very early on Monday morning, I think it was about 3.30 am, Miss Skipper heard the same sounds in the school, so she went down and was there till 7 am with

for one to take Blasio's place."

William Nagenda joined the team at Gahini. In addition to making up, in part at least, for the gap left by Blasio Kigozi, it began a partnership between William and Joe Church that was to last for many years and involved many thousands of miles of travelling together.

In July 1936, occurred a most startling event, the account of which opens "Fire in the Hills', the story of the beginnings of the Ruanda Mission. At Gahini the hospital and medical outreach was in the hands of Doctors Joe and Decie Church and nurse, Mildred Forder (later Mrs W Church). The church work was supervised by the Rev. Cecil Verity while the educational side was headed by Dora Skipper, helped by a recent arrival, Joy Gerson (later Mrs Berdoe).

It was in the girls' boarding school where, at the end of July 1936, the most dramatic happenings occurred. Joy Gerson wrote: "I will try and give you a rough sketch of what has happened in the girls' school this week - there is no doubt at all that God has been doing a very very big, deep, real work there; there is no doubt too, that Satan put up a desperate fight for the girls' souls, but he was defeated. This is how it started.

"On Sunday evening we had the usual hymn singing and prayer time for the whole school. It was a quiet and peaceful time. After our supper we were having our own prayer time, when we heard a noise in the school, which in the distance sounded exactly like a Bank Holiday crowd on Hampstead Heath. As we got nearer we heard shrieks and cries and inexplicable sounds. We got into the second compound over the hedge as the gates were locked (it was about 9.30 pm). There were girls here and there watching, but the main body of girls were in one of the school rooms.

"Miss Skipper could hardly open the door and when she did she could hardly stop being dragged inside. The girls seemed to have gone mad. Some were on the floor. They

Christians came round ... after supper, and said that they too had seen a similar vision in the church ... We felt the power of God in that meeting that evening and we wondered if God was allowing us to see the literal fulfilment of the promise of Joel 2:28 - 'Your young men shall see visions ...'"

The year 1936 opened with an evangelistic mission in January at Mbarara, in south Uganda. It was notable for two reasons: It was led by four men from different language areas, Blasio Kigozi from Buganda, Yosiya Kinuka from Ankole, Paulo Gahundi from Rwanda and Dr Joe Church from England, working together in deep fellowship and preaching the Gospel with great power. And it was marked by such a new and deep sense of urgency and danger that a new topic was added to the preaching messages, "the state of perishing of the sinner before God".

Within a few days, Blasio Kigozi suffered an acute fever and, despite all that could be done for him, he died at Mengo Hospital in Kampala, less than a fortnight after the Mbarara convention.

The death of Blasio Kigozi had a profound effect on many people in the Gahini and Kabale areas, but on none more so than his brother-in-law, William Nagenda. "Both had been privileged with a good education judged by the standards of those days," wrote Dr Joe Church. "William had gained a diploma from Makerere College before it was raised to a degree-conferring institution and he had a good post as a government clerk. He was a truly saved man but he did not have the vision and zeal of his brother - until Blasio died. He immediately offered to the Bishop of Uganda to go to Rwanda where his brother had served.

"He was unknown to any of us but when we were asked by the Bishop at the committees which station would like to have him, my hand went up because I knew that he was a convert of Nsibambi. God was answering our prayer

Missionaire Protestante) to pay poll-tax on his cows. While there he began to witness and rouse his friends. An invitation came to us at short notice to hold a weekend mission. I think that I have never seen such a spiritual hunger and expectancy. We were speaking almost all day. Great things happened afterwards. The lady missionary in charge began by courageously standing up after the Morning Service on the following Sunday, and openly confessing to coldness and anger; whereupon four more, one a notoriously bad and back-slidden Christian, did the same. There was great joy and a time of reconsecration and decision for Christ has continued. Many had grown so cold since their baptism that they had ceased to read or carry a Bible."

A mission to Uganda was planned to celebrate the Diamond Jubilee of the Church in 1937, and students from the Theological College at Mukono would be taking part. First, however, they wanted a 'mission to the students'.

On the way to Mukono, in June 1936, Dr Joe Church and his team stopped at Mbarara where a remarkable incident occurred. As recorded by Joe Church, "Many had gathered to meet us on our way to Kampala and a gathering had been arranged in the church for 5 pm. We all spoke and we made an appeal when a thing happened that I had never experienced before. A man began to cry out and howl at the top of his voice. I was alarmed and made people sit down. The man continued weeping, lying on the floor. I called him up to the chancel to say what he had experienced. He was one of the most trusted Christians, a government interpreter. He stood beside me weeping and in halting words gave a moving testimony. He said that he had seen a vision of Christ in the church and he saw the awful state of the lost and was overcome with grief for his own past. He asked his friends to help him, but he could not stop crying out. Later some senior

to the district around. "There are about 250 bush schools in this mountainous part of Western Uganda, between Lake Edward and the Ruanda border. A movement of the Spirit - a Wind of God - came blowing through these little companies of Christians drawn from the wild Bakiga tribe, and in places it became almost a mass movement. Churches where there had been only a handful of children learning to read, were suddenly thronged with a congregation of several hundreds. Many began to have dreams and see visions. There appeared for the first time, absolutely spontaneously, the phenomenon of 'trembling', i.e., the violent shaking of the whole body during prayer or when repenting of sin. We have seen this often since, but it was unknown to us previously. Convicted men and women would tremble violently, and even fall to the ground, being unable to kneel any longer. This was accompanied by remorse and weeping, and when peace of mind came it disappeared.

"The inevitable 'tares' appeared also, almost at once. A few began to imitate, sometimes almost innocently, and this entailed many visits to the district by Mr. Barham; but they were willing to learn, and now everywhere things have settled down to what seems to be steady growth. In some places large crowds of men and even old women went out preaching, and in one of the districts, although there had been no special teaching about the Second Coming, the idea spontaneously arose that Christ was coming back this year. They sent in for advice to Mr Barham as to the planting of their crops. ... On looking back nearly a year, it is encouraging to note that in every case, with careful teaching, they have been willing to learn and have avoided the dangers."

"Early in January, 1936," wrote Dr Joe Church, in his 'Call to Prayer', "one of our evangelists, who has recently had a very definite experience of conversion, went to his own home (near a Mission Centre of the *Société Belge*

2 "I will put my Spirit within you"

recently been converted, returned to his home at Kabale for his annual month's holiday, and caused surprise by going round to all his old friends and telling them of his new life, and that he could no longer go and drink with them as he used to do. This left a deep impression, as it came at a time when Kabale station seemed to be dead spiritually, and Mr Barham was considering and praying much about how to deal with this condition and had contemplated having some kind of mission. It was just at this time that Blasio wrote the letter ... telling of the experience that he had had in that week of waiting upon God for power. The letter seemed to come as a direct answer to the prayers of the leaders at Kabale, and they sent an invitation to us at Gahini to conduct a ten days' convention for all the 300 evangelists and the school teachers of the Kigezi district. News of blessing at Gahini had spread, and there was a longing on the part of many of the leaders at Kabale that they should share in it too. There was only about a month in which to prepare, and much time was given to praying over the message and choosing the leaders. ...

"The convention was held at the end of September, 1935, and the scheme was that which had been followed at Gahini. We took a party of about ten Africans chosen from several different stations, men on whom God had laid His hand ... They came primarily to do personal work, but could be asked to speak when necessary.

"At Kabale, Blasio was the 'Peter' of the band, speaking the Word with boldness ... We worked on the scheme that we had followed at Gahini. The day began with a blackboard Bible reading, and the subjects for the different days in order were: Sin, Repentance, the New Birth, Separation, the Victorious Life, the Holy Spirit. A deep and abiding work of conviction began which has continued unabated up to the time of writing."

That 'deep and abiding work of conviction' then spread

The influence of Blasio Kigozi at Gahini extended to every section of the work there. "Sin loomed large in his preaching," wrote Dr Joe Church, "and he was more than ever urging repentance and a coming to Jesus Christ for release from the burden. There was much conviction, and in May, 1935, there were many conversions at Gahini. The preaching of sin is never palatable to the natural man, so this renewed zeal and aggressiveness on the part of Blasio caused a fresh outbreak of opposition to him. It arose, partly, it is true, because there were some indiscretions ... in their zeal to witness and to do personal work, junior hospital orderlies had often approached or 'tackled' senior Christians. The idea of a senior church worker being spoken to by a junior hospital boy was more than some could bear." [Awake.21]

A strong bond had grown up between Blasio Kigozi, Yosiya Kinuka and Dr Joe Church. Their combined witness led to a wave of evangelistic zeal in the hospital and schools at the centre and teams went out to the neighbouring district.

Testimony to the quiet work that was going on in homes was given by the Rev. Yohana Bujindiri who lived at Kayita, not far from Gahini. "The work of revival began with the hospital workers, slowly, slowly," he said, "When we went to learn at Gahini we used to spend the day there at Yosiya's or Blasio's. We loved what they said and started to enter into it."

Rev. Chrysostom Habyara was particularly helped by Blasio Kigozi. As a student in the Evangelists' School, Blasio, the Head, sent them out with other men and women, like Jesus "sent out His disciples. It was a wonderful time. Blasio loved the Banyarwanda from the beginning but he changed then and was just full of such peace and love that others were made thirsty."

"In June, 1935," wrote Dr Joe Church, "one of the hospital workers, Kosiya Nkundiye, by name, who had

Chapter 2

"I will put My spirit within you."

At Kabale, in south-west Uganda, and Gahini, in Rwanda, the first two mission centres of the Ruanda Mission, the major activities centred on the hospitals and the evangelist training schools. It was from these that medical safaris and evangelistic teams reached out to the districts around them. The more recently opened church centres at Shyira and Kigeme, in Rwanda, were still in their early stages of development and Buhiga and Matana, in Burundi, were opened in the course of 1935.

In charge of the Gahini Evangelists' Training and Primary schools was Blasio Kigozi (later ordained). "In the spring of 1935," wrote Dr Stanley Smith, "overwhelmed by a sense of failure in his work for, after a term of spiritual apathy in the Evangelists' Training School, six had left following a strike, Blasio Kigozi was driven to his knees. He spent a whole week of solitude in his house, eating very little, studying his Bible and praying. He prayed for power; God's answer was to show him more his own weakness. He came out a changed man: still cheerful, laughter-loving, happy in his home and his baby son, but now with a new urgency in his message, a new fearlessness, and a new power not his own. The Evangelists' Training School became a different place, and a wave of fresh blessing swept over Gahini and its district."

meeting on Saturday afternoon at which those who were to go on these evangelistic efforts were chosen. Concurrently, a deep desire for prayer grew up and increased, until at times it caused trouble in the various departments of the work. Prayer meetings and hymn singing went on continually, often late into the night, or starting at three or four o'clock in the morning. But in spite of the annoyance that this epidemic of midnight singing caused at times, it seems certain that the need and desire for prayer were spontaneous and were blessed of God."

At Kabale, Rev. Lawrence Barham and Rev. Ezekiel Balaba were teaching in the Evangelists' Training School. Both felt a deepening sense of the need for God to break into their 'biblically sound teaching' with His 'breath of life'. Encouraging new signs of spiritual life among the students began to appear in 1934.

It was with a mixed sense of, on the one hand, sadness that there was not more evidence of spiritual life among the many who attended church services and were learning the truths of Scripture, and, on the other hand, expectancy in the light of the signs of evangelistic zeal on the part of some Africans and their desire for prayer, that the year 1934 came to an end. Had the work of the Mission continued like that, it would still have been successful in the sense of many people being reached with the Gospel in medical, evangelistic and educational outreach. There would not, however, have been anything special to record which was different from what was happening in many other mission areas. In 1935, however, remarkable things began to happen around the mission centres of Kabale, in Uganda, and Gahini, in Rwanda.

avoid it as he will flee from a leopard, by instinct. Each story took some five minutes, because the African has to start almost from the day of his birth in narrating an experience, but some wonderful stories of God's saving power were told. Three at least were born again through dreams. One dreamed that he saw Mr. Verity coming to his kraal on a motor cycle and that he was afraid because he knew he was coming to ask him why he wasn't working for God in his distant village. Another dreamed that he had developed gangrene of the tongue from smoking too much, so his pipe was thrown away and he stepped out for God.

"Many others stood up and said they were convicted at these meetings, many of bad living and adultery, many of bad drinking, and in each case they promised in God's sight henceforth to step out on the new life with Christ. So we rejoiced to feel that the Word had gone home to their hearts. We had to stop them when it was dark at 6.30 pm. It seems definite that we were guided of God to have this extra meeting. These native Christians should all have been on their way home, but many had been praying with a real burden for a move of repentance, and many laid themselves down that night rejoicing that it had come, and others at peace under the care of their new found Saviour."

In the years 1929 to 1934, there were other small indications at Kabale in Uganda and at Gahini in Rwanda that were later to be seen as precursors of revival. The team at Gahini of Dr Joe Church and Yosiya Kinuka (later ordained) was joined by Blasio Kigozi, the brother of Simeoni Nsibambi.

Dr Joe Church wrote: "It had been a custom at Gahini since about 1933 to send out parties of evangelists into the district, especially on Sunday, and for the weekend to more distant places. Blasio and Yosiya had become the leaders of the keen section, and they had their own special

offered up for a real movement of conviction, but up to the last meeting there was no very obvious movement going on. I was a bit disappointed, and found some of the Hospital workers felt the same, so we had two hours of real prayer before dawn on the last Saturday morning, praying especially for a spirit of conviction. Unknown to me, Geoffrey Holmes had felt the same and had told all the Convention to stay on for another day, especially to pray and not go away empty. The extra Prayer Meeting began in the Church at 3 pm on Saturday afternoon.

"After half an hour of the usual formal prayers at which the African can excel. Kosiya Shalita slipped out and asked me to come. He said he could not stick it any longer. People were praying these beautiful long prayers, but many of them were hypocrites, he knew it, and they needed to be broken down before God. He wanted to go back and ask Mr. Holmes to stop the meeting. We talked outside and agreed that nothing but the Spirit could break men's hearts and that we must have faith that the words that had been spoken, almost entirely as Bible readings, would bear fruit during the days of the Convention.

"We had been pressing Repentance, because we knew that that is perhaps the hardest thing the African can be called upon to do before God or men. A remarkable thing then happened a few minutes later. While everyone was bowed in prayer, a native Christian got up and began confessing some sin he had committed and then all sat up, and it seemed as though a barrier of reserve had been rolled away. A wave of conviction swept through them all and for two hours it continued, sometimes as many as three on their feet at once trying to speak.

"You must get the African setting to this. The African is not afraid to stand up and speak in front of others, for half an hour if you like, he loves it, so this was not so remarkable, but what he hates and does all in his power to get round is to repent of sin before his fellows. He will

had been taught about the power of Christ to save and deliver, and he yielded his life at last to Him.

"Yosiya Kinuka arrived back at Gahini a new man, and now between him and Joe Church began a fellowship in Christ which God has used beyond anything that could have been dreamed of then. There was first much to put right, including some misappropriation of hospital money and property, and then all barriers were down and a completely new relationship came into being. The once proud, aristocratic senior dresser now called all his fellows together and repented openly of stealing, telling them of his new life, and warning them concerning their own state. It was not to be expected that this would be well received, for petty pilfering and secret drinking were general among them all, but their hatred, slander and threats he answered only by prayer and love, until, one by one, almost all of them were also converted, and Gahini hospital became an entirely new place. Hidden sins were openly confessed, and costly restitution was made. Then a burning zeal for others began to appear, as they went among their fellow Christians testifying to what God had done in their own lives, and challenging them about the sin of which the missionaries might often be unaware, but which were well known to the African community."

Another indication of what was to come occurred in 1933. Three conventions were held in that year, a 'Keswick convention' for missionaries at Kabale and two for Africans. The last of these was held at Gahini.

"On Tuesday, the day after Christmas, our Convention began, the first we had ever had at Gahini," wrote Dr. Joe Church. "There were three addresses each day, at 9 am, 11 am and 3.30 pm, which were so arranged as to form a sequence to last over the days, as follows: Sin, the Holiness of God, the Second birth, Repentance, Faith, Prayer, the Holy Spirit (three addresses), and the Second Coming. There had been and there was much prayer

done a heroic work during the famine, and were still nursing the sick with a faithfulness which only the grace of God made possible. Yet now they were restless and dissatisfied, and no one more so than the senior assistant, Yosiya Kinuka.

"This man, a Muhima from Ankole in Western Uganda, had been among the earliest patients in Kabale hospital. He had come there as a young lad, scarcely able to walk from the ravages of a tropical disease for which his people knew no remedy, and had found healing. Later he began to work as a dresser in the hospital, and having eagerly learned to read, was baptized, with a good head knowledge of Christianity, but without ever having met Christ as Saviour and Lord.

"He volunteered for Gahini hospital before it began, and was Joe Church's right hand man throughout the famine. After a further period of training at Kabale he returned to Gahini, and it was then that friction developed between him and the doctor, whose attempts at this time to draw the hospital staff to share in the evangelism of the district were hotly resented. Yosiya Kinuka felt that since he was already doing what he was paid to do, no more should be required of him - certainly not the work of an evangelist. At last he decided to give up Christian work altogether, to return to his own country and get another job. Dr Joe Church suggested he took a holiday first, and arranged for him to go to Kampala in Uganda to stay with Simeoni Nsibambi.

"He went. His time with Nsibambi, to whom he poured out his troubles, left him deeply challenged, yet he set off for Gahini again with no change in his intention to leave. But as the lorry bumped along the road, Nsibambi's words came back to him, "It is because of sin in your own life that the hospital is like it is." God's convicting Spirit brought home to him the truth about himself, and as, for the first time, he saw his need, he remembered all that he

mad!' I asked what she meant and she said that he was going about everywhere talking to people about their souls and that he had only just then left her gardener! Doubts began to haunt me a bit. Kind and well-meaning missionaries more or less told me that the African was not ready for the deeper teaching of sanctification and the Holy Spirit, and that I ought to confine myself to the evangelising of the heathen in Ruanda before 'interfering' - that horrible word! - with the Christians of Uganda."

Simeoni Nsibambi gave up his government job of sanitary inspector, sold his motor-cycle, and began a life of daily personal witness in the streets, shops and hospitals, of the big town of Kampala, the capital of Uganda ... Undoubtedly Something happened at this time which changed the course of his life, and personally I put that down to The Mysterious Fire that resides within the pages of the Word of God."

Of that event, Dr Joe Church, wrote: "I have often referred to this time in my preaching in later years as the time that God in his sovereign grace met with me and brought me to the end of myself and thought fit to give me a share of the power of Pentecost. There was nothing very spectacular, nothing ecstatic; it is easy to become proud if one has received a special gift. The only special gift is the experience of the transforming vision, of the risen Jesus Himself."

One of the Africans who was converted through Simeoni Nsibambi's testimony was his brother, Blasio Kigozi, later to hear and obey a clear call from God to go to Rwanda and serve Him there.

The second event occurred at Gahini, in Rwanda, where Dr Joe Church was in charge of the hospital: "During 1930, the hospital became outwardly transformed, but the African staff were not happy. These young men, many of them highly born, not bred to do any work, still less the menial and often revolting tasks which fell to their lot, had

had touched him and he said that he wanted more. He said that he was seeking for something that he knew he had not yet attained."

That Mugandan was Simeoni Nsibambi. He was the son of the District Chief of Busiro. Well educated and working for the Kabaka of Buganda, he had had high expectations of being selected to study overseas. However, in 1922, he was passed over in preference for another man. This brought him great disappointment. It was then that he had a vision in which he heard a voice say, "Salvation is better than studies abroad." God began a work in him which he likened to the reviving power that Pilkington had received in 1896. He became an evangelist at Mengo Hospital, Kampala, and witnessed to many both inside and outside the hospital.

Dr Joe Church continued the story of his meeting with 'this quiet, humble man'. "We arranged to meet at 2 pm the next day with our Bibles. I had been going through the References on the Holy Spirit with the Scofield Reference Bible at Gahini, so we started on this, at the beginning (Gen 1:2), "And the Spirit of God moved over the face of the waters." We got as far as Pentecost and I well remember his face as we knelt to pray; he was moved with excitement, and absolutely claimed this life of victory. He insisted on coming again the next day at the same time. We carried on from where we had left off on the day of Pentecost in Acts to Revelation. He there and then completely surrendered his life and claimed, at all costs, this life for which he had been seeking. We talked about practical details and I happened to mention the phrase 'One by one band', suggesting that he should speak to one person about Christ each day.

"I went on to Nairobi, Kenya, and returned there after about a week. I remember being met by one of the missionaries at Namirembe, near the Cathedral, who said to me, 'What have you done to Nsibambi? - he's gone

This movement was not *revival*. It bore the hall-marks of a supernatural work as thousands appeared to be inexplicably drawn into the church centres and so made open to hearing the Gospel, but there was not that deep, lasting work in the hearts of people which indicates a true work of God. The powerful call, expressed by that witch-doctoress, to 'worship God', good though it may have been, was ineffectual because there was not the prior call to repentance from sin. True worship can only be offered to God where there has been reconciliation with Him. The short-lived mass activity in Kigezi served as a warning against false spiritual movements.

Three years later the Rev. Lawrence Barham wrote, "It has come home to us lately how desperately low the spiritual standard is here in the Kigezi district. We have been brought, one by one, to realize the state of things, and have been seeking God's face to find out where the failure lies. We believe that God has put this hunger in us because He means to satisfy it. We believe God is going to give us a big new blessing and a growing longing for the things of God."

"Before they call, I will answer," God said to Isaiah, and that proved true in Africa. Two incidents occurred, one of which happened two years before Lawrence Barham's letter and the second a year later, to which may be traced the beginnings of God breaking through in remarkable ways.

The first of these, in 1929, was recounted by Dr Joe Church: "After having been at my new station for over a year, I returned to Kampala, Uganda, for a holiday and to get stores. I went to the Cathedral on Sunday morning and after the service I met a well dressed Mugandan outside who wanted to speak to me. His motorcycle was standing there and he spoke fairly good English. He said that he had been at a meeting that I had addressed on my way through to Ruanda in November, 1927. Something

relatively few in number. For the majority, the transition from a deeply ingrained animistic bondage to the spiritual liberty of reconciliation with God and the indwelling of His Holy Spirit was too great a step and a nominal acceptance of the Christian truths, baptism with its sign of a new, usually biblical, name, was sufficient. It was this 'skin-deep' conversion which was worrying for some missionaries.

The great concern for a deeper working of God in the lives of those who became, at least nominally, Christians, led one missionary, the Rev. Jack Warren to make a plea, in 1927, for a 'Week of Prayer and Humiliation before God' and another, Dr Joe Church, to issue a strong 'Call to Prayer' in 1928, addressed to both missionaries in the field and to those who supported the work in the UK.

A month before that second 'Call to Prayer', a remarkable incident occurred in a remote part of Kigezi, in southwest Uganda, which upset the steady progress being made there. A sorceress claimed to have heard Jesus call her one night commanding her to urge people to worship God. "Using her considerable influence she threatened the people among whom she lived with severe punishment if they did not also go to 'the Worship' to learn about God. The effect among the superstitious people of the district was very powerful. Thousands flocked to Sunday services, usually in the open-air, as simple church buildings proved inadequate to contain the crowds."

Bands of untrained volunteers were sent out from Kabale to teach the basic truths of the Gospel to the expectant gatherings of people. After about a year, the crowds began to lessen and, as far as could be discerned, little remained of spiritual value. Dr Algie Stanley Smith commented on this remarkable movement: "There is no doubt that the Spirit of God was moving in the hearts of multitudes of people, it made the Mission believe in the possibility of a supernatural work of God among uninstructed heathen."

evangelists who taught the catechism classes during the week also led the church services on Sunday and prepared candidates for baptism and confirmation. The term 'readers' applied to those - men, women and children - who attended church services and catechism classes or were being prepared for baptism or confirmation.

All this represented a considerable amount of work. It also required a close cooperation between missionary and African - white and black, as well as between missionary and missionary in the differing areas of medical, school and church outreach. 'Work' and 'relationships' were the two areas which demanded all the physical, spiritual and mental energy which the missionaries could muster.

Despite the problems and various forms of opposition, the early missionaries were never in any doubt that God had called them to the peoples of south-west Uganda, Rwanda and Burundi, with the simple Gospel of reconciling salvation to whoever repents of their sin and trusts in Jesus Christ. Given that certainty, they tackled the problems which arose in pursuing that task - the physical problems of disease, poverty and lack of adequate facilities and equipment, the mental and spiritual problems of loneliness and ill-health, negotiating between the black and white cultures, coming to terms with the 'ruler' and 'ruled' distinctions which prevailed in a colonial climate and facing Roman Catholic intolerance. At least the physical climate was favourable. Despite being within a few degrees of the equator, the altitude of these countries ensured a healthy mixture of sunshine and rain.

Right from the beginning there was encouragement. Not only did a number of men and women from these countries respond to the Gospel but they then gave themselves to God in a missionary zeal which led many of them to leave their own homes to go elsewhere and cooperate with the missionaries in their outreach to the needy in both body and spirit. These were, however,

founders of the mission were medical doctors and it was natural, therefore, that the medical side should be foremost in evangelistic outreach and that future recruits should also be predominantly medical - doctors and nurses. Although 'church planting' appeared to come last, as one of the early missionaries, Dr Godfrey Hindley, stated, "We were there to build an African church", and it was to this end that both medical and educational aims were pursued.

It was soon recognised, however, that despite apparent success in terms of mission centres established, hospitals built, schools opened and numbers joining the churches, the results were, in fact, discouragingly superficial seen from the spiritual point of view. The Gospel was being proclaimed in simple, biblical terms and the Bible was being taught as God's authoritative word to sinful men and women ... and yet the evidence in the spiritual lives of those who claimed to accept those truths was, in general, sadly disappointing. This was not unusual, however, and many mission fields reported a similar state of affairs. There were, nevertheless, exceptions and God was clearly at work in some Africans. This was reflected in their devotion to serving others in hospitals and schools and in evangelistic outreach to places beyond their home areas where the Gospel was not known.

From 1921, in increasing numbers and places, a healing work was carried on under very difficult circumstances due to prevalent diseases, poor hygiene and rudimentary medical facilities. Hospital and medical safari staff were trained from those with little educational background. School teachers and evangelists were also trained for the steadily increasing number of catechism classes in which evangelists taught 'readers' of all ages to read, write and understand the Bible, and for elementary schools where children were taught the basic so-called 'Three R's' - reading, writing and arithmetic, plus Scripture. The

Chapter 1

Preparing the way

The story of the beginnings of the Ruanda Mission is told elsewhere. It's missionary activity began in early 1921 when Dr and Mrs Len Sharp and Dr and Mrs Algie Stanley Smith began medical work at Rugarama, one of the hills on which the town of Kabale is built in southwest Uganda. In the years that followed, a hospital was built there, schools were started in the district around, the training of church teachers was begun, a 'leprosy settlement', as it was called in those days, was established on Bwama, an island in Lake Bunyoni, and medical evangelistic safaris reached a wide region.

Visits to Rwanda began in 1922 and these led to the starting of the first mission centre in Rwanda at Gahini (1925). In succeeding years, mission centres were established at Shyira and Kigeme, (1932), in Rwanda and, in Burundi, Buhiga and Matana (1935) and Buye (1937). The last, at Shyogwe, in Rwanda, was started in 1946. In Uganda, Kisiizi Hospital was opened in 1958.

Missionary activity followed a well-tried pattern, sometimes likened to a three-legged stool: medical outreach, educational support and church planting. Both the

God worked half a century ago.

It would be impossible to give credit for every contribution incorporated in this anthology of praise. Particular thanks are due to Miss Doreen Peck and to Miss Joan Hall for access to their recorded discussions with Africans. It is largely from these that African testimonies have been drawn.

The affirmation of this record of revival as a *precious heritage* of a group of people to whom God was pleased to grant this privilege, does not lie in the remarkable manifestations which they experienced or witnessed, still less in themselves as special people in any way, but in the amazing grace of God as He worked in ordinary human lives, and in the great truths He made so vitally real in them.

Uganda, the Protestant Church of Uganda and the Roman Catholic Church claimed approximately equal numbers of members. In Rwanda, the Roman Catholic Church was predominant, numbering over 50% of the population. The total membership of Protestant Churches represented less than 20% of the population and of this number probably a third belonged to the Seventh Day Adventist Church. In Burundi the Roman Catholic Church claimed 60% of the population. Protestant churches numbered about 7% of of the population. Of that number one-fifth belonged to the Seventh Day Adventist Church. As the revival directly affected only the evangelical churches, the numbers touched were of the order of 12% of the population in Rwanda and 6% in Burundi.

However, the influence of the Protestant Churches was far greater than would be expected from their minority status. This influence was most marked in the homes of Christians who experienced God's reviving power. A particularly notable outcome was the emancipating effect of revival on the status of women.

It will become clear, however, that although the amazing ways in which God worked in revival can only be described in superlatives, the numbers of those who experienced God working in this way were numerically small when compared with the total Christian communities, when that term includes both the Roman Catholics and the Seventh Day Adventists, and even smaller when compared with the total populations of these countries.

This does not in any way detract from the fact that to see God working in such amazing ways in people, irrespective of race, tribe, colour or background, and to share in that work, was an inestimable privilege.

An added value to this account has been the testimony of African brothers and sisters in Christ. It is only relatively recently that there has been an impetus to record for future generations the memories of those among whom

the differences observed between the ways in which those truths were expressed in Africa and in Great Britain. This led to the 'message of revival' often being understood as referring only to the aspects which were considered as different from normal experience, such as the 'open confession of sin' and the challenges of 'walking in the light with each other'. It will be seen from what follows that the 'message of revival' was, in fact, the essential, central truths of the Gospel without which it is no Gospel at all.

A further point must be stressed. This account of the events of revival shows very clearly that that experience was a shared one, shared between missionaries, but much more importantly, shared with African brothers and sisters in Christ.

When, in 1938, the Rev. Lawrence Barham, one of the leaders in the early days of revival in Kigezi, was moved to Buye, in Burundi, to begin the pastoral training of church teachers and clergy there, the reviving work did not cease in Kigezi. On the contrary, it gained in momentum. God continued to work in amazing reviving power when there was no missionary directly involved at all. Far from the missionaries being jealous of this continuing revival without their direct participation, they rejoiced to see God confirming and vindicating *His Word*, not *His workers*. It was where God's saving Gospel was proclaimed in *its fullness* that God worked in *His fullness*.

An historical review at this time is also appropriate in order to put into perspective the extent of the influence in the 1990s of the revival which God graciously gave in the 1930s to 1950s. It is easy to exaggerate both factually and by implication.

It will be noted, for instance, that revival only affected the Protestant communities of Uganda, Rwanda and Burundi. Very rarely was the Roman Catholic Church in these countries touched although both represented large numbers of those who called themselves 'Christian'. In

to ignore. This was expressed in 1946 by Dr Algie Stanley Smith, one of the founders of the Mission, after experiencing a decade of revival: "I think God is wanting to say something to our time through what He is doing in Ruanda. Certain vital truths are being emphasized which seem to be inseparable from a Revived Church as we are seeing it."

This does not mean that the Mission claimed a unique revelation or experience from God. Far from it! However, God is the same 'yesterday, today and for ever' ... and *everywhere*. When He works in one place, it is good for those in other places and of another generation to take note.

Although the missionaries who witnessed revival were unanimous in rejecting any claim to an exclusive, unique experience, they were united in proclaiming, not the events or manifestations of revival, but the truths which those happenings underlined so dramatically. In revival God did not teach new truths until then unknown; rather He impressed on Christians the old, biblical truths to a much greater intensity. In becoming vitally real, the old truths became, for those who experienced them, *new*, in the sense of being understood and grasped more fully for the first time. It is that *renewing experience of biblical truth* which was at the heart of revival, as experienced in those areas of Africa where the Ruanda Mission was working.

Here a problem had to be faced. How could they describe or refer to what God was doing in the revival they were experiencing without placing a wrong emphasis on the dramatic manifestations which abounded? The course adopted was to play down the dramatic events and concentrate on the truths which God was so clearly vindicating and calling that the 'message of revival'. Unfortunately this was often interpreted, not as the central truths to which they gave strong testimony, but to

those concerned. At different times and places during the last three hundred years many groups of people have been similarly privileged. Even more important has been the fact that revival has widened the bounds of fellowship to all who share the reconciling work of the same Saviour. There has never been any desire to limit the revived fellowship to the privileged few although a tendency to this has had to be withstood at times.

Those early missionaries who were privileged to experience revival in its initial stages were joined and succeeded by others. These, although working alongside their senior colleagues, did not see, at first hand, the same dramatic manifestations nor experience their immediate effects. Later still, new missionaries found that the term 'revival' began to take on an historical aspect. It was the 'revival which had happened in the past'.

In the geographical areas in which the Mission worked there have also been political and church developments. The countries of Uganda and Ruanda-Urundi (as it was then named), gained their independence to become the republics of Uganda, Rwanda and Burundi. The Anglican churches there, all initially in the Diocese of the Church of Uganda, have since become part of either the Anglican Province of Uganda or the Episcopalian Provinces of Rwanda and Burundi. Churches of other denominations have also become indigenous self-governing bodies.

The single significant fact that emerges from these developments is that there is now a new generation for whom the 'revival' of many years ago is history. More recent mission-partners and younger Mission supporters may well wonder what history has to do with the present-day situation.

It is the strong conviction of many missionaries who saw God working, either in its earlier or later stages in this area, that the story of revival as experienced by them and their African colleagues, is one which it would be foolish

Introduction

For many years, missionaries of the Ruanda Mission (CMS), now the Mid-Africa Ministry (CMS), have referred to 'Revival' as a very precious part of their heritage. For those who were actually there in south-west Uganda, Rwanda and Burundi, when God was working in the special way we call 'revival', in the mid-1930s and 1940s and for those who shared in its later stages and immediate aftermath in the 1950s and 1960s, this heritage had a very personal significance. The impact of what God did in those early days among the Africans and Europeans in those countries was to reach much further afield and become known as the East African revival.

In Great Britain, the 'Ruanda revival', as it was often called, was associated with the term: the 'Ruanda message'. All efforts to disassociate the name 'Ruanda' from the 'message' failed and, sadly, the content of the so-called 'Ruanda message' often became distorted. Nevertheless, within the Ruanda Mission, among its missionaries and supporters, the reality of the truths which revival underlined so vividly, experienced then and to this day, made them very precious. For them that experience is, in truth, 'a precious heritage'.

This experience of God's reviving power has, however, never been considered as being in any way exclusive to

Revival -
A precious heritage

H H Osborn

N APOLOGIAN